# John William

## and the

# Omnipotent Indigo Orb

&

A modern-day fairy tale In a fantasy realm where the real and metaphysical entwine, the fate of existence hangs in the balance.

•

HOWARD R. GORRELL

# CONTENTS

# Chapter 1:
# Northern Greenland

Shards and fragments of my life flickered in the tomb of a cockpit as I plunged toward the Arctic ice. The F-16's mighty engine seized, and the instrument panel went dark. The displays were out, the backup gauges were dead as were all three radios. I must have been in free fall, but there was no sense of motion. There was no sound, nor a speck of light—the sky itself seemed to have vanished.

Instead, I found myself in another place and time: thirty years in the past, pulling my childhood friend Malcolm in a toy wagon along the cobblestones of a back alley in Swindon, England. We were perhaps three or four years old. The wagon's wheels rattled and squeaked. The faster I ran, the wilder became Malcolm's laughter. When we reached the main street, jet planes were flying overhead. I said, "I'd like to fly a plane someday, Malcolm."

"I would too, John Willy," he said.

This was not a dream. At least I didn't believe it was. The images were in 3-D, stereoscopic color. It was not a hallucination, nor a delirium spawned by oxygen deprivation. And I felt certain my vitals had not been compromised. How could this be?

Then I was back in the . . . real world? Still the jet fighter plunged. Although I had been above 40,000 feet, I realized my time on this earth had whittled down to seconds. At my present speed, whether I struck ice or ocean, it was unlikely I would feel a thing. As I tried to gather my thoughts and reason out some plausible explanation for what was happening, old memories flooded my consciousness, and with a wink and a blink my blessed return to tangibility transcended into a parallel existence. Having no choice, I let the barmy thoughts flow.

I saw my mother's kind smile and bright brown eyes. I felt my father's powerful hands as he tossed me high and set me gently on the ground. All around were the faces of friends and family, long lost but never forgotten. And the animals—both our pets and the strays that roamed the neighborhoods—that held a special place in my heart. I was there, as real as anything, hugging my old sheepdog Neal-boy. We can give love to and feel the love of an animal in the same way we can with another person. We can miss and long for places and things now part of the past just as we can for friends and family.

Then there was that rascal of a cat: a grey, striped tabby with yellow- green eyes as big as saucers and a curiosity that would take her away for days at a time on what I imagined were the most wonderful adventures. Such imaginings were probably just my way of hiding from worry over her—no doubt a similar experience to what was happening right now. Next, I was in the kitchen of my childhood home. I heard the cat door flap open and there she was, teeth clenching a small green lizard—or was it a toad? I don't quite remember. My mother scolded, "Katrina! You cruel thing. Take it back outside!"

And so, my imagination ruled the moment as the aircraft continued to fall. When a person knows they are about to die, it is common for their life to flash before their eyes; in theory, this is a way of searching our memories for a way to save ourselves.

A blinding flash! I was in a cockpit again but no longer careening toward the Arctic Ocean. To my great surprise, I was soaring over a vast span of sand—the Iraqi desert. From six o'clock, a missile from an SA-14 Gremlin roared past, clipping my right wing, and sending me spiraling into a nosedive. Impact was inevitable. Unable to trust my instruments and displays, I reduced thrust to an idle and labored to coordinate the aileron and rudder. Leveling the wings was critical, my only chance. Gratefully and humbly, I admit it was luck rather than skill that allowed me to stabilize, descend, and skim over the rolling dunes. The Iraqi guard closed in from the east, three Humvees of Marines from the west. Clearly outnumbered, the Iraqis held off. The Marines destroyed the damaged fighter and hauled me out of there. On our way back to base, one of the guys playfully punched me in the shoulder and handed me a small pack of sunflower seeds. A simple gesture that meant a great deal. I kept the gift as a good luck charm.

Inexplicably, the curtain closed on my memory matinee, leaving me in absolute silence, stillness, and darkness. Why hadn't I struck the ground? Maybe I had smashed into the ice or waves. Maybe it was all over, and I had been delivered into the great unknown. What was next to come?

There it was! It was beautiful: the aurora borealis—at least I thought that's what it was. And I was again in the pilot's seat of the F-16, all systems go. The HUD matched up with my helmet readings and appeared reliable. My mission picked up where it had left off. How and why these strange things had happened, I neither knew nor cared. I was just glad things were back to normal.

I'd been sent up from the Thule Air Base in Northern Greenland to search for the elite of the elite, an F-22 Raptor, which had been dispatched to search for a missing weather reconnaissance plane—at least that was the official story. The northern lights wavered in the distance; the flowing, shimmering bands shining in colors I could not name; the view left me breathless. Suddenly, they were gone, every trace swallowed by churning black clouds. A wind rose with demonic fury, straining the fighter at the seams. Rivets shot like bullets and sheet metal peeled back, exposing the craft's naked innards. It felt as though the frame was buckling. Blinding bolts ripped the horizon, and thunder roared like a million lions. The breath of an arctic demon encased the hull in ice. The nose dropped, and I was once again in freefall.

To be certain, I was wide awake and well aware . . . no dreams, no imaginings, no hallucinations. This was all very real. The plane quaked as ice began breaking away; a huge chunk bounced off the windshield. Despite the damage, at least I had a fighting chance: the instrument panel was up and running, and I was able to establish some maneuverability. Out of habit I tried to contact Thule and then remembered that white noise and an occasional crackle was all I'd heard for most of the flight. Turbulence rose and would soon bury the Richter scale. I had to get below the storm.

Risking another spiral, I dived deep and steep. The G-force was tremendous; it felt like the threads of my flight suit were unraveling. The displays blinked and then flashed, sparked, smoked, went black, surged back on, went dim, then out. In primitive panic, I hammered on the instruments. When I twisted the stick, there was no response; it may as well have been a piece of licorice. Another blinding flash. The stick responded. Miracles do happen. Incredibly, there was no evidence of damage from the ice storm. It was as if some weather poltergeist had pulled a practical joke.

The F-16 was handling well. Still, I dared not press my luck.

Bringing the plane down was imperative, but the coast of Northern Greenland was nowhere in sight. Again, I tried contacting Thule. Again, white noise hissed and static crackled.

Ice landings were reasonably routine, but I needed a nice, flat floe, the lengthier the better. I knew my search-and-rescue mission was over. If the "weather" plane or F-22 had run into what I had, they could easily have been on the ocean floor. As I looked for a suitable floe, I thought about how none of this made any sense. When I left Greenland, the sky was perfectly clear, and the midnight sun blazed gloriously. So, what had happened? Had I been swallowed by a black hole? Did I cross an interdimensional bridge? Had climate change taken a quantum leap? Was I astral projecting? Was I dangling from some string-theory lanyard?

Just as I began thinking I could make it to the coast, the hydraulic gauges went limp. Warning lights flashed. A jet doesn't use a lot of oil, but what it does use is crucial. There wasn't an ice floe—small, medium, or large—in sight. I had the option to eject, but even though the surface temperature of the Arctic Ocean isn't as cold as one might think, hypothermia would set in very quickly. My addled brain estimated I was cruising at about 500 mph.

Buzz, hum, pop! The instruments flashed back on—all displays. My speed was 450. Greenland should have been in sight, but all that lay ahead was choppy ocean. The hydraulics looked good, but at this point, I trusted my instincts more than my instruments. In fact, the northernmost coastline might already have been visible had it not gotten so foggy. And that fog was not only thickening, it was also beginning to glitter and sparkle. That's when I realized it couldn't be fog. It was distortion—a wavering ribbon stretching over a gelatinous sea—a mysterious atmospheric wall rising more than fifty thousand feet. Its consistency seemed much denser than water vapor, and it kept changing from glossy opaque, to a swirling spectrum of colors, to nearly transparent, to not there at all.

Suddenly, I caught a glimpse of the coast—it was close! There was an all-encompassing shimmer and another brilliant flash. The landscape that had once been behind me now lay ahead. And there was something moving toward me. It was small and it was coming fast—jet fighter fast. And that's just what it was: not the missing F- 22, but another F-16. Maybe they'd sent somebody up to search for and rescue me. The fighter was headed straight for me; it seemed the pilot was deliberately taking a direct line. In that vastness of sky, this maniac was on a collision course. When I banked, he banked; when I dropped, he dropped. An Arctic kamikaze. As I squinted through my face shield, I saw that the aircraft looked familiar—very familiar. It was my own F-16, and the pilot . . . was me!

At nearly 500 mph, I smashed into a duplicate of myself and was swallowed by the shimmering wall. Everything was white, like I'd flown into a bowl of milk. Just as suddenly, I was out of the milk and into an envelope of diffused light. The light grew brighter and brighter. The sparkling clouds thinned. Below me were mountains, green valleys, rivers, and a large body of water to the south.

Suddenly, the engines coughed and sputtered. The fighter lost speed. The dashboard dinged and flashed a red light, telling me the engine was leaking oil. The F-16 stuttered, dropped, and then leveled out; as I entered a cloud bank, the jet began to shake in the turbulence.

A snowy mountain peak appeared out of nowhere. As I skimmed over the top, something landed on the left wing and began to move toward me. At first, it appeared to be a man, but as it drew near, I saw a green frog-like being dressed in a waistcoat with flapping tails and a ruffled cravat. There was something tied to its back that looked like the sort of small surfboard a lifeguard might carry, but it was shaped like a lily pad. The frog thing leaped from the wing and landed dead center on the windshield; its suction-cup fingers spread out against the glass. The creature stared at me with shifting, googly eyes, and its mouth opened and closed as if it were gasping for breath. The expression on its face was a bizarre mixture of fear and glee.

Ignoring my inexplicable passenger, I looked for a place to land. It was getting darker. I was losing altitude. I was past the mountains and over a body of water. The hydraulics system was failing. The oil temperature was high, the pressure was low. The engine chugged, the whole craft shuddered, and the tail had caught fire. Apparently cognizant of losing its ride, the frog creature unstuck itself from the canopy and jumped high and away. Pulling out the sides of its waistcoat to form sails, it glided down toward the brine.

Meanwhile, smoke filled the cockpit. No miracles this time. Having no choice, I gnashed my teeth and ejected, shooting out almost horizontally as the F-16 plummeted. The chute obediently popped out and trailed away, quickly billowing like a whipped cream cloud. Far in the distance, the fiery jet splashed into the waves.

Beneath a velvet black ceiling, I drifted in a direction that I decided to call south. The stars appeared fuzzy and swollen as they flickered and glowed, which I put down to a flow of warm, moist air. And most bizarrely, in an area that should have been encased in ice, I floated in the amniotic warmth of a tropical night.

All things considered, setting my boots on solid ground was

the number one priority—perhaps a life-or-death priority.

Squinting till my eyelids ached, I spied a narrow stretch of beach that lay at the hemline of a forest. As the F-16 sank beneath the waves, I drifted toward dry land. "C'mon, give me a break!" I said when a mild wind pushed me away from the shore. The farther I went out, the closer came the waves. Finally, the breeze let up and I landed in the water, but I was at least a mile away from land. Swimming in my flight suit was going to be an ordeal, but the water was surprisingly warm, almost like a backyard pool. Things could have been much worse, so I counted my blessings. I detached the chute, inflated my vest, tossed my helmet, and kicked my way toward the beach. Thankfully, the frog creature was gone, and I was even more grateful that most of my faculties had returned.

With my buoyant vest and all the air trapped in my flight suit, the swim to shore was a slow endeavor. I felt like a human life raft. My boots were waterlogged and extremely heavy. I considered taking them off and looping the laces around my neck, but it would still have been like dragging an anchor. I felt like letting them sink to the bottom, but I knew I would need them when I reached land.

A side stroke with a strong, coordinated kick turned out to be the ideal method of propulsion. The water had looked a little choppy farther out, but close to shore it was completely calm.

About every five minutes, I floated on my back to rest and looked up at the stars. Where was Orion? The Big Dipper? Cassiopeia? Even at the top of the world, the constellation would have maintained identifiable patterns. But these stars were different. Totally different. Some were very bright. Some blinked off and on in a rhythm, like chaser lights. It was abnormal, unnatural. This was not the sky I knew. But at least the glowing spots lit up the beach and outlined the treetops, which looked to be mostly evergreens. Greenland has lots of evergreens along its coast, but from my present perspective, Greenland may as well have been on Mars.

Seeing that there were only a couple of hundred yards to the beach inspired me to pick up the pace. If these were not earthly waters, unearthly fish probably lived in them. I couldn't help imagining what sort of aquatic life might be swimming below. I knew it was salt water because I'd gotten a big nose and mouthful when I first landed. Could there have been a fifty-foot shark looking up at me at that very moment? Was a giant squid about to fling its tentacles around my neck? Maybe some prehistoric thing was out there—an Elasmosaurus, a Kronosaurus. Such horrible thoughts. Sometimes I hated my imagination; I wished there were a way to unplug it or switch it off.

Of one thing I was certain—the faster I got out of the water, the better. As I imagined the turbines of the Batmobile kicking in, I picked up speed. Soon my boots touched and dragged along the sea floor. After finding my footing, I realized the sea bottom was cluttered with a great deal of debris that had likely drifted in with the lapping tide. Lord only knows what was down there—probably things with big, sharp teeth. I strode out of there like I was jumping hurdles and running a steeplechase.

On the beach, I knelt and unlaced my boots, then set them aside. Off came my vest and flight suit, which I let fall around my ankles. Thankfully, I wasn't wearing MAGs; out of the water, they would have weighed a ton. While scanning the beach, I removed my T-shirt and skivvies to wring them out. My plan was to start a little fire once I got to the tree line, not for warmth, but to dry my gear and clothing. As far as warmth, I estimated the air temperature to be at least 70, maybe 75 degrees Fahrenheit. It was autumn in the Arctic, but I felt like I was on a beach in Tahiti, half a world away from Greenland.

There were a couple of protein bars and a water pouch in my flight suit, but I wasn't all that worried about finding something to eat and drink. I was at the doorstep of a coniferous forest, the best environment for a person to live off the land. I had no doubt there was plenty of fresh water, for I'd seen rivers and streams from the air. It was funny—the sky was clear, so the moon should have been visible, yet not a silvery sliver was anywhere to be seen. And those strange, unfamiliar stars

. . . they really had me puzzled.

I put my skivvies and undershirt back on. When I turned to gather up my flight suit, it was gone, and so was my vest. Had I absentmindedly wandered away from them? As I started my search, I noticed drag marks in the sand, going all the way back to the water. Something had to have taken my gear. Something quick, something silent. I scanned the gentle waves, hoping to see my clothing floating on top, and found nothing. My Beretta, knife, compass, tube of maps and flight documents, fire, food, and medical supplies now belonged to the denizens of the deep. Without my flight vest, all I had were my bare hands, wits, and training. Exasperated and with reluctance, I contemplated my few options. Clad only in undershorts and a T- shirt, I picked up my boots and headed for the woods. The sand beneath my feet was dry and slightly warm, a pleasant sensation.

Glancing back with the faint hope my belongings would wash to shore, I saw nothing but the gentle rolling of the sea.

## Chapter 2:
## The Woodlands

For some odd reason "The Owl and the Pussycat" poem popped into my head, but at the edge of this wood, no piggy wig stood on the sandy loam giving rise to the tall grass; sparse, slender birch and alder trees; and scant underbrush at the edge of the forest. Clad in soggy undergarments, I pulled on and laced my heavy boots. My decision: To search for a ready entrance, a pathway or road; or to blaze a new trail into the frontier. An established route might well harbor unfriend- lies; on the other hand, if I stayed alert and did plenty of 360- degree sweeps, following an established trail made far more sense than fighting my way through branches, brambles, and brush. Above, the radiant quasi-stars supplied enough light to see in the outlying terrain, but the pine, fir, and cedars farther into the woodlands were dense. I knew the deeper I went, the darker it would get. Waiting for daylight seemed my only choice, so I started to search for a place that provided cover and a wide, multidirectional view.

As I searched, I also gathered some golf ball-sized rocks and found a sturdy, rule-of-thumb stick with the keenest of points. Winding my way through the saplings and weeds, I spotted a welcome glade and what appeared to be an unobstructed pathway into the woods. As I leaned against a tree, some pine-smelling sap stuck to my shoulder. I scraped it off against the bark of another tree and then sat in the loam, among the itchy pine needles. Astern, glints from the stars danced over the sea. Ahead loomed the dark woods. Everything was crackling dry; the lightest step on the forest floor would amplify by ten. As far as I could tell, the whole world was asleep. But I dared not sleep. The thieving thing that had taken my clothes might set its sights on me next. And there was no telling what might lie ahead. For me, morning could not come soon enough.

To stay awake, I sought the comfort of memories—longing for the fond, casting out the foul. I pondered the events that had led me into this incredible predicament. An American army brat born in England, I had been enamored of the jet fighters roaring over the RAF base in Brize Norton. At the enlightened age of six, I knew I wanted to be a fighter pilot, to soar above the seven seas and touch down in all four corners of the earth. Back then, I dreamed of the thrills and perils of flying combat missions. Eventually, those titillating dreams came to pass. But there was no joy, no thrills, just lamentations of death and flames of destruction. The prophetic words, "Beware of what you wish for," haunt me even today. Over time, the words of Chief Joseph— "I will fight no more forever"— became my banner, and I became a test pilot. As an engineering specialist, my job was to evaluate and analyze the features and functions of new types of aircraft. But personally, I was a little old- fashioned—no spike-pounding rock driller could ever replace my trust in a faithful F-16.

A noise. I snapped to. Birds. The chirping of birds. Perhaps, while lost in my thoughts, I'd dozed off. I stood and turned full circle. A soft, soothing light bathed the distant ocean and beach. But this was not morning light, not in the normal sense; it seemed synthetic, artificial. When I looked at the sky, a painted luminescence spread toward the horizon, and there were dark patches—not clouds, more like smudges on a wall. Standing and staring, I happily realized my skivvies were nearly dry. Rejoice in the little joys of life, I thought. My boots were still damp, but not too bad. The birds nearby stopped chirping, but I could still hear twitters in the distance, little sounds from little birds. Listening to them was somehow comforting. I deemed bird friends an upgrade from no friends. It was a silly thought, but a welcome one.

After my passage through the shimmering curtain above the Arctic Ocean, verisimilitude lay asunder. That I had astral projected to another planet or into a new dimension was as good an explanation as any. Yet most of my mental references and anchors indicated I was still on Earth. Looking around the glade, I felt a familiarity, a sense of belonging. Trees were trees, bushes were bushes, and woods were woods. And again, best of all, I stood at the threshold of a thriving forest, which meant water and wildlife. As I approached, I could see a slew of branches and brambles had been recently cleared by a machete or something similar. This assured me there was intelligent life in the vicinity, and that life had tool-making skills. I looked for footprints, but the soft soil and pine needles were not suited for leaving impressions.

In all fairness, I suppose it's not that odd that someone who'd escaped a bizarre death twice in a matter of minutes would have some irrational thoughts. But this was a time to be serious and sane. At least I had my caveman weapons—a couple of rocks and a nice, sharp stick. As I looked back at the beach and the sea one last time, my gaze lingered on the horizon, where the lower bands of milky blue blended into a dome of nebulous white. The grey smudges I had noticed earlier remained, and there was no sun. But there was a noticeably brighter cluster of light in a direction I had decided to call east. At this point, I typically would have made a detailed plan of action. But all I could do was head north and try to find the entity that had brought me here. I figured that was my best chance of finding a way home.

After a little more pondering, I accepted things for what they were and headed down the trail and into the forest. Fortunately, enough light filtered through the trees to provide a passable view. Farther on, the trail curved in a direction I decided to call north in relation to the brighter light of the "eastern" sky. When the mountains I had flown over to the north came fully into view, I would have a fair grasp of my bearings.

Although the trail itself was adequately lit, the forest on either side was quite dark. As I made my way deeper into the woods, the distant chirping of birds faded. Then, a crow began to caw. I saw it! A big, black crow sitting high on a branch, likely warning its brethren of my approach. Another crow appeared, and others cawed among the trees. Louder and faster, the caws rose to a cacophony. Then there was a sudden flutter of wings, and all went silent. No doubt something else had entered the woods. Something the birds found far more threatening than me: a fox, a bobcat, maybe an owl or hawk.

A rustling came from behind me. Then a thump. More rustling— ahead of me this time. I looked deep into the trees in every direction. Visibility was ten, maybe fifteen feet at best. But something or someone was out there. And they were watching.

Another big decision. I could backtrack to the beach, where at least I could see my stalkers approach, or I could continue along the path I was on—this was my preference. But was I walking into a trap? Should I take a stand right where I was? All I wanted to do was find a way home. If I could make a friend along the way, that would be fine. I'd welcome any help I could get. But if somebody out there wanted to fight, that was fine too. All the sneaking around was putting me in a bad mood. It was time to open a channel of communication.

"Hey!" I said. "Who are you? Show yourselves!" I waited. "I mean no harm. I'm just passing through."

A rustling and bustling were followed by a thud, as if something had jumped from a tree. Shadow shapes filled my imagination. I thought I saw a huge, hairy hand pulling on a cedar branch. Next came a glimpse of wild red eyes and the flash of a hideous face. My imagination again? The cedar branch had moved, I was certain of that. But had I really seen those fierce, red eyes? I decided to follow the trail with my shoulders back and my head held high—like I owned the place. I said, "Listen up, folks. There's an old saying in my neck of the woods— 'If you're coming, then come on!' Any takers?"

No takers. Maybe my tough guy act had worked. With my improvised spear at the ready, I watched my back with every step. All I could hear were the twigs, dry grass, and pinecones crunching under my feet.

Rounding the next bend, I came upon the end of the trail. It opened onto a stretch of tall grass and a sporadic clustering of trees. There were some apples on the ground. I picked one up and took a close look. Very tempting. I took a small bite. Delicious. Four apples later, I took account of a small hill that blocked the view ahead. As tasty as those apples were, their sweetness had given me a terrific thirst. I felt certain water couldn't be too far off. Grass so thick and green had to have been fed by creeks and streams. My spirits on the rise, I ran to the hilltop. Below me was an endless field of plush, green fescue and what appeared to be bright yellow daffodils nearly ten feet tall.

To the south sprawled a dense forest; to the north, the terrain rose and fell like the braes and dells of Scotland. I knew that while there was no way I could have been in Scotland, Greenland was still a remote possibility. There is a gigantic canyon beneath the ice sheets of Greenland that spans the entire country. CGI maps have been developed, but the actual landforms have never been explored due to the sealing sheets of ice, two miles thick at the center. Could I be under a dome of ice? If so, light from the sun could not have penetrated. What was the widespread illumination? And again, there was the perplexing heat: This far north, at this time of year, the air should have been windy and extremely cold, yet it was placid and pleasantly warm. There should have been no fog, yet there was a heavy fog bank beyond the next rise of hills.

Quietly talking to myself as I took everything in, I reached back to history in hopes of some answers. Admiral Richard E. Byrd was one of the first scientists to explore the North and South Poles over land and by airplane. In 1947, he noted in his Arctic journal that he and his crew had once flown over an area of forests, mountains, lakes, vegetation, and animal life where they should have seen nothing but ice. Low on fuel, they were not able to land or linger. At the first opportunity, they returned to the mysterious location, but all they found was ice. Was it a hoax perpetrated by zany scientists; evidence of a hollow Earth; a collective hallucination; or a matter of verified fact? The observations of Byrd and his crew have never officially been explained. But the speculation and skepticism live on.

To this day, the North and South Poles present many conundrums. The north wind gets warmer as you near the geographical pole. Warm northerly winds sometimes blow over the Arctic Sea for hundreds of miles. At the poles, the snow sometimes falls in colors such as pink, yellow, green, and blue. Supposedly, this is caused by the presence of algae and pollen, yet the evidence of this source of life is unknown.

Above 82 degrees latitude, compasses can give inconsistent and inaccurate readings. Icebergs float in salt water, yet they are composed of fresh water; massive glaciers are the source of these islands of ice. But if the glaciers in a world beneath the Earth's crust were fed by subterranean waters, they'd be part of a water cycle independent of the surface world. No such cycle is known to exist. Leaving the woodlands behind, I must admit, at this point, I was flummoxed.

# Chapter 3:
## Of Mist and Mirrors

With my spear now a walking stick tucked under my arm, I headed north beneath the soft glow of a sunless sky. Venturing into the unknown had its perils, but it also promised high adventure. As I reached the top of another hill, the air felt humid; when I reached the bottom of the hill, it was steamy. Suddenly, the ground rumbled, and a column of boiling water shot skyward—two, maybe three hundred feet high. Thankfully, when it rained down upon me, it had become tepid. I realized the fog bank I had seen was steam billowing from ground spouts. So much for the mystery of the warm air; it was likely caused by magma flowing deep beneath the ground.

Again, the earth trembled, and another geyser blasted up. Intuition told me to continue north, which meant negotiating the thermal springs. This would be tricky, for the steam gathered in pockets and the terrain was only partially visible. My next decision: Navigate the geyser field and risk being scalded to death, or turn back and find a safe way around.

My last verified location was off the coast of Northern Greenland. I was headed due south at the time. Returning to the point of the atmospheric distortion that brought me here was the most sensible course of action. Right or wrong, I decided to follow the logic. Home was north, and the shortest distance between me and home was a straight line. There was no sense in doing further analysis. I had to make it past the geysers.

As the steam rolled, a swirling window opened; it exposed boundless fields of tall grass and a span of rolling hills. Aware another geyser would soon blow, I broke into a full run through the steam and around the vents. Only two boiling craters remained. The earth again trembled, and one of the geysers spewed in short bursts. The ever- trembling ground foretold the coming eruption. Just after I passed the irritable vent, the ground rolled and knocked me flat. Scrambling to my feet, I felt a blast of hot gas slap me on the back as the geyser blew. Running like a man possessed, I heard the sizzling liquid splashing closer and closer. The splashes faded to soppy plops. Reaching the grass, I sprinted on, leaving the fury of steam spouts far behind.

Atop one of the nearby hills was an outcropping. This became my destination; it would serve well as a point of reference and an observation platform. As I waded through the waist-high grass, there was movement ahead. About twenty yards in front of me, the grass parted—something was heading straight for me. After taking an evasive step to the right, I felt a chill cross my temples when the oncoming party adjusted its path. I backed away and circled left. It followed. No more running, I swung my sharpened stick like a machete to clear a space around me and backed farther away.

Soon the reddish-brown head of a massive snake emerged from the grass; it was a constrictor of some sort, and I was its prey. The snake's tongue flicked out and slithered back repeatedly. I froze and held my breath, but the huge reptile continued to close. A stone about the size of a cantaloupe was half exposed in the soft soil. Digging feverishly, I freed the stone and hurled it. Though I'd aimed for the head, the rock struck the reptile in the side, which provoked a hiss and the exposing of its wicked, saw-edged teeth. This maneuver merely spurred on the attack.

When the snake whipped into a final rush, I sidestepped and landed a jab with my stick right on the end of its nose, then another to the back of its head. Deterred by the blows, it circled away. As it veered off, its massive tail swept my legs clear out from under me. Flat on my back, I could see nothing but grass. I listened for movements. The snake had to be out there somewhere. Taking a firm hold of my spear, I warily rose to my feet, fully expecting to be face-to-face with the slithering thing. But it had not returned to attack. Instead, the mottled mass undulated west toward the encroaching forest, no doubt in search of an easier mark.

Encountering a twenty-foot reptile can sharpen the eyes and put points on the ears. My ears tuned in to the sound of a geyser bursting back in the distance. My eyes fell upon a surprise and a curiosity. The rock outcropping I'd noticed earlier was a structure. As I quickened my pace, ever scanning for snakes, the formation ahead gradually took shape. It was a pyramid, but not Egyptian, nor was it of Aztec design. A ziggurat! A style of temple first introduced to Mesopotamia by the Sumerians, with a long, rectangular base, steep slopes, a winding stairway, and a flat, unadorned top. I hurried up the hill to take a closer look. It was ancient. Its hardened blocks were cracked and crumbling, its mud and bitumen glue had long washed away. But it had been majestically constructed; its mass alone upheld its integrity. Though it was likely uninhabited due to its condition, it would at least make a temporary shelter. Standing at its base, I was in awe. When I touched the stones, I felt a blood rush, a spine- tingling connection to an age six thousand years in the past. My heart pounded, and I struggled to relax and catch my breath.

Beyond the hills, diaphanous drapes of sparkling rain sprinkled over the fields. A crash and a rumble echoed from the sky. Having no idea why, I'd always loved lightning storms: the jagged bolts and timpani drums. But the sound I'd just heard had not been thunder. It had to have been volcanic activity, but there were no mountains in view. As a fireworks lover, I felt cheated. Such a vast curtain of rain, a rumbling sky, yet not a single flash of lightning.

When I reached the top of the next hill, I glanced back. There stood the ziggurat, high above the dissipating vapor. Indulging for just a moment in its magnificence, I could not help but wonder about its history. Who had built it? And why were there no other ancient structures or relics in the area? It was just standing there, a lonely mass of rock that must have once meant so much to so many.

Ahead, the tall grass gave way to a mossy moor, and in the middle of it was a splashing fountain. Over the spongy, mossy terrain I jogged, in my T-shirt, underpants, and soggy combat boots. I could almost taste the artesian delight. But I took all due caution when I reached the wellspring. I had seen one like it in Athens—a wide-brimmed ivory goblet with a tall column stacked in the middle of the bowl. Well over six feet, four spouts sent steady streams into the ample basin. The base was marbled alabaster, and it bore a golden plaque with the engraving: Jungbrunnen. My smattering of German included jung (young), but brunnen eluded me. Brun meant brown in French, but that didn't make any sense. So, I reasoned that brunnen meant fountain—perhaps a fountain built in dedication to children. I let the water splash on my hands and gave it a taste. It was cold; it must have been glacial. The taste was almost sweet, and as pure as snow. I leaned toward one of the spouts, opened wide, and guzzled away. Gulping till I thought my stomach might burst, I stepped back to watch the torrent that continued to rage in the north. The massive drops should have been pounding those mossy fields like steel mallets. But there was no sound, no sound at all.

At that moment, my weary brain realized I wasn't watching rain; I was looking at that same vast, translucent ribbon that had slung me into this realm at the edge of nowhere. And in that moment of revelation, the wavering wall gave way and became a panorama of green hills and fields, a distant span of steaming geysers, and a replica of the ziggurat I had passed earlier. To top it all off, there was a man walking toward me, a man wearing only underwear and boots. I appeared to be headed toward a mirror as wide as the horizon and as high as the sky—the same reflective phenomenon I had passed through in the F-16. A grand hope arose—if I passed through it again, maybe it would return me to the world I knew. So, I kept on walking toward myself.

Slowly, the reflection faded into a ribbony translucence, a cloudy coverture obscuring all that lay beyond. I had to take the chance. I had to blindly delve into this thing I had decided to call the Miribon (from the words mirror and ribbon).

I reluctantly drew closer to the strange shroud until I was one step away. When I touched it, there was no sensation, no evidence that it was either energy or mass. When I wafted at the milky mist, it stirred not in the slightest, apparently not obedient to physical law. Taking a deep breath, I stepped inside and was enveloped for less than the bat of an eyelash. I thought I was walking forward, but I wasn't sure. Emerging from the mist, I was treated to a distinct change of scenery.

I now beheld a snow-capped mountain range, probably the one I'd flown over before abandoning the fighter. I stood in a wide valley with forested foothills on either side. The floor of the valley reminded me of the Australian outback. Up ahead was a rocky stretch, and I could hear the rippling of water—a stream or creek, I suspected. My feet became tangled in weeds, and I nearly fell. When I looked down, my skivvies had dropped around my ankles; they, not the weeds, had tripped me up. Somehow my clothing had been stretched to extremes when I passed through the Miribon. I was swimming in my boots, and my T-shirt touched my knees. The skivvies were a lost cause, so I tossed them. Though the boots had become an encumbrance, they were a necessity, so I laced them tightly and clomped along like a cart horse.

I knew I could eventually make a pair of sandals from pine bark, binding them with either spruce roots or my own boot-laces. After clomping my way to a rocky stretch, I decided enough was enough and headed for the woods. I had my choice of evergreen: pine, cedar, spruce, hemlock. As I neared the forest, I spotted a dead tree with a board attached. Duly excited, I hurried over and found words carved into the plat-ter. No need for translation, the message was in English

—Beware: The North Woods.

What first came to mind was my episode in the woods to the south, the shadowy stalkers who would not come out to play. Were they watching me now? Had they been following me? I had to assume so. I decided to look for a bigger stick, and that was when I noticed a narrow, unkempt road, well-pounded by hooves and deeply rutted by wagon wheels. Heavily over-grown in places, it probably hadn't been traveled in years, maybe decades, but it was better than clomping along in the middle of the scrubby prairie lands.

I kept one eye on the woods while the other took in the beauty of the distant mountains. Since I'd flown over these moun-tains after penetrating the Miribon, I reasoned this northern portal would extend from ground to sky just like the one to the south. I also reasoned I would eventually come to a town or settlement; someone had to have engineered the road and built the wheeled carts. In a village, I could likely find work and procure provisions for my journey home. It was likely the creatures that had followed me through the woods were, at best, Stone Age folk, who would have been of no practical as-sistance. But the fashioners of the road and wagons might well be helpful.

With my next step, whether by fate or providence, I spied a short, sturdy stalk of wood. As I reached for it, it seemed fate had smiled again—it was a shillelagh! Ornately fashioned, about thirty inches in length, with a solid, knobby end and well-spaced finger grips, fortuitously preserved with some type of lacquer. Perhaps there was an Irishman or a leprechaun nearby. I would have been most pleased to make their acquaintance.

Employing a whistle-past-the-graveyard strategy, I strolled at a leisurely pace, softly singing the Old English madrigal "Early One Morning." My voice sounded sort of high-pitched. Nerves, I supposed. At the start of the second verse, the lyrics echoed in harmony. The strange counter melody ended when I returned to the verse. As I repeated the chorus, I stopped in my tracks—a voice even higher than mine rang from the woods. It was a female voice, with a lilt and well-honed vibrato. Stepping from behind the trunk of a mighty pine was a woman dressed in nut-brown tunic and tights. Around her neck was a royal blue neckerchief. Her ears were atop her head, her eyes were wide and yellow green, and long whiskers sprouted above her lip. When she smiled, her fangs caught my eye. For all the world, she resembled a striped, gray tabby cat in the body of a human female.

"Hello, little boy," she said and purred. "You've certainly strayed a long way from home."

Completely astonished, I felt my thoughts freeze. For the life of me, I could barely generate a thought. Finally, I mustered a lame reply. "Y- you speak English."

"I speak five upper world languages: French, German, Russian, Spanish, and English, along with my native Ultranian. I also meeeeowwww." She tried to suppress a laugh, but it got away from her.

Regaining my poise, at least somewhat, I said, "You're right—I am a long way from home. But why did you call me a little boy?"

"I have eyes. Bright green ones—you must have noticed." She leaned forward with a mocking stare. "I assure you, where I'm from, everyone would call you a little boy—a lad, garçon, muchacho, junge, mal'chik—your choice."

"Miss Cat, I will have you know I am a captain in the United States Navy, thirty-four years of age, and all of six-foot-two."

"More like ten years of age, and all of"—she tipped her head—"a good smidgen under five feet, I should think."

"What?!"

"Indeed, I could place a bowl on your head and enjoy a ladle of soup." She stepped forward and reached out with her paw-hand, which was furry at the back and padded on the palm.

When I put my hand up to hers, it looked like a child's. "You're a giant!"

She glanced at the sky and then placed her hands on her hips. "Gracious me. You must stop being so silly and tell me why you've strayed so far from home."

"So, you think I'm being silly. OK, how's this for silly. I flew my jet fighter through a weird, cloudy wall, nearly crashed into a mountain where a Froggie-Went-a-Courtin' guy jumped onto my plane and shoved his fat, ugly face against my windshield, then jumped way out into the sea. Following which, I too jumped into the sea while my burning F-16 crashed into the waves. How's that for silly?"

"Not silly at all. I simply didn't realize little surface world boys were allowed to pilot great big airplanes."

"Stow the 'little boy' bilge, lady. I haven't insulted you in the least. What if I called you an old hag cat lady?"

She laughed, took another quick glance at the sky, and said curiously, "So that's what happened to Parnie. He leaped into the sea. Hmmm . . . oh, and yes, referring to me a giant was a bit of an insult."

"Yeah. OK, poor choice of words. Anyway, when he was in the water, that frog thing climbed onto his little surfboard and jumped about two hundred feet in the air."

"Drat. I'd hoped his little lily pad contrivance would be a bust. Most disturbing. He'll likely reach the island in a day." She glanced again into the strangely glowing sky.

"Parnie, lily pad, island? What are you talking about? And why do you keep looking up at the sky?"

"No time for stories, laddie. You've got to show me how you came through the Coverture. And we must hurry!"

"Coverture? Oh, you must mean the Miribon. Yeah, I can show you, but what's the big hurry?"

"Show me. Quick. We must run." Again, she glanced skyward. "Kick away those gumboots and let's be off." She picked up what looked like a bo staff from the ground, left the road for the scrublands, and nodded for me to follow.

Casting my fate to the wind, I knelt, unlaced my boots, and did my best to keep up in my bare feet. She paused from time to time until I nearly caught up, and then she bolted off with the speed of a frightened deer. Bounding over the prairie without footwear hurt like H-E double hockey sticks. But there's no hiding courage, and this cat had plenty. That was the main reason I followed. The cat had a truck load of confidence, and I knew she could handle herself. But she was scared—and that scared me.

When the cat lady neared the Miribon, she stood in defiance, brandishing her bo staff in the manner of a Shaolin monk. As I approached, she waved me away and yelled, "Walk along the Coverture. Find the place where you entered—the exact spot." So, I turned west toward the woods. Keeping a cautious distance from the wavering curtain, I scanned the ground for my boot prints. If the Miribon had been transparent, from where I was standing, I'd have seen the children's fountain and the ziggurat on a distant hill. But the screen remained cloudy, sometimes shimmering, sometimes reflecting like a mirror.

Shuffling along at a steady pace, I carefully scanned the ground. I had to be getting close to my entry point. At two hundred yards, I looked back and saw the cat waving her staff, desperately trying to get my attention. She was shouting, but her words were too faint. I waved back and kept looking, finally catching sight of my boot prints at the edge of the wavering passage. When I turned and headed toward her, she jabbed her staff in my direction, pointing to the trees. She raced toward me yelling, "Go back! Stop! Go back! Hide in the woods!"

She looked at the sky. So did I. Hundreds of feet in the air soared an ancient chariot, drawn by four white horses. Dropping dramatically in altitude, the vehicle turned in our direction. At the reins was a tall, slender figure whose tendrilous black mane flowed wild as the wind. The cat turned her full attention to the oncoming chariot. Her bo staff whirled like the blades of a fan. In a triangular battle stance, the cat thrust her bo like a Zulu lance. Still more than 100 yards away, I ran, shillelagh in hand, to stand by her side.

In a near vertical dive, the chariot descended and leveled off just a few feet above the prairie, then streaked toward the cat. Slowing gradually, touching down gracefully, the horses rolled the chariot to a stop, about ten yards from the feline. The chariot's driver was a woman with lily-white skin, scorching red lips, and long, blue-black hair. She was beautiful until she smiled, showing some wicked- looking canines. With the clap of her hands, the horses' eyes closed. She stepped from the chariot dressed in golden light armor, drawing a scepter with a claw-shaped end from the sheath on her back. She pointed the wand directly at the cat and said, "I am very disappointed with you, Katherine."

"You had best go home, Piranda. The toad is gone, and you know you can't pass through the Coverture."

"Then how did the toad pass?" "He has the Orb slice."

"You allowed that cretin to lay his webbed hands on the crystal?" "We made a bargain."

The woman laughed with disdain. "You trusting little fool."

"Precisely what choice did I have? Trust him or remain your

slave forever."

"You were never a slave, Katherine. And I offered you freedom for allegiance a dozen times—thrice a dozen times!"

"Pish, posh, and fiddle dee. You're fathoms more deceitful than the toad could ever be."

The woman's eyes narrowed. "Enough of your nonsense! You're coming home!"

"Hah. Without that slice of Orb, you've only tricks and lollipops." "Do you say you will fight me then?"

"Go home, Piranda."

Piranda's armor and knee-length boots vanished; she was covered by shaggy, ashen fur. "Your sister misses you." And with that, Piranda was no more. In her place, a Smilodon, a saber-toothed tiger, glowered and began to circle. Resigned to battle, the smaller cat sighed and faked a lunge with her bo. The Smilodon growled, "You are my pet, and I do not wish to harm you. But you are being very naughty."

"Go home, Piranda. The Orb is gone. You'll never get it back."

The Smilodon grumbled, "I'm growing impatient, Katherine." The huge cat readied to pounce.

Katherine charged and swung her bo; it flashed like lightning and snapped in two as it shattered the saber-tooth's fangs. Piranda reappeared, sitting in the dust, one hand covering her bleeding mouth. She garbled a few words, spit some blood, leaped into the air, and became a hovering wasp. The insect was the size of a rowboat; its abdomen wore a sheath of black and yellow; its lethal stinger curled and pulsated. The wasp took a beeline, with Katherine dead in its sights. All six legs struck the cat, knocking her backwards. Her head struck the rim of a rotted stump. Weaponless, woozy, she struggled to rise. The wasp spiraled upward, then attacked from high noon. Katherine's legs were like rubber, and she fell flat on her back. Hovering, stinger aimed at the cat's chest, the wasp threatened to strike.

Still twenty yards away, I threw the shillelagh, missing the wasp by an eyelash. But the distraction gave the cat just enough time to grab a dead branch. As the stinger plunged, the cat blocked the venomous spike. The wasp dropped and fluttered in the dust, grounded with its stinger lodged in a log.

"I found the exact spot," I said as I helped Katherine to her feet. We ran toward the Coverture as the wasp fought to free itself. Halfway to our sanctuary, we glanced back and were horrified at the sight of Piranda's new mutation—a huge, black arachnid whose eight legs moved four times faster than our two. It was on us in no time. The cat had no bo and I had hucked my Irish cudgel into the brush. Piranda knew she had us. Her spidery form rocked back onto its abdomen, her hairy forelegs spanned at least five feet and reached toward the sky. Her whiskery fangs jutted like the tusks of a boar. This spitting image of a giant funnel-web spider dared us to move. The first to flinch would feel its wicked bite.

Katherine whispered, "When I dive for its belly, you make your run." "You won't stand a chance!"

"I'll roll aside and jump on its back—I know what I'm doing!"

Stepping back, I nearly fell over. My bare feet had stumbled across a rusty pipe wrench; it was surrounded by scraps of copper tubing. I picked up the wrench and whispered, "OK, I'm ready."

The cat dove. The spider plunged. I drew back to throw the wrench. The cat rolled away. The spider spewed a viscid gob of web, which glommed onto Katherine's legs. I hurled the tool end over end, striking the center of the eight glossy eyes. As the spider crumbled, Piranda appeared, downed, dazed and bleeding from the brow. I helped the cat pull and scrape the gooey web from her legs, and we ran toward the Miribon. Piranda sat in the dust, head in hands, rocking and moaning. When she looked up, she screamed, "Katherine! Katherine!"

We ran all out, dreading thoughts of the witch's next transmutation. Adventure glanced back. "She's given up. She's returning to her chariot."

"Why doesn't she transform into something?" I asked.

"The Orb's essence is fading. She can't manage another change." Closely heeding the grassy strip along the base of the Miribon, I said, "Hold up! That's it." I pointed with a circular motion.

The cat said, "Are you absolutely certain about the location?" "Yeah, I can still see some of my boot prints. This is the exact spot."

"You do realize there's no guarantee as to where we'll end up," she said.

I nodded.

She nodded and reached out. I held the cat's hand and we delved into the cosmic corridor.

## Chapter 4:
## Piranda of Nidge

Once more on the moor, I was overjoyed to be on familiar ground. The cat and I hurried toward the fountain. We both glanced back to see if Piranda had followed. She had not. Reaching the fountain, the cat said, "You're certain this water is safe?"

"I sure hope so. I'll bet I drank a couple of gallons."

She eyed the engraving on the fountain's base. "Jungbrunnen." She chuckled. "Fountain of Youth." She looked me over from head to toe and then sighed, "That explains a lot." She shook her head knowingly. "You say you're a captain, the pilot of a great airship—a grown man of thirty-four years."

"That's right." I furrowed my brow. "You have a funny look on your face."

"And it isn't any wonder." She raised her padded foot to the bowl of the fountain and began to wash the spider's web from her matted fur. "You, my dear fellow, have consumed enough of this enchanted water to have taken at least twenty years from your true age—you are, indeed, a little boy."

"Not possible."

"Open your eyes—take account of yourself."

I looked down and wiggled the toes of my tiny feet. When I extended my child-like hands, I noticed a scar I'd sustained in a barroom brawl had disappeared from my left forearm. I said, "You're right. I have the body of a small boy. No more than nine or ten. But I have all my memories—all my thoughts, experiences, and knowledge."

The cat winked.

Assessing myself from head to toe, I said, "I'm going to have to grow up all over again."

"Maybe you'll do it right this time," said the cat with a mischievous grin.

"Very funny." I returned the grin, and then pointed. "You've got a clump of web on your tail"

"Ugh, disgusting! Pull it away—please."

Being very careful, I lifted the end of her tail and picked at the sticky web. She piped, "Don't be shy lad, rake it right the way off!"

Milking away the goopy glue, I said, "That witch-lady, Piranda, called you Katherine."

"Yes, Katherine Knutson, that's my given name. But to celebrate my new life, my life as a free woman, and a free cat, I am changing my name. From here on, I shall introduce myself as the Adventure Cat. Adventure, that's who I am, and that's what I'll be."

"Well, my name's John. John William Newman, and I'm a captain in the United States Navy—that's who I am and that's what I'll be." I reached out my hand. "Nice to meet you, Adventure."

"Nice to meet you, John." My blue eyes and her green eyes met. We shook to a lifetime friendship.

"So, who was that horrible woman?"

"To keep the dismal tale brief, she is the High Priestess of Ultrania. Under the pretense of homage and loyalty to the crown, Piranda of Nidge bided her time. She was sorely disgruntled with her lot in life, despite being the second most powerful inhabitant of the North Unterlands. After Queen Danya passed in a fateful birthing ordeal, King Yegor alone maintained the prosperity and peace of Ultrania's Golden Age. But he proved to be too good for his own good. Piranda usurped the throne. He now lives in exile on the Isle of Woe. Piranda now cows all beneath the imperium of a worthless sphere of amber glass. She calls it the Orb of Nidge. In truth, it's the orb of nothing."

"She's a total fake?" I said.

"A second-rate illusionist at best. But she is quite clever. She has always made the best of her ineptitude."

"It's hard to believe she runs the show with no real power, no black magic, no skills in witchcraft."

Adventure nodded. "I agree. It is hard to believe. But she had everyone fooled, including the king. And she did have some unique knowledge, which can be far more dangerous than the sharpest of swords. She knew of a of crystal hidden in the Aurium Mountains on Ultrania's eastern border—the stuff of legends and nonsense to the rest of us."

"And she eventually found this crystal?"

The cat let out a long sigh. "Unfortunately . . . yes. Convinced the mystic Orb of Andes was no myth, she implored King Yegor and Queen Danya to venture stakes in caravans to the mountain caves where boundless treasures reposed deep within the caverns. She claimed her reasons to be academic, and in the sole interest of recovering historic relics and artifacts. But it was really the Orb she was after.

"To my great dismay, I was the knight appointed to lead the fateful expeditions. One cold night, as the servants and soldiers slept, she crept past the guards. A mile into the caves, the light of her lantern fell upon an indigo crystal and her hand clutched a slice of the Andean Orb.

"When I awoke that very night, I found her gone. Immediately, I organized a search. I had warned her of the perils of going out alone." The cat paused for a moment and sighed heavily. "But Piranda did as Piranda pleased. Calling her strong-willed would be as a lion to a flea. When I found her, not knowing she had found the crystal, I admonished her for ignoring our protocols. I questioned her motives and judgement. She then spitefully poked me in the chest with the wedge of Orb and muttered, "Koshka." At that instant, for the all the world to see, I was spell-cast into this halfling form. At that moment, I became the lowly drudge of a so-called omnipotent sorceress."

"Omnipotent?"

"Hardly, but she had us all fooled. Lying, cheating, stealing, intimidating, manipulating, conniving—these are her true powers. And they are quite formidable."

"The weak and the cowardly often rise to power through such tactics. It has happened throughout history. . . And you said the toad man now has the Orb?"

The Adventure Cat rolled her eyes. "Speaking of the weak and cowardly." Her exasperation was building with every thought, with every word. "Yes, Parnelius Wermbom, called Parnie by most, now has one quarter of the coveted Orb. This leaves Piranda, the pretender, with only her wits, a paralyzing stare, a soul-shredding voice, a smattering of black magic, and a few charlatan's parlor tricks

—such as the worthless ball of glass she calls the Orb of Nidge. To their miserable misfortune, the masses have no hint of the truth. They full-heartedly believe in the phony woman and her fake bauble. Fed by Piranda's torches, the orb beams nightly from the high window of her imposing tower. And nightly, the subjugated gather and gaze up in awe as her infiltrating spies draw the hopes, fears, and dreams from their minds. The next day she spoon feeds it all back to them so they'll think their thoughts and beliefs are her own."

"Basically, telling people what they want to hear," I said. Dictators, autocrats, con artists—they've used that trick for thousands of years. So, when all's said and done, when it comes right down to it, who is this phony witch? What's her backstory?" I asked. "Where did she come from? How did she come by flying horses? And with no discernable aerodynamics, how the heck does that chariot stay in the air?"

"Here's what I can tell you: She is called Piranda of Nidge. It means 'Piranda from Nowhere.' She came through the Coverture—so say the Mentorians, our order of intellects and soothsayers—on a chariot drawn by flying horses, which you have seen. I suppose it was in much the same way you arrived in your flying ship."

I sat down, taking a moment to think about what I'd heard. "Hmmm, let's see. Considering everything else I've seen around here, I guess some weird sort of things like that could have happened. But how did she go from chariot jockey to High Priestess? That was quite a promotion."

"According to historical scrolls, she established a stronghold in the mountains, luring her followers with baubles, bits of gold and silver, worthless runes, and promises of hope and glory. She was very patient with her scheming. It took more than a hundred years, but her minions grew stronger and became a threat to the Ultranian Kingdom. In a predicament and against his better judgement, King Quashnik, Yegor's great-great-great grandfather, appeased her with the title and privileges of High Priestess."

I did the math. "Criminy. In that case, Piranda of Nidge has got to be three, maybe four hundred years old."

Adventure said, "She claims to have been born over seven thousand years ago in a land called Mesopotamia." The cat's eyes narrowed, and a slight growl came into her voice. "But she lies, and lies, and lies upon lies—so who knows!"

I nodded sympathetically. "Yeah, saying you're seven thousand years old and were born in ancient Persia would seem to be stretching the truth a little." I sarcastically added, "I suppose she got her witching powers from a genie."

The cat perked up. "Yes, how did you know?!"

I bumped the heel of my palm against my forehead. "It's from an Arabian fairy tale. If you release a genie from a lamp, they give you three magical wishes."

"You're spot on about the genie and the lamp, but a djinn gives you only one wish. And Piranda wished for a flying chariot."

"Even after everything I've seen, I find that scenario really hard to believe."

Adventure raised one eyebrow. "Perhaps we'll cross back through the Coverture one day and the two of you can discuss the issue."

"No, thanks. That's a lady I'd just as soon never lay my eyes on again."

With a huff and a haughty lift of the chin, Adventure said, "I can't say the same about the rotten old shrew. She and I still have business."

"What about this Wermbom character?" I asked. "What's he up to?"

"He's up to no good; I can assure you of that. Parnelius Wermbom was the smarmy, snooty curator of the Ultranian Royal

Museum. I came to know him well because he insisted on being part of every Aurium excavation caravan. That sneaky little rodent knew what Piranda was up to long before any of us."

"So, he wasn't always the toad thing I saw?"

"No, not at all. He was once a man. Not much of a man, but a man just the same. Piranda turned him into a toad after he tried to steal her precious slice of Orb. Testing his loyalty, she deliberately left it unattended, and he foolishly took the bait. With one wave of her hand, Piranda turned him into a warty, toadish wretch. She imprisoned us in her tower to serve at her pleasure for the rest of our lives, always under the threat of being transformed into something frightfully repugnant—a worm, a bug."

"Well, I'm sure glad you found your way out of that situation. And I guess I should warn you about another situation up ahead. I passed through a bunch of steaming geysers on my way north. It was kind of dangerous. A person could easily get scalded to death walking through that area."

"Good to know. We'll find a way around."

"I think following the tree line would be our best bet."

Adventure gave a slight bow. "Then feel welcome to lead the way, Captain Newman."

The woods stood a quarter mile to the west. Walking the moors and grasslands barefoot was tolerable, but I knew I would eventually meet up with rougher terrain. Adventure too favored a stop in the woods so she could fashion a new bo staff. At the edge of the forest, she used a penknife to carve out some thick slices of pine bark while I dug for spruce roots. She then turned to the task of crafting a new fighting bo. She was very finicky, rejecting limb after limb for the slightest imperfection. As she moved deeper into the woods, I asked, "Aren't you at all concerned about those creatures in the woods. I'm almost certain they've been following us?"

"Twarvian trolls," she said. "Yes, they've been following. But they're smaller than you are, perhaps a little stouter, but really quite small— and very hairy. Have no fear. If one draws near, I'll tweak his nose and take a willow switch to his backside."

"How many do you think there are?"

"On the north side, they usually scout about in small bands."
"So, they're not dangerous?

"Not to me. But they'd happily drop you in a pit and bake you like a little gundy."

"Gundy?"

"A tiny wild pig. Their favorite."

My stress level kicked up a notch as I peered through the branches. The shadows started playing tricks, so I moved into the open to finish tying my pine moccasins. Adventure voiced a long, frustrated sigh and joined me in the clearing. She eyed my new shoes.

"Not bad," she said. "Not bad at all. They'll take you a mile or two."

"Did you give up on the bo staff?"

"Nothing to bother about. Besides, I have these." She curled her fingers, extending five razor-sharp claws, then displayed a sly, satisfied grin.

"Those ought to do the job."

"Pity you lost that fancy walking stick of yours."

"A shillelagh. It was authentic. In beautiful condition. . .it was just lying there in the grass. And that pipe wrench— tripping over that thing was unbelievable!"

"You can find all sorts of things in the unterlands—probably on either side of the Coverture. Sometimes they simply seem to fall out of the sky."

I glanced up at the pale blue ceiling. "Do you think that witch lady will try to find a way to follow us?"

"She won't try crossing the Coverture, not without the Orb. She knows the danger. And she's also learned not to underestimate me. That was Piranda's big mistake. She turned me into a lower form of creature, but she left me with a cat's strengths—stealth, quickness, night vision, sharp teeth and claws, and a tail for precise balance. I bided my time. It took more than a year, but finally I pounced and divested the rotten old thing of her ill-gotten prize. And after his amphibious conversion, all Parnie Wermbom could do was jump and swim in the manner of a toad. But after latching on to the crystal, that changed considerably. The sly devil snatched it when I looked in on Piranda after locking her in the tower's keep.

"Pondering my next move, my mind was in a jumble, and I'd casually set the crystal on a table. The toad grabbed it and ran off. Ordinarily, I'd have caught him in a wink, but on his first leap he sailed high into the air and came down some fifty yards away. On his second jump he sailed even farther. He'd reached the mountains before I'd gone a mile. Apparently, that's when he hitched a ride with you. Fortunately, the slice of Orb he held took you both safely through the Coverture."

"I didn't see any sign of an Orb when he was clinging to my windshield. You say it's a slice?

"Yes, it looks like a wedge of orange, but it has a very dark violet color. The stories and legends sometimes refer to it as the

Indigo Orb."

I nodded and we walked in silence for a while. Taking the woodland route increased our walk a mile or two, but at least we avoided the geyser garden. Seeing the ziggurat up close piqued Adventure's curiosity. She eyed the structure all the way up the hill and said, "Such a peculiar pyramid. So long, so many stairs, and no peak at all."

"Actually, it's not really a pyramid—it's a ziggurat. Sumerian, I think."

"I am not very familiar with the architecture or the people. But it is a handsome structure."

"I fully agree." I pointed southwest, toward a patch of forest. "That's the spot where I left the woods. The seashore is about two miles beyond."

"Heading for the shore without a ship would be a useless trek. I'll need a sound vessel to catch the toad."

"You said his destination is an island?"

"The Island of the Valgars. Parnie's after another slice of the Orb. There are four in all. I'm surprised he has the courage. He must believe the Orb slice he already has will protect him."

"And if he finds all four?"

"He will have powers beyond those of any ruler, witch, sorcerer, or god. Powers beyond the imagination. And he will use them in the cruelest of ways. He's been ridiculed and humiliated all of his life because of his peculiar appearance and even more peculiar attitude and mannerisms. He's become hateful, vengeful, vindictive, spiteful toward all—toward life itself."

"And he means to get even."

"Oh, much more than to get even, I assure you. Some of the ideas that spin around in his head—absolute madness."

At the base of the ziggurat, we stopped to catch our breath before climbing the winding stairway. "You said Parnie the toad was headed to the Island of the Valgars. What are Valgars?"

"Bird people—at least twice my size," said Adventure. "Before the Coverture descended on the land, Valgars would wing their way to our shores for food, and by that, I mean people. The Valgars gobbled up the people of Ultrania by the dozens. The greatest armies could not drive them off. They stayed till they had their fill, then flew, fat and happy, back to their island home."

"You saw them?"

"No. These things occurred hundreds of years ago. That's the one good thing about the Coverture; it took form well north of the island —no more Valgars. I've only seen pictures in books and paintings on walls. With their talons they could tear a tiger to tatters, with their beaks they could crush great stones."

"Formidable," I said. "How does Parnie Wermbom plan on taking an Orb slice from people like that?"

"By learning to use his slice. That's the only sense I can make of it. He believes the Valgars to be dumb creatures. He believes he can master the power of the Orb and lay them all to waste. But I suspect if anyone gets laid to waste, it will probably be Parnie Wermbom."

At the top of the ziggurat, we could see miles and miles of treetops, the canopy of a vast forest, a spacious intermingling of evergreen and deciduous giants. Quickly, the cat walked toward the structure's edge. She stretched her neck and pulled at her whiskers. She pointed. "There. Look there. Coming out of the west, following the tree line."

"Yes, I see it. A road. It's got to be."

"And quite wide, I should think, if we can see it from this far off. It looks well-kept too."

With unbridled enthusiasm, I said, "Infrastructure maintenance—a sure sign of civilization. Let's go!"

Adventure paused and turned to me. I saw her swallow a lump in her throat. She placed a hand on my shoulder and blinked away a tear. "Had I my druthers, we'd journey as one. But I can move much faster on my own, and I must find the toad before he obtains the Valgars' slice of the Orb. So, it is here and now, Captain John William Newman, that I must bid you adieu."

I nodded acceptance and sadness filled my heart. "I could never keep up, but I can follow your tracks," I said. "You're as fine a person as I've ever known. If there's a way I can help, I'll offer my hand. Any threat you face, I'll have your back."

"I know you will, young Captain." She tousled my hair, patted my shoulder, and bounded down the stairs. The cat reached the bottom of the hill in no time. I watched her race over the fields like a feline F-16. And I believed that somehow, somewhere, we'd meet again.

# Chapter 5:
## Twarvian Trolls

Before moving on, I had to consider the possibility that the Indigo Orb might truly exist. If an enigma such as the Coverture could swallow me and my F-16, an entity powerful enough to end all existence should be lent at least a little credence. The most exacting sciences of physics and mathematics have been challenged by baffling concepts such as string theory in the study of time, space, matter, and energy. Enough substance has been gleaned from the research to challenge long-held perceptions of the universe. Many myths and legends have been found to have a basis in fact. Just as the opening of Pandora's box released the curses of evil and destruction in the world of mythology, could the Indigo Orb do something of the opposite and draw the Earth, the galaxies, the universe back within itself in the world of physical laws? According to the Adventure Cat, such were the ramblings of the mad toad Parnelius Wermbom. By procuring the entire Orb, he believed he could hold all of existence in the palm of his mottled green hand.

I thought over what I knew of the Orb's metaphysics. A portion of the crystal gave a witch the power to transform matter, gave a toad man the ability to jump hundreds of feet in the air, and facilitated transport of a person through a distortion in time and space. If a courageous knight, like the Adventure Cat, feared that the Orb may be a doomsday device and was willing to risk her life to retrieve and contain it, then I as a soldier was under the same obligation. At that very moment, I decided to postpone my journey home and join the cat's quest. On my honor, I pledged to stand and fight by her side until all Orb-related matters were resolved.

Which side of sanity I stood on was of no consequence. I was in a different world where different rules applied. Reality had become fantasy, and fantasy was now reality. I figured I could wander around in a Dali painting just as well as the next guy. Tennessee frontiersman Davy Crockett once said, "Be always sure you're right, then go ahead." At this point, I believed I was right.

Determined not to take a tumble in my ungainly bark sandals, I stayed close to the wall as I descended the stairs of the zig-gurat. Adventure was no longer in sight, but I knew where she was headed. Moving at a respectable rate considering my foot-wear, I followed the path of the cat as closely as possible. A bit of a breeze picked up, blowing dirt and debris over her tracks, but her destination was the main road, which I felt would be easy enough to find.

When I reached the road, I found it to be smooth and soft on the surface but solid underneath; it reminded me of a well-groomed baseball infield. To take full advantage of this fortuitous avenue, I slipped off my sandals and sprinted all-out until I came to a fork; both directions led into the forest. There were two signs: Morningtown 12 mi. and Kearn Harbor 6 mi. The cat had said she needed a ship, so I considered the harbor route. But I presumed she also needed authorization to justly appropriate a vessel, and she needed the aid of a good crew. Assuming Adventure had employed similar reasoning, I took the path to Morningtown.

A dozen yards into the woods, her footprints reappeared. I picked up my pace; if I could maintain it, I figured I'd reach the outskirts of Morningtown in seven, maybe eight hours— hopefully before dark. Little did I know, this part of the forest was infested with Twarvian trolls. This was their heartland.

***

As I tended to my own considerations, I was unaware of the two fellows walking the trail from Kearn Harbor, on a mission to gather medicinal mushrooms and fill flasks of water from the Jungbrunnen. Eventually, I would learn they were residents of Morningtown. And though I would consider them peculiar at first, in this world within a world, they were ordinary people, no different than you, me, or the Adventure Cat. To this point, their mission had been pleasant and routine, but that would soon change.

***

Dressed in woolen tunics, trousers, and deerskin boots, Golly Gorki and Brutus Petronski lollygagged down Horse Muck Road, a shortcut from Morningtown to Kearn Harbor. Golly was a tall, portly, dog- faced man, and Brutus was a long-nosed, pointy-eared elf. Golly's hair was long and shaggy; Brutus's hair was pixyish. Golly had the red-nosed complexion of a fellow who enjoyed his ale. Brutus's hands and face bore a slight seafoam tint. The pack on Golly's back held two large gourds filled with water from the Jungbrunnen. Over Brutus's shoulders hung two bags, each half-filled with sominous mushrooms. Each man had a Roman broadsword on his hip.

"We'll have to go through Bog Hollow for more mushrooms," said Brutus.

"Nay, we've enough for this trip."

"The burgomaster needs four bags to the brim."

"We'll not go to the Hollow, elf. There'll be trolls about." "They won't be near the bog—you know they hate the bugs."

"Eee! Gadflies!" Golly shuddered. "Even I 'ate the ruddy bog and bugs!"

"But the hollow's full of mushrooms," insisted Brutus. "It's the only way. We can have the bags filled in a piff and a puff."

"We'll not. We'll end up in a bloody bash." "Maybe, maybe not."

"No maybe! We'll 'ave to do a load of thumpin' to get out o' there with our skins."

Brutus rolled his eyes. "Such a bluster. You're turning into a right cow, Golly. A right old cow."

"Right then—I've said me piece. It's to the bog! God 'elp them bloody boogers! And God 'elp us!"

"Jolly good. Jolly, jolly good."

***

From both sides of the road, hidden eyes followed my every step. But I had a decent weapon. I'd found a length of stick: smooth and straight, dry and old, but not brittle. Hearty oak.

Although that incredibly delicious water had turned me into a little boy, I still had my hand-to-hand combat skills. If Twarvian trolls were as small as I'd been told, I felt confident I could hold my own against one or two . . . maybe three. My main concern: there were probably a whole lot of them out there, and they would almost certainly be armed. Earlier, Adventure had described their main weapon as a knobby-ended cudgel with spiked pegs lodged in the brunt. She said she'd never had to fight Twarvian trolls because they were shy and fearful by nature; at least, that had been her experience. She had, however, fought Farthingale trolls, who were much larger beings. She'd described them as having thick brow ridges, angled cheekbones, huge, wide noses, teeth too big for their mouths, and short, brick-outhouse bodies. Neanderthals, to my mind; fortunately, they lived well to the east in the thorny Farthingale Forest.

When I thought back to the beach and woodlands and my first encounter with the Twarvians, these locals were behaving in much the same manner: following almost silently, keeping out of sight, showing no sign of aggression. But back then, there were only a few; now, I sensed there were perhaps fifty, probably more.

The woods were dark, dense, and spread out for many miles. The forest was my frying pan, and the curious eyes of the little wood trolls were coals in the fire. After leaving the beach, I'd had the stature of an adult, very likely a deterrent. But now I was a little kid. Though I was about their size, I had a child's bones, ligaments, muscles, and tendons. The adult trolls would likely have a great deal of strength for their size. I was not going to underestimate them in any way.

Walking tall, shoulders back, chin level, stick at the ready, I ostentatiously scanned the trees. Such a showy display would have been laughable in any other setting. But these fellows were somewhat dim-witted—at least that was the view of the Adventure Cat, who I surmised was well on her way to Morningtown; in fact, considering her fleetness of foot, she was probably already there.

The nervous caw of a raven broke the silence. The bird landed on the gnarled branch of a dead tree, twitched its wing, tipped its head, cawed again, and flitted away. Always a little superstitious, I took it as an omen or warning. Such thinking probably had something to do with Poe's poem.

I scanned the trees and tapped my stick against the ground. I flashed glances in random directions, fixing a gaze from time to time. When I came to the next bend, I was wary and tense, but the way was clear. I relaxed, but just a hair. Water. I could hear it flowing. A lot of water, probably a river. Ahead were weeping willow trees, their droopy branches trailing to the ground. Beyond the somber trees was a stone bridge, ancient-looking and covered with moss.

# Chapter 6:
## Mossy Bridge

The dark waters of the Stork River flowed swift beneath an ancient stone bridge. The structure was covered with moss, lichens, and toadstools that exuded a foul, musty smell. Beyond the bridge were more willow trees, weary under the burden of their weeping limbs. With oak stick at the ready, I tested the integrity of the walkway with a few tentative steps; it seemed a solid base, spanning perhaps forty feet and rising on each side to the height of my chin. I had no doubt this construct had faithfully served the populace for well over a hundred years.

Just as I thought I might venture unmolested for the rest of my trip, two stumpy, bearded, grubby little men appeared at the end of the bridge—Twarvian trolls. Clad in tanned loincloths and vests of fur, one held a black-tipped, ember-hardened spear, the other had a knobby wooden club. The puny, hog-nosed scrubs grinned with rotten teeth. Their approach was cautious yet menacing. To my surprise, they grumbled a few discernible words.

"You get here," said the spearman. Was he asking me to come forward or where I had come from?

"Stick, you drop! No fight," said the other.

There was no way I was going to drop my stick. They may have had the strength, but I had the skill. These men were clearly not offering friendship, so I said, "Back off!"

They mumbled to each other, then chanted, "Gundy, gundy, gundy!" They began hopping from one leg to the other. One said, "Me kill." The other said, "Me cook."

With the end of my stick, I pointed at each. "You kill? You cook?" They gawked. "Me bash your brains out!" I was cheek-clenching scared, but I couldn't stifle my laugh.

They shook their weapons. "Gundy, gundy, gundy!"

PO'd as PO'd could be, I yelled, "Gundy, gundy, double-gundy!" I tried to scare them off with theatrics: a front kick, side kick, and awkward spinning back kick. I whirled my stick like a majorette's baton. None of it worked. They charged, I charged. I jabbed the first troll right in the forehead and knocked him flat. I smashed the other in the jaw, sending him into the side of the bridge; he dropped to one knee. My way was clear, but just for a second. Another troll appeared at the end of the bridge. He had a clamshell necklace, was bare chested, and had animal-claw mitts; he wore face paint, and his hair was pine-tarred to a sharp point. He looked sort of like a punk rock musician, but instead of a guitar, he held a sea-shell axe. Another troll rushed in beside him. Then another.

By now, the first two had struggled to their feet. When I turned to run, at least a dozen trolls blocked my retreat. Holding my stick parallel to the ground, I turned and knocked the first two trolls backward, then charged the punk rocker. I swept away his hatchet, he slashed out with his claws, I dropped and leg-rolled him. As I popped up, he grabbed my leg, digging his filthy, sharp fingernails deep into my skin. A heavy blow struck the back of my neck. I staggered, stumbled, fell and was out cold.

When I came to, my hands and feet were bound, and I dangled from a roasting spit like a slaughtered hog. The two trolls carrying me had a bounce to their step as they sang, "Gundy, gundy, gundy." Groups of others, fore and aft, sang too. Some with high voices, some with low. It sounded like a discordant, cultish choir. Now the two that bore me chimed with an alternating chorus: "Me kill. Me cook. Me kill. Me cook." They sang and laughed, laughed and sang, all the way to their camp, where they promptly dropped me beside a roaring hearth.

Never in my thirteen years of military service had I been a captive. Under normal circumstances, I would have been questioned, and in accordance with the Geneva Convention, I would have given my name, rank, and serial number, as well as my date of birth (a little detail usually left out in the movies). In addition, my captors would have had to treat me in a humane manner and afford me all considerations given to a prisoner of my rank. Unfortunately, I was captured by subterranean trolls who made it clear all they cared about was "kill, cook, eat." At one point, a particularly brutish fellow bent down, and nose-to-nose, blurted with unbridled fervor, "Eat. Eat. Eeeeeat!" His sulphury breath could have stripped paint from a wall, and I was able to detect the alcohol fumes of some pungent, blackberry hooch.

As the curtain of night descended, the merriment had progressed to its second stage—food procurement and preparation. At the hearth, a troll scooped orange embers into a huge clamshell. In the distance, the cooks appeared to be digging a deep pit. Back home, we used to bake potatoes under the ground; we dug a hole about a foot deep, dropped in some coals from the barbecue, covered them with about an inch of soil, added les pommes de terre, then filled in the hole. Not in my most insane imaginings would I have envisioned myself as one of the potatoes. Too bad they didn't have some aluminum foil; it would have been over with a lot faster.

***

Climbing up through the reeds of Bog Hollow, Golly and Brutus paused to hide their gourds of water and burlap bags of mushrooms. Keeping to the woods, broadswords drawn, they made their way to Mossy Bridge. Crouching low as they crept over the stones, they could see the silhouettes of trolls off in the distance, dancing before their ritualistic fires. Waving their spears and cudgels, the trolls chanted, "Gundy, gundy, gundy!" while hopping up and down and side to side.

From behind a mighty pine, Golly whispered, "What the 'ell does gundy mean?"

"Something along the lines of hooray is my bet," replied Brutus.

"Oi! Sayin' 'hooray' about chewing meat from the bones of a wee lad twists me stomach in knots."

"Mine as well."

"A right 'appy lot they are. How many would you say?"

After a moment's reckoning, Brutus said, "A score and a dozen, if one."

"About right."

"It's an hour yet till full dark. We won't be able to sneak in."
"Nay, we'll 'ave to make a run."

Brutus looked at the sky. "The sprites seem weary."

Golly surveyed the heavens as well. "All but to the east. Common enough. We'll have a dark one."

"Finally, a little luck."

"We'll let 'em get their fill o' swill and wait till they drag the lad to the oven."

"Just a bit of a lad, but he gave them a good thumping with that stick."

"Aye, that he did."

"We'll need cover." Brutus eyed the foreground and pointed. "That clump, the ivy and brambles."

Golly assessed. "Should do."

"A hoot, a holler, and a wave of swords should drive them to the trees."

"Aye, in this dark, they won't know our numbers—not right off." "If the lad's game, we'll hold them off at the bridge."

"Aye, if we 'eave a few o' them yawbaws into the Stork, they'll soon think twice."

***

Rolling logs and boulders closer to the fires held most of the trolls on the shy side of slumber. Tipping back cannikins of blackberry grog and belting out songs to the night sky was making them all good and hungry. With a heft and a grunt, two of the brutes hoisted the spit pole to which I was bound onto their shoulders and carried me toward their underground oven. Smoke reaching up from the smoldering pit grabbed me by the throat. My lungs seized as they dropped me, feet first, into the hole and raised the pole to its full height. Hurriedly, they filled the pit with dirt and rocks until I was buried up to my neck. They packed the dirt using sticks and their wide, flat feet.

The heat soon became unbearable. I could not see, I could not breathe, my flesh felt afire, and my head was about to explode. "Gundy, gundy, gundy!" they chanted, over and over and over. But then the chanting stopped. Barely conscious, I could hear yelling, shouting, whooping, hollering, a squeal here, and a scream there. Next came a trampling sound as a stampede of trolls passed on either side. Before passing out, I heard: "They won't be fooled for long. You dig and I'll stand guard."

A jostling and jolting brought me back to consciousness. I found myself in the embrace of two powerful arms, being carried like a baby. The pace began to slow, and I was gently placed on my feet. "Can you stand, lad?" said a soothing voice. When I looked up, the face of an enormous dog man looked down. "Can you stand?"

"Yeah, I can stand," I said. "Thanks. Thank you." The dog man let me go.

A strange little man handed me a stick. "Here, take this spear."

Through my dry throat I rasped, "Yeah, OK, I know how to use it." "We know," said the two.

The three of us stood at the threshold of Mossy Bridge and watched the flames of the trolls' hearths wane. The trolls themselves were gone. The two strangers looked me over, as I did them. The little one had a long nose and pointy ears, a classic storybook elf. And as for the dog man, the first words that came to my mind were big oaf, but I certainly did not voice them.

"I'm Golly," said the dog man. "This is Brutus, me best mate." The elf winked.

Brain on autopilot, I said, "I'm Captain John William Newman, United States Navy."

"Eh?" said the dog man.

The elf chipped in. "No time to be fibbing to us, lad. Surely you can see we're in a bind."

I sighed. "Yes, I'm sorry. I know how it looks. Once we're in the clear, I'll try to explain."

"Aye," said the dog man. "I'll be all ears."

"As will I," said the elf. "And no more fibbing—that's final!" "No more fibbin'," I said.

With a quick nod, Golly told us to step backward onto the bridge. "Watch the back, Brutus. And lad, keep your eyes peeled all the way 'round."

Brutus said, "I wonder what they're up to?"

"Come on," said Golly. "Let's get across. We'll sum things up 'cross the river."

When we reached the other side of the bridge, I could not contain myself. "Just you two?" I glanced around. "You two alone drove them off? There must have been at least fifty of those little guys."

"We thought forty," said Brutus.

"But maybe fifty," Golly said, nearly boasting. "We tricked the little wags," said Brutus. "They knew not our force," said Golly.

Brutus raised his eyebrows. "Tippling away with the fairies, they were."

Golly raised his sword. "And they've long feared the steel."

I paid a nod of respect to the sword and said, "Well, they know our numbers now—a force of three—and only two have the steel."

"Aye, granted," said Golly. "Let's stand back, take a good look."

There in the dark of night, a dog man, an elf, and a little boy stared across the fields, peered into the trees, and gazed along the riverbanks. Out there, in the pitch-black forest, lurked a tribe of little men—hostile, hungry little men. A hundred, two hundred, we did not know. And so, weapons in hand, we turned and walked the leaf-laden road to Morningtown—prepared for the worst, hoping for the best.

"Dead quiet," said Golly. "Is that good?" I asked. "It's bad," said Brutus.

Golly cleared his throat. "Aye, lad. It's bad."

# Chapter 7:
## At Rope's End

So scant was the light filtering through the trees that I couldn't see more than a few feet ahead, but Golly and Brutus were ambling along just fine. "If it gets any darker, we'll all be blind," I said.

"Not me," said Brutus. "Elves see quite well in the dark—though I haven't a clue as to why."

Golly said, "I could smell my way through the woods even if I was blind. It's the dog in me, I suppose."

In a comforting tone, Brutus said, "Just follow us, little lad. Stay close."

I said, "Gentlemen, please realize I am not really a little boy. I'm an adult, just like yourselves. And I'm a combat-tested military man. You needn't coddle me—"

Golly cut in. "Eh, eh, eh. No fibbin'—that was the bargain." Brutus added, "Keep the trust, lad. Keep the trust."

"You can trust me. Guaranteed! Believe me, I don't want to look this way. It was the water, from a fountain, just north of here."

A burst of laughter. Quickly suppressing the levity, my companions stopped short. We all scanned the darkness; all was still. Golly looked me over and said, "Gumpfries and gadflies, Captain, you surely did have your fill."

"I did. It was so delicious. I'd become so dehydrated that I just kept guzzling away."

Brutus said, "A few more swallows and—" "You'd 'ave been a pile o' dust," said Golly.

"Yeah, I know, I'm pretty lucky . . . but I want you guys to realize, I still have my mind—all of my thoughts, my memories, my knowledge. That's all still there."

"Good to know," said Golly. "We'll treat you as the man you be." "And a fine figure of a man as well," Brutus said, followed by a titter.

As we entered a glade, I looked up at the unfamiliar stars. "Too bad there's no moon tonight."

"Moon?" said Golly.

Brutus said, "Yes, Golly. Remember your studies. The world above has a sun and moon. And the ball we all live on flies around in a never-ending emptiness."

"Oh, yes, yes, I remember the lessons. Some believe it—not

me. Not sayin' I know the truth of it all, but I do know I'm not flyin' 'round the heavens on some great blue ball."

I had no intention of arguing with a six-and-a-half-foot-tall dog man. "You mean those lights up above—they're not stars?"

"We call them sprites," said Brutus. "Tiny creatures that can grind light right out of thin air. Pretty interesting what they can do."

"Amazin'," said Golly.

"Photoluminescence," I said. "Fireflies use it to attract mates."

Brutus explained, "Here in the unterlands, they light up the sky. In the day, most are awake, and the sky gets quite bright. But like all things, they too need to sleep, and that's when the nightlighters raise their heads."

"It seems like they were brighter a couple of days ago," I said. "Winter draws nigh," said Golly. "That's the way of it."

"Aye," said Brutus.

Golly tapped me on the shoulder. "There's a good-size log yon. Let's 'ave a bit of a sit."

Plopped down in the woods, under the sprites, in the cool of a night breeze sounds idyllic, and it would have been had I not known we were deep in the heart of troll country. Neither Brutus nor Golly were certain why the trolls were allowing us to pass without at least some minor impositions. They told me that one reason may have been an informal, unspoken truce that had spontaneously materialized some time ago for reasons of practicality. Morningtowners had business to attend to, and so did the trolls; over time, both sides realized avoiding each other had led to an efficacious productivity. This was also the primary reason the roads were in such good condition. The trolls, imitative by nature, maintained the road to Morningtown, and the townspeople kept up the roads to the harbor. The events surrounding my capture and near execution (by being baked) had provoked the first pugnacious tiff in years.

"No activity out there at all," I said. "It's looking like we may be in the clear."

Golly sighed. "Best not lower the guard just yet. Seems them imps were right set on making a meal of ya, lad."

Brutus said, "It's us they should be raving at, Golly. We've ruined a grand feast—at least in their eyes."

"None of this is your fault, guys," I said. "They probably don't want to fight any more than we do." Cracking my knuckles and flexing my neck, I added, "But I'd feel way, way better if I still had my side arm."

Golly and Brutus gave me a curious look. Golly said, "Oi then, you 'ad three arms?"

Brutus looked me over. "Where was it? On the left or the right?" "How'd you lose it?" said Golly.

I finally realized their meaning. And they weren't joking. "I did not have three arms—just these two." I held both palms up. "A side arm is a weapon. A gun. It shoots small pieces of metal."

"A blunderbuss!" said Golly. "I love me a blunderbuss."

"Not for me," said Brutus. "They're far more trouble than they're worth. One shot and you're done. A dozen trolls would be bashing your head."

"My gun was a little fancier—a Beretta—fifteen shots."

Golly cleared his throat. "Too bad you lost it, mate. It might have saved us all a lot of bother."

"Where's it gone?" said Brutus.

"It was stolen. Just after I left the water, I pulled off my heavy gear and left it in a pile. I only looked away for a few seconds."

"So, you were quite near to the water?" asked Brutus.

"Yeah, I had just walked onto the beach. I was maybe fifteen feet from the water. There were drag marks."

Golly and Brutus exchanged glances. Golly nodded to Brutus. "Mermaid?"

Brutus confirmed, "Mermaid." "Mermaid?" I said.

"They'll steal anything, given half a chance," said Brutus. Golly added, "And proper sneaky they are."

"Mermaids. You mean beautiful women who have tails like fish?"

"To my mind," said Golly, "they have fish tails right enough, but I'd 'ardly call them beauties."

I glanced at Brutus, who shuddered. "Hideous, wretched-looking things they are!"

"What about mermen?"

Golly said, "Ain't none—far as I know." "Never heard of such," said Brutus. "So how do they reproduce?"

"What's that you say?" said Golly.

Curiosity piqued, I said, "How does there get to be more mermaids? Who are the fathers of the children?"

Golly recoiled. "Don't look at me. Oi!"

Brutus shuddered again. "Nor I, Captain! Please—let's not speak of it again."

The expressions of my companions changed from revulsion to concern. Golly raised his nose and sniffed. "Last of the sap's flowed. It's a bit strong today. But there be trolls—and not far off."

"Many?" said Brutus.

"An 'andful close. Umpteen further off." "Draw swords then, eh?"

"Stay your hand for now, elf. No worries just yet."

"If we maintain a steady pace. How long will it take to reach Moringtown?" I asked.

"About five hours in the dark," said Brutus. "Four if it was daylight."

Golly stood and scanned the area. He turned left and right sniffing the air. "There's still trolls about," said Golly. "Best we be on our way.

. . keep a sharp eye out."

With each step, my bare feet were sinking a little deeper into the turf. "The ground's getting kind of spongy," I said.

"We're near the bog. That's the way of it," said Brutus.

"And the leaves," I said. "These are mostly evergreens, but the leaf layer—it must be a foot thick."

Golly said, "Lots of brush through here. It's like a great hall, the leaves pile up."

Looking ahead, Brutus pointed and said, "There's the spot. Shall we take up the load?"

"Nay," said Golly. "Let's get the lad to the inn."

"The sominous are sure to spoil now that we've picked them."

"We'll soon return. I'll ask Arkle to ride us out to the junction." Golly tapped his belly. "And I could do with a little extra walkin'." He sniffed again. In a low tone, he said, "Slow and easy, Brutus. Draw your blade."

Suddenly, the ground beneath us moved and leaves flew all around. We fell onto one another, suspended in a net a few feet off the ground. Trolls rushed from the trees with long vines and coils of braided twine; they lowered us and quickly joined our net to a second net. We were tightly tangled, barely able to twitch our fingers. Conch shell horns blew hollow and loud. The trolls reprised their earlier chant: "Gundy, gundy, gundy!" They dragged us through the leaves, poked us with spears and sticks, and doused us with a foul-smelling liquid. When we protested, they roared with laughter and hit us with clubs; understandably, we slipped into silence. Our tormentors continued these antics all the way back to Mossy Bridge.

Using the sharp edges of oyster shells, they sliced at the netting just enough to pull the broadswords from the belts of Brutus and Golly. They took turns sinking the blades into tree trunks and fallen logs. "Chop, chop, me can chop," each troll would say. At first, they were cooperative with each other, but before long they started to argue. It seemed the swords were highly prized. In the end, a troll with a berry-stained face and a shark-tooth necklace demanded possession of the weapons. He must have been their chief because there was no argument—that was the end of that.

Carefully, they cut away the netting around our hands and feet, binding them tightly before pulling us free. Golly's great strength proved formidable. When they freed his right arm, he struck out, sending two, three, four trolls sprawling. A heavy club struck the back of his head. The dog man lay still.

"Are you all right, Golly?" Brutus called, and then took his own beating. He too lay still.

Skull-shaped stones lined the top of the bridge, each having its own ghoulish visage. Long vines were looped over three of these ornaments, and the ends of the vines were tied around our ankles. Coming to, Golly and Brutus moaned and mumbled. At least they were alive, but I suspected our final doom was only minutes away. We were all bound tightly and completely helpless. Six trolls lifted Golly and lowered him, head-first, into the river. Brutus was next. Still groggy from the blows, they would soon awaken to the horror of their fate. As the trolls lowered me to the river, I saw the vines of the others being pulled by the current, but the bindings held fast. I could hear the trolls chanting as I went under. There would be no escape.

# Chapter 8:
## Down River

About ten minutes before submersion, when it was clear to me what the trolls intended, I had started oxygenating my blood. Breath control—taking in slow, deep breaths, holding a few seconds, then slowly releasing the air—was part of my military training. Three and a half minutes was the longest I'd ever gone without air.

The water was relatively warm, which made it easier to relax. Shaking my right wrist, tugging a little, twisting a little, I was able to stretch the binding fibers. With one last twist and pull, my hands were free. After a few bends and flexes, I was able to jackknife tight enough to reach my feet. But the twine held fast; it had furrowed my flesh. No matter how much I twisted and tugged, no matter how deep I dug with my fingers, I was unable to loosen the knots.

The river was inky, and I couldn't see either Golly or Brutus. Two minutes probably more had passed. Though I was growing faint, I was certain something had touched my feet: debris floating by, plants growing up from the bottom, the tail of a fish? Then something grabbed my ankle. I felt a rhythmic sensation and the pain and pressure around my ankles eased. The twine was coming loose. I kicked twice and my feet were free. My arms scooped back water like mighty wings. My head burst up through the surface and I gasped for breath. Back floating, I drifted with the current, conserving energy and taking in the precious air.

There was a splashing ahead. And a voice. "Help! Help me, Golly!" All I could see were shapes and shadows along the bank, but I was sure it was Brutus. All I could do was swim toward the sound, which was growing faint. "Golly! Golly, I'm going under."

"Brutus?!" I shouted.

"Captain?" called the fading voice. "Captain?'

Spritelight reflecting off the river revealed the faint shape of a bobbing head. Swimming all out, I finally reached Brutus. But he was no longer moving. His body was limp. Slipping beneath the current, I wrapped him in a cross-chest carry as we flowed into a stretch of rapids. There was nothing to do but ride them out. With my hip under him, I took most of the pounding. He still wasn't moving, but I could feel the slight rise and fall of his diaphragm. As the water calmed, I side-kicked toward the bank.

The sky had brightened just enough for me to see the outline of a big man, standing next to a huge tree. No mistaking that gent—it was Golly. Then I spotted someone moving toward the river's edge. It was my friend Katherine, the Adventure

Cat. She stepped into the water and helped us to shore. Brutus coughed, spit up water, and fought for breath. Golly cradled Brutus in his arms and placed him beneath the maple tree. Adventure and I followed. As I leaned back against the tree, the cat struck flint sparks onto a nest of grass. Soon a fire blazed. I rested my eyes for a moment and then drifted off to sleep.

When I awoke, it was morning. Golly and Brutus were eating berries, and the cat was roasting a fish over the flames.

"Where are we?" I said.

"Down river, not far from the harbor," said Adventure. "Any trolls around?"

"Not to worry, Captain," said Golly. "We'll not see trolls 'round here."

"There'll be a cart comin' soon," said Brutus. "They'll give us a ride to town."

"At the bridge . . . how'd we get free?" I asked.

Adventure set her breakfast on a rock and held out her pen-knife. "A gift from my father. Seventh birthday. It's saved my skin more than once. And last night, it saved yours."

"I remember. You used it to skin bark off a tree." "Indeed, I did."

"So, Cat, your knife'll write down words?" Golly asked.

"Hah, no, not at all," said the cat. "In days of old when people wrote with quill pens, they'd have to sharpen them from time to time before dipping into the ink."

"Aye," said Brutus. "And they used their penknives." "That's the long and short of it," said Adventure. "Well, I just learned something," I said.

The cat went back to finishing her breakfast.

I asked her, "Are you both a knight and a frogman?"

The other three looked puzzled. Adventure posed, "Frogman? Whatever do you mean?"

"The work you did underwater. The way you set us free. That's the sort of thing Navy frogmen do." The three looked at each other and shrugged. I added, "One of my best friends was a frogman." "What witch did it, then?" asked Brutus.

"Witch?"

"Yeah," said Golly. "What witch turned your mate into a frog-man?"

I rolled my eyes. "I see . . . sometimes I forget where I am." I stood and stretched. "Where I come from, some sailors train to perform special operations underwater: find things, fix things, rescue people. They're called frogmen."

Adventure laughed. "So, he's just a normal man, then, not part frog. It's just a name—that's quite funny!"

Golly and Brutus still didn't seem to understand.

Adventure clawed away a piece of her breakfast and offered me a bite. I gobbled it. She shared the rest.

"Why did you come back? How did you know we'd been captured?" I asked.

"Because I know the ways of trolls—the Twarvians as well as the Farthingales. As I neared Morningtown, I began to think about your chances. I shouldn't have left you but stopping the toad has become an obsession for me. If he finds the second piece of Orb and learns to use it, the power in his hands could be almost limitless. What he could not control, he would destroy."

Most humbly, Golly said, "Beholden we are to you, Cat." He put his hands on his hips and tipped his head. "But 'ow did you know we were under that river?"

"The conch horns," said Adventure. "The Twarvians of the north do much the same. They pour oil on their captives to keep the skin from shriveling. They break their arms and legs and stake them down in the rapids to tenderize the flesh. I was fairly certain they'd soften you up in the current."

Brutus said, "Why didn't they break our arms and legs?"

"I suppose they were in a hurry. Quite hungry, I should think," said the cat.

"Bloody lucky for us—all the way 'round," said Golly.

In hopes of gaining more insight into our plight, Brutus asked, "So, Miss Cat, what's your take on the Orb? We've heard all sorts of stories. Where did it come from? Why was it broken into pieces? How many pieces of this Orb are there?"

"Four wedges in all. Together they form a perfect sphere," said the cat. "The toad stole the northern slice from Piranda. The western wedge is said to be on the Island of the Valgars, which is where the toad has gone. The eastern wedge is said to lie in the clutches of a stone gargoyle that guards a passage to the surface world. The final slice is said to be in the southlands— but no one knows for sure. As for its origin, it's from some- where in the oberlands, the surface world. Some believe its creator quartered it and hid the pieces here in the unterlands to protect all creation from its evils."

Golly wafted his hand and said, "I 'eard similar prattle, from all sorts, most of 'em drunk as lords. Storybook tales for little children.”

Adventure’s tone became a little stern. “Take care, Golly. In truth, the Orb is very real, and it is very dangerous.” The cat stood and began to pace. “It must be kept out of the toad’s hands at all costs. Once joined, the Orb could command powers of all heavens and earth— forces unimaginable.”

“Oi,” said Golly. “You’ve a convincin’ bearin’, Miss. You’re scarin’ me a bit. Me ’eart’s poundin’ for wantin’ to go and find the ruddy thing.”

Brutus chimed in, “Me as well. We’ll all lend a hand if you like.”

The eyes of the cat, the elf, and the dog man fell upon me. I raised my hands to welcome the invitation. “By all means, count me in. I wouldn’t miss it for the world.”

Adventure waved us near the waning flames. “Hands in,” she said. We joined hands above the embers. “Knights we are, one and all!” We raised our fists and cheered. “Hey yo!” said the cat.

“Hey yo!” said we all.

The dog man and the elf led the cat and me away from the riverbank, through a fringe of woods. We ended up at the side of a cobblestone road. As we walked, Brutus and Golly bickered and bantered like an old married couple. Adventure was quiet and pensive. I took in the sights, sounds, and smells of the countryside. Before long we heard the rattling wheels of a wagon, out of the east, returning from the harbor.

"Here's our ride," said Brutus. "I knew it wouldn't be long."

"It's Arkle!" said Golly. "I've rode his bloomin' cart many a time, all about the land. Arkle, me, and Brutus—barn builders we are."

"Indeed," said Brutus. "I've helped raise a barn or two. And Arkle's a good man. A right good man."

After cordialities, the four of us piled in the back of Arkle's wagon. Rolling jovially along what Arkle called Horse Muck Road, we talked of the witch, the toad, and the Valgars. Adventure and I also learned a few things about Morningtown and its mysterious burgomaster, Stanislaus Korkunia.

"We'll need a sound ship," said Adventure. "The storms of the northern seas can thrash a common craft to splinters. I doubt the storms to the south would offer more consideration."

Arkle reined in the horses, and the wagon eased to a stop. "You'll 'ave to go north for a ship," he said. "The two in Kearn Harbor were set afire and adrift two days past. Lighthouse keeper saw it right off, sounded the horn, shined the light. But it happened too fast. What's left of 'em is strewn over the rocks. All's not lost though. The Duchess was tucked away safe up in Cutlass Cove. She's plenty seaworthy."

"Sounds like one of Parnie's stunts," said Adventure. "He's a rotten little wag, but quite clever. He knew I'd find a ship and follow. Thank goodness he missed the ship in the cove."

"It was hidden up north for a reason," said Arkle. "Now you know why. One thing's for certain, I'd best never get me 'ands on the blighter. I'll scrag the life out of 'im."

"All right then," said Adventure. "I'll be asking the powers that be for loan of the Duchess. But I'm a knight, not a sailor. I'll need a captain and a sound crew."

"I can pilot a ship," I said.

Arkle smiled through the gap in his teeth. "Aye, you're game, wee lad. But it's no job for a boy.

"I'm not a—"

Adventure chimed in, "A man's what we need, and a man's what we'll have." The cat gave me a wink.

Brutus said, "All's well, Arkle. You know Golly and I have sailed with the merchants."

"And I've sailed the Horn!" I said.

Skepticism showed on the faces of Golly and Arkle. The dog man said, "Ta for the offer just the same, Captain. But that tout holds no water here. We sail ships, ships of resin-soaked wood—not horns of tin."

Arkle added, "I 'ad no clue a horn could even float."

"Nor I," said Golly. "The horns 'round here would fill with water and sink right to the bottom, they would."

"But they can be proper fun to play," said Brutus. He pretended to play a trumpet and made tooting sounds. Everyone laughed but me.

Adventure consoled, "Never you mind, Captain. We'll have a post that suits you."

A little disgruntled, I said, "Fair enough. I'll help in any way I can." Then a thought came to mind. "I've been wondering about that witch, Piranda. What if she were to fly that chariot thing to the island and lay claim on the Orb?"

"She'd never chance it. The Coverture extends to the spritely skies and runs west well past the island," said Adventure. "Without a wedge of Orb, the Coverture could take a person anywhere. Up until now, we did not realize the Orb could provide safe passage to the south. Poor old Piranda missed her chance."

"She doesn't sound like much of a witch to me," said Golly.

"Not at all," said Adventure. "She calls herself High Priestess, but she's a charlatan! She has her flying cart, a few carnival tricks, and that's the whole of it. But she is very, very sly. Had me fooled for a time, I'm ashamed to say."

The cat took a lengthy, weary breath. "The story goes that she appeared out of thin air on a flying chariot drawn by four white steeds. She could have cups and saucers rise from a table, make birds vanish and reappear, flick bits of fire here and there. She said she could summon demons at will. The king was fooled, the queen was fooled, the court was fooled, the knights were fooled. Now she has all of Ultrania convinced of her sorcery. The truth is, without that slice of Orb, she's no more of a High Priestess than a chamber maid."

"Admittedly," I said, "there are a lot of despicable people of the surface world that can connive and lie like champions. I've been burned a couple of times."

"'Ow bad were the burns," said Golly. "Looks like you've healed up quite nicely."

Brutus said, "Water from the Jungbrunnen can heal wounds and burns. Maybe—"

"All right, all right. That's enough you guys. I didn't get burned by a fire."

"Gadzooks, Captain. How else does a man go about gettin' burned?

"It's an informal way of talking. Burn refers to a loss of some kind when someone tricks or cheats you out of something."

"Ah," said Brutus. "There's a sucker born every minute, eh?" Golly said, "Oi—watch your language, elf!"

I said, "The saying fits all right. I'll probably be sorry I asked, but where did you hear that phrase?"

"Not hear," said Brutus. "I read it. In a book about a circus man named Barnum. People think he said those words, but he didn't.

Nobody knows where they came from."

"The words hold truth. People did dumb things in the good 'ol days, and people still do dumb things nowadays. I guess we'll never learn."

"There will always be foolers and there will always be fools," said Brutus.

Adventure said, "That's the way of it in every haunt and hollow." She cleared her throat. "And to finish up with matters concerning Piranda—aside from what I've already shared, I have no knowledge or explanations."

"I suppose it doesn't really matter," I said. "She's stuck on the other side of the Miri—I mean, the Coverture."

"Aye," said Golly. "The witch can do nowt. It's them Valgars we'll have to battle."

"Ah, the bird people," I quipped. "Why don't we just pluck their tail feathers?"

Brutus wagged his finger and chided, "Not a matter for jest, young man. The Valgars are not to be trifled with."

Arkle cleared his throat and offered a historical perspective. "Hear me now, all. As the eldest of us gathered, I'm the lone soul who's seen a Valgar, and I hope to never see one again. Giant bird people they are. They can fly to the top of the world and dive from the sky like shots from a cannon. With them huge, pinchy nibs they can snap a man in two with a single bite. Hear me now. If that froggy fellah or dodgy witch sets foot on their sand, they'll both end up rags of flesh at the end of pointy beaks."

We soon passed a sign that read Morningtown 2 Miles. Gradually, the pines and firs thinned, revealing open fields of cornstalks and cattle. Scattered about were barns, haystacks, silos, cottages, and windmills. The busy farmers waved and shouted, "Guten morgen!"

"How big a place is Morningtown?" I asked.

With sweeping arms and sculpting hands, Brutus panto-mimed the geography. "It's the whole countryside. West to east, it stretches from the Cerulean Sea's coast to the Farthingale Forest, and from the Coverture in the north to the Fever Jungles of the south."

Oblivious to our discussion, Adventure primped and preened. She adjusted her tunic and brushed the dust from her leggings. When she swished her tail, her eyes flashed. "Ewww, a snotty gob!" she said, plucking off a wad of web we'd missed earlier and flicking it away. Clearly hoping the rest of us hadn't noticed (we had), she brightened and pertinently posed, "So lads, how does one go about commissioning a ship?"

"A word from Burgomaster Stanislaus," said Golly. "That's all we'll need."

"Aye," said Brutus. "He'll have us loaded up and on our way in no time."

"And I will be most grateful," said the cat. "He must be a well-respected man," I said. "We all love him, Captain," said Brutus. "And he loves us," said Golly.

"A man from the surface at that," Brutus added.

"Is that so?" I said. "I'm really looking forward to making his acquaintance."

Golly chuckled. "And he'll be atingle with delight to meet a dashing captain and a lady of the knighthood!"

# Chapter 9:
## Morningtown

At the edge of the village, the crimson words WELCOME TO MORNINGTOWN were emblazoned on a forest green archway. The sculpted stone bridge stretching over what Brutus called the Myna River was an architectural masterpiece featuring animal shapes from forests, jungles, deserts, oceans, and farmyards. Entering the town was like stepping into the Dark Ages, somewhere around AD 700. Most buildings were stone and brick topped by conical roofs of timber and clay, but there were also houses and shops of stucco and wood with woven thatch roofs—anachronisms compared to the mechanical clock in the town square and the tall gas lamps lining the streets. Peripheral art and architecture also posed a perplexity: Ancient Greek and Roman, Medieval, Renaissance, Colonial, Old Western, Victorian, Gothic, Asian, as well as unique eccentric forms. There was a town hall, a library, a museum, a livery, a laundry, and a little red schoolhouse. I longed for a leisurely walk from one end of town to the other, but that luxury would have to wait.

Patrolling the street was a truncheon-wielding Keystone cop. Elves rode boneshaker bikes. There were horses hitched to posts and alongside watering troughs. "All is well!" called the town crier, ringing his bell with every step. He was dressed in buckles and black, like a Mayflower pilgrim. No matter how many times I blinked, these images would not go away. This multicultural mosaic was both time-diverse and fully tangible. And there could not have been any friendlier people, above or below the crust of the Earth.

"This place is—all over the place!" I said.

"Glad you like it, Captain," said Golly. "We just call it home."

As we passed an idle bandstand and marketplace, I pointed and bellowed, "Holy smokes! You folks actually have operational pillory stocks."

"Seldom used." Golly smiled, "Been in 'em once myself—and I deserved it!" He and Brutus rollicked with laughter.

Arkle continued along a cobblestone street called Fashion and turned right onto Dean Street. He rolled up to the Morningtown Inn and we deboarded. "I'm off for a load of wood," said Arkle, and we waved him on his way.

The big clock beneath the inn's eave showed 8:51. The heavy door creaked as Golly pushed it open and we stepped into the lobby, which was full of elves, gnomes, and dog people who could have posed for Tyrolean postcards. Next to the crackling fireplace was a full suit of plate armor. It caught the cat's eye, and she snipped. "Shoddy, clumsy clanker. I much prefer chain mail." In response to our glances, she said, "Pay no mind to my cheek. I'm just a bit weary."

"Need a catnap?" I said.

"You mind your own cheek as well, young man."

At that moment, Burgomaster Stanislaus Korkunia of Morningtown appeared from an arched doorway. He was portly and bespectacled, with a shocking mane of white, and clad in the braces and britches of a field worker. He took a puff of his curly pipe and said, "My, my, my. Well, well, well. Who have we here?" His accent was muddled:

German, English, and perhaps . . . southern Italian? "Brutus, Golly, you both look well." He looked Adventure and me over, then cocked his head. "Tell me, gents, with whose presence are we graced?"

"Here we have Adventure," said Golly.

"An enchanted cat," said Stanislaus. "How delightful!"

"And this little lad—oh goodness! I mean this young man—we call Captain," said Brutus.

"Pardon?" said Stanislaus.

Brutus explained. "He drank too long at the fountain. He didn't know—"

"Gracious me!" Stanislaus extended his hand, and we shook. "It's all right, my good fellow. Time heals . . . in one way or another. In a few years, you'll be right as rain."

"I sure hope so," I said. "In any case, I'm Captain John William Newman, United States Navy."

"A mariner—stalwart, steady, and courageous. I am honored, sir," said Stanislaus. "So, what's your business here, Captain?"

I nodded toward Adventure. "I'm here to help her."

Adventure said, "And I'm here to ask for your help, Burgomaster. I need a ship, and the need is dire."

"Dire, indeed," said Stanislaus. "Sounds as though we'd best get to it. I'll put a call out to the council and advocates."

The burgomaster bid us follow him into a spacious parlor. At the center of the room was a circular dining table surrounded by fifty finely crafted chairs. We chose seats facing a beautiful display of artwork—paintings and sculptures from civilizations known and unknown. As we admired the gallery, the room slowly filled with townsfolk of all sorts: elves, dwarves, gnomes, pixies; dog people, pig people; elders, shopkeepers, guardsmen, workmen; and a strange little fellow with impish features and marbly skin. I was told he was the only goblin in all the land.

Once all were present, the Adventure Cat, sometimes fervent in her rhetoric, provided a backstory that kept everyone on the edge of their seats. Standing tall, gesturing in earnest, she spoke in words both fearful and bold. She became most impassioned whenever referring to the Orb.

"Without intending to trepidate, I must sound a desperate call. The Andean Orb is not a myth. It is not the stuff of legends. When I held the northern slice in my hand, it became warm and buzzed like a nest of bees. It was as though it were alive. From a single wedge of the crystal, Piranda the witch gained the power to transform living things. She turned the nattering fishwife of a relic hunter, Parnie Wermbom, into a croaking, warty toad of a man." She gestured toward herself with both hands. "And I assure you, my mother did not give birth to a cat!"

Laughter ensued. Adventure paused as tea and biscuits were served. The cat pulled and twisted her whiskers.

"Jest though I did, the truth outdoes the jest. Wedge of Orb in hand, I was able to transport Piranda to the dungeon of her priestess tower. And when Parnie the toad man got his hands on the crystal, he was able to leap, with little effort, to the top of a mountain. That's how he eluded me."

"Where's he gone?" asked the strange little goblin in a helium balloon voice.

"'E's crossin' the Cerulean," said Golly. "To the Island of the

Valgars to fetch the western lump o' the glass."

Gasps rounded the table. Murmurs and mumbles followed. Adventure raised her hand and waved. The room became silent.

"Yes, yes, it is disturbing," she said. "And I do fear the toad will become more and more powerful with each slice he finds. As you can imagine, this poses a threat to all we know. Though the western slice is sentried by fierce bird men, these creatures have not the desire to fathom the Orb. They are simply guardians. Should the toad somehow divest them of their charge, these birds of prey might easily become the prey themselves. Possessing the northern and western wedges, the toad will surely leap his way east to pilfer the third slice."

With grave concern, the burgomaster asked, "Has this Parnie Wermbom fellow gone mad?"

"Mad indeed," said Adventure. "More so by the day, by the hour. He rambles on about summoning the fires of the Seven Calderas to lay waste to the surface world because it has been tainted and poisoned by the oberlanders. He'll rant, then shout, 'I'll cleanse their world with flame.' Then he blathers about ruling the unterlands forever."

Adventure stood and strolled around the table. "Should the toad assemble the Orb's quarters—north, south, east, and west—he may well have the power to crush all beneath his heel." The cat beseeched, "For the sake of the mortal substance and hallowed spirit of all living things, the toad man must be found, and he must be vanquished. My friends and I need a ship. And we must sail on the morrow."

Calmly, the burgomaster offered assurance. "Your words rival those of a saint and sage, dear cat. And I know all too well the ominous and threatening nature of the Orb. Morningtown does have its share of doubting Thomases, but most of us believe. There'll be no challenge to you having a ship."

Adventure sat down for a well-earned rest and sipped at a flagon of ale. "I'll set out a list of provisions within the hour."

"And a crew?" said the burgomaster. "We have the saltiest sailors ever to brave the waves."

The cat nodded appreciatively. "Ta just the same. I've all the crew I need. Golly and Brutus as first mates, and Captain as a captain. He's a pilot of the air as well as the sea. If he says he can sail, then sail he can. He may look a wee lad, but he's as good a man as any."

"Hear, hear!" said Brutus.

Golly clapped and barked, "Accolades, accolades!" Applause clattered all around.

Out of obligation and necessity, I rose with strained dignity (wearing nothing more than a filthy, knee-length undershirt) to set forth my motives and intent. "I'm sure you've all heard by now of my mishap at the fountain. But rest at ease, I'm a military man of a dozen years and I've proven my worth in both diplomacy and combat. I feel I owe my life to the three here beside me: Adventure, Golly, and Brutus. And I do hereby pledge loyalty and devotion to these friends and their homelands. I freely and gladly offer my knowledge, skills, and experience as a man and a soldier to serve and defend the people of this realm. While I am a man of peace, I am bound to uphold justice and to fight for freedom. As we've learned through the centuries, freedom is not free—it only lives as long as free people fight for its honor." With that I sat.

The burgomaster said solemnly: "As I peer about, I see the cat shall have her ship. Any nays? Speak now and without cost to name or reputation . . . On with it, then. In my time here, I've said little about the Orb. No need—it was of no concern. As many have suspected, I came to this land through the Coverture, as did Captain Newman. But what no one knows is that I came not from the surface. I came not from this world at all." Stanislaus paused for the murmurs. "The Coverture reaches forward to eternity's end, and it reaches backward to the dawn of the void. To think our world smaller than a grain of sand is both to think not enough and to think beyond excess, for such thoughts lie not in the woken mind—they swirl about our deepest thoughts, and among the dashes of our dreams."

Out of the quiet spoke the strange goblin. "I too hail from a distant realm!" Others stood to say the same. An impromptu moment for revelation and confession had raised its head.

The goblin continued, "No matter how small, how great, how frail, how mighty, each grain on the beach is its own. It is a mountain, it is a wisp of wind, it is as wretched as cruelty, it is as treasured as love; it is one, it is only, it is many." The goblin sprang high, whirled around, and plopped back into his chair.

Stanislaus then shared a final bit of wisdom. "To see within and without another's eyes is to know the truth of oneness and to accept our destiny. For each one and each only is due a just claim to all that is. Let us embrace what we have, what is here and now, and take hold of the notion that the rights of one comes with a responsibility to all. As a grain of sand has the right to lie upon a beach, we have the right to dwell upon this Earth, and we have the responsibility to care for it, to protect it. For within all existence, this is our common ground . . . this is our home."

***

I have come to believe there is no greater reverence than the silence of a listener. An embrace, a handshake, a touch on the sleeve, a friendly nod, a kindly smile—how often we forget that these simple things show the best in us. And isn't it strange how the best in us can bring out the most in all of us, especially when times are the darkest? Alive, dead, lost within a dream— it didn't matter anymore. This was my world now, my life, and I meant to make the best of it.

Adventure, Golly, Brutus, and I were assigned rooms on the inn's second floor. Baths were drawn. Our new and neatly folded attire was placed on the ends of our beds. Golly, Brutus, and I were given silly-looking sailor suits, but Adventure insisted on brown tights, a grey tunic, and a royal blue silk scarf. My Napoleonic bicorne fit perfectly, but I couldn't stand the thought of wearing it, so I said it was too big. We were treated to a wonderful meal in the parlor: roast beef, Yorkshire pudding smothered in onion gravy, boiled cabbage, and carrot wheels. We merrily washed it down with (perhaps too many) flagons of burnt umber ale.

Then it was on to the warehouse. We'd been offered a ride in a grand silver coach, but I suggested we take an after-dinner walk. It was a beautiful afternoon, and the streets were bustling. The word was out; we were celebrities. Shopkeepers stepped outside for a vigorous wave. Maids wearing wooden clogs smiled and shyly looked away. Wide-eyed faces gawked from the windows of the school. Crossing the next street up, the town crier called out, "Ten to two and all is well." His bell clanged and he called out again. A young lady carried blooms of peonies from a garden shop and displayed them on a board-walk table. We were so very glad we'd decided to walk.

At the warehouse, Burgomaster Stanislaus stood on the load-ing dock, directing workers, and inspecting goods. "Standard fare for a lengthy sail," he said, pointing to a cartload. "Go around back and we'll check the manifest."

"Right-o!" said Golly. "Have you found the maps?"

"Maps galore!" said Stanislaus. "You're more than sure to find your way."

Before entering the warehouse, we paused to enjoy the Myna River's placid repose. It flowed past the inn and warehouse, making a downstream turn northeast toward its source in the Crooked Mountains. The trees along the banks blazed in yel-lows, reds, and shades of orange. Leaves fell and were whisked away by the wind like little magic carpets. Squirrels busily gathered acorns. Starlings chirped as they lingered near their nests; soon they'd wing off to southern retreats. A racoon peered over the bank with a fish in his mouth. Possums scut-tled over a rugged stone road.

The four of us roamed the warehouse looking for items for personal use. To my mind, the next best thing to a Beretta would be a high- tech slingshot; unfortunately, this required rubber tubing or synthetic power bands, which I thought unlikely to be part of the local arsenal. Adventure was testing the tension of some recurve bows. Though I preferred a less cumbersome weapon, I figured a bow was my next best bet. On my way to the recurve display, I spotted a box of shiny ball bearings. Above the box was a shelf covered with slingshots. They had strong wooden frames, secure leather pouches, and thick bands of natural rubber. I appropriated two. Broadswords and daggers were Golly and Brutus's weapons of choice, but one item caused a bit of a row.

"I'm telling you, Golly," said Brutus. "You don't need jeweled handles."

"Oi, you choose your blade, I'll choose mine," Golly said. "Any road, that eagle's claw on your pummel looks bloody daft!"

"What's bloody daft are those glistery gewgaws. On a half-dark night, a glint'll give you straight away."

Golly brooded. After a moment, he thought better of his choice and changed it for black stiletto. "I'll 'ave this one then. Are you 'appy now?!

"You're a smart lad," said Brutus. "And a right good lad, me old mucker." He slapped Golly on the back.

We walked the aisles and rummaged in the bins. From time to time, Adventure would tell Golly and Brutus to drop a toy or trinket; however, Golly did insist on the acquisition of a blunderbuss. Finally reaching the reference den, we gathered around a table covered with books and maps. We perused and passed around the materials for well over three hours. I could tell Adventure was getting impatient, so I cleared my throat and presented my thoughts.

"Other than us not having a viable picture or description of the island itself, the maps are highly detailed, and the ships' logs were written in depth. The books confirm that the sprite sky patterns have been constant for centuries and provide reference for adequate navigation. As for the island, we can use logic, scientific parameters, and common-sense speculation about what we might find."

"Agreed," said Adventure. "Historically, we know ships have been lost to storms and Valgar attacks. The attacks ended long before I was born, and to our good fortune, the storm season is waning fast."

Stanislaus held up a map. "These things considered, it appears the voyage from Morningtown's coast to the Forbidden Reef should be a pleasant three-day sail. But according to the logs and journals, no ship sailing beyond the reef has ever returned. No wreckage has ever been recovered. We know the Coverture, even though it wavers, comes nowhere close to the reef. And the ship logs note the reef waters are mostly 'as calm as a summer pond.' The fate of the lost ships remains a mystery—they simply vanished."

"No one's gone near the reef in fifty-odd years, Burgomaster," said Golly. "We may all be feared o' nowt."

Brutus put a finger to the tip of his long elf nose. "Granted, Golly," he said. "But we should fear the bird men, storms, sea beasts, scatterings."

Golly shrugged and folded his arms.

"What are scatterings?" I asked.

"They're like rags and shreds torn from the Coverture," said Brutus. "Quite small, but step into one and you're gone for good. They don't hang about long—that's the best of it."

Golly said, "One popped up in the marketplace a couple o' years back. We built a box 'round it. A week's time, it was gone."

"Mysteries abound, and the perils are many," said Stanislaus. "You wouldn't be the first to sail beyond the reef, but you'd be the first to make it home."

Adventure stood and placed her hands on her hips. "We all know the dangers, and the dangers forbode. Anyone who wants out—there's no shame. No shame at all."

I stood and reached out my hand. Adventure did the same. Golly and Brutus joined us. We touched fists. Adventure said, "Hey, yo!"

"Hey, yo!" said we all.

Adventure pointed west and shouted, "Off and away!"

# Chapter 10:
## Asail, the Duchess

Stanislaus, my not-so-motley crew, and I watched from the loading platform as workers transferred our provisions from hand trucks to boxcars at the back end of a single rail train. The mechanical aspects of the vehicle were much like the workings of a railroad hand car. Eight rowers powered the engine car. They sat in two rows, churning hand cranks in rhythm to activate a construct of gears, chains, and differentials on each side of the rail. Crewmen could switch from rowing to pedaling whenever they liked. The external appearance of the cars resembled olden-days San Francisco trolleys.

I was told that elves had perfected steam engines many years past, but they had not applied the concept to transport locomotion, mainly because of sentimentalism and tradition. It reminded me of the quartz crystal paradigm of the mid-20th century when the elegant beauty and magnificent precision of mechanical Swiss watches fell prey to the economic practicalities of vibrating specks of silicon. I found Morningtown's indifference to monetary worship to be quaint and endearing. When I mentioned this to Stanislaus, he said, "To find contentment, we needn't covet coin. And I propose the most treasured of contentments owes to knowing that wealth comes in many forms."

As I contended with contentment, Golly studied the sky. "The blinkin' sprites are blinkin' out. Two hours till dark."

Stanislaus said, "It's a day's ride to Cutlass Cove, even with twice the rail crew. Fortnights will pass before the Wind's Maid and the Sea Witch can sail. But the Duchess is a fine ship and the fastest of the three. She'll make good time in weather foul or fine."

"It's a pity our times are so troubled," said Brutus. "It's custom to have a sendoff before a ship sets out. The oom-pah-pahs and the twirling skirts; the free-flowing stout and pickled eggs—now that's the life!"

"How I do love the polka," Adventure sighed. "It's been too, too very long."

"Be all the more fun when the ship comes in, lass," said Golly. "Best we get some rest."

"I'm for that," I said. "That feather bed back there at the inn looked mighty comfortable."

"Go rest, then," said Stanislaus. "You can leave for the cove at first light."

With droopy eyes and dropping chins, we spoke hardly a word on the way to the inn. Retiring on arrival, we slept soundly through the night until we woke for a breakfast of poached eggs and freshly baked bread.

When Golly saw Brutus's little elf hand pull a hefty chunk from the bread loaf, he joshed, "Eh, Brutus, lad, that looks like a lump o' somebody's back step."

Slathering le pain with butter, Brutus said, "Bugger off. Let your meat shut your trap."

With eyebrows raised, the cat and I exchanged glances. Adventure jumbled two more eggs and sopped them up with bread. The coffee itself was strong enough to weigh an anchor; we each had two cups. The servers plucked up our plates, and a bowl of fruit was placed on the table. We each took an orange, an apple, and a pear. Niceties spoken, we hastened to the single rail and were off.

Behind the engine trailed one passenger coach and two boxcars, but no caboose—speed was of the essence. We each enjoyed the comfort of a seat to ourselves. We did our best to relax, taking in the sights and the lay of the land, but nothing could keep images of the Forbidden Reef from invading our thoughts. My imagination summoned a vision of the two taloned hands, gnarled and demonic, that reached up through the water forming a macabre passage. Try to find another way around and we'd run aground on the jagged coral, having most of our keel ripped away.

Judging from what we'd learned yesterday, from the reef, it would be a day's sail to the island, which was said to be ever shrouded by volcanic smoke and ash. No one knew of the island's length, width, or any of its landforms. It was thought to be tropical and mountainous, but that was speculation. Daydreaming about white sand, azure waters, and swaying palm trees was wonderful, but the notion of bloodthirsty bird monsters circling above did much to taint the image. So, I would banish the thoughts, clear my mind, and indulge in the visions of paradise until the horrors crept their way back in.

The words of Shakespeare's Hamlet came to mind. "To sleep, perchance to dream—ay, there's the rub." A field of roses has its thorns, a field of dreams has its nightmares. At least the single rail afforded a lazy, quiescent ride.

Golly's curiosity broke the silence as he solicited advice from an expert. "Oi then, Adventure, how would a fellah go about fightin' one o' them Valgars?"

Adventure searched her thoughts. "The closest I've come would be scaring off ground goonies. They're destructive, ill-tempered birds— and quite large. But they're awkward and flightless. If they don't run away, you wait for one to kick, then chop off a leg. Most times all you need do is shout at them and they waddle off, honking and squawking all the while." The cat took pause. "Other than Piranda's clumsy giant wasp antics, in all my years . . . I don't recall ever staving off an airborne attack."

"Not even dragons?" I asked.

"Hah! Dragons," Adventure laughed. 'Oi, what drivel and tripe," said Golly.

"Goodness, Captain!" Brutus said. "Do you think you live in a fantasy land?!"

I looked around at my extraordinary traveling companions and thought—discretion, discretion. "Ha, Dragons, indeed! What a crazy thought. Looks like the jokes on me."

"Aye, and you're a good lad, Captain," said Golly. "Now back to the point at hand. 'Ow would you go about fightin' one o' them flyin' beasties?"

Without hesitation, I advised, "Get 'em in your sights. Focus on the main body mass. That's my training. And though I would prefer to 'fight no more forever', I must admit I've always preferred a clean shot to the beak."

Stanislaus chimed in, "Now, now, now. Let's hope it doesn't come to all that. Think stealth. Look things over, be sly, sneak in and sneak out."

"Always preferable," said Adventure. "In fact, my favorite tactic."

"Aye," said Golly. "Make your play and steal away." "Poetry now, Golly?" said Brutus.

Golly stood for a recitation:

Through dashes of dreams As you swoop and swoon You'll see a shadow

Across the moon

"Lewis Carroll?" I said.

"Golly Gorki," said Golly. "This dog man once cobbled a song for the kiddies."

"Oh please, not again," said Brutus. "Not that it's a bad song; it's just that I've heard it a hundred and fifty-thousand times."

"Never mind that, you scalawag,' laughed Golly. "I know it's your favorite." Brutus waved him off.

Up ahead a herd of horses grazed in an open field. A few were active: running, jumping, kicking, rearing. When I saw one bite another on the neck I said, "Looks like there's a couple of mean ones out there."

"They're not being mean, they're just playing," said Adventure. "When horses play fight, it shows a strong connection and affection."

"Ah, good, I'm glad they're getting along."

"They move so gracefully," Adventure said with admiration. "It's as though they're dancing to a beautiful melody."

"You know, I think a little music might be just what we need," I said. I glanced at Stanislaus. "We could use a good song about now, Burgomaster."

"How about one we all know?" said Stanislaus. "A song about horses!" said Adventure.

An elf at the back of the car strummed a ukulele and said, "'Stewball' is a good one'?"

"'Stewball' it is," said Stanislaus. "Sing along if you like." In a rich baritone, the burgomaster rendered the sentimental tale of an old racehorse. By the second verse, we had all joined in.

Amid a meadow of lilacs and edelweiss, the single rail slowed to a stop. As a new rowing crew replaced the old, we continued to watch the Appaloosas graze. I looked over the back of my seat to Adventure and asked, "What sort of horses do Ultranian knights ride?"

"Volsheks," she said. "They are much like the Arabians of the oberlands. I've always loved to ride."

"I'm mostly a city boy. I'm embarrassed to say I've never ridden a horse. That's one of the things I want to learn to do when I get back home."

Adventure nodded toward the field. "Well, don't start with Appaloosas. Too high-strung. Though not all, I suppose. Just like people, every horse has its own temperament."

The coxswain boarded the passenger car to apprise the burgomaster of the progress and ongoings. "About a mile off, 'round yon bend, we'll roll down an easy grade and be in sight of the bay. The Duchess is docked, ramps locked in, ready to load. Be there in an hour—more or less."

Stanislaus beamed. "Commendable work, Coxswain! Most commendable. Plenty of light, plenty of time. We could want for nothing more."

"Sit tight. And we'll get on with it," said the coxswain. Within the minute, the engine bell clanged, and we were on the move.

All cheered when Cutlass Cove came into view. The Duchess was anchored and bound securely to the docking cleats. The unloading and loading went like clockwork. Adventure directed the workers to stack the crates and roll the barrels to the center of the deck, near the cabin. Stanislaus made certain the boxcars had been emptied and then helped the workmen uncoil the docking ropes. Golly and Brutus hoisted the anchor. I hauled in the loading plank, and Adventure closed the cargo door. As we stood side by side, I initiated a salute.

"No sense in standing on ceremony," said Stanislaus. "You've a job to do. Our fate is in your hands." He took up a length of pole and helped the workmen push the Duchess away from the dock. As we drifted with the tide, all on shore waved and hollered, "Fare thee well!" Then they boarded their ride, turned around at the wye, and were on their way home.

The Duchess was a fine ship, and we were proud to serve as her crew. I gave Brutus and Golly pre-sail checklists while I appraised the integrity of the sails, masts, rigging, and steering. Adventure inspected the cannons; she wheeled them around and locked their brakes—one mid-port, one mid-starboard—and placed two small barrels next to each, securing them with rope. One barrel held gunpowder; the other contained a finely ground, greenish dust made from sominous mushrooms—they called it slumber dust, the burgomaster's special recipe. We were each given a pouch of the stuff to wear on our belts. The dust was portioned into small packets of wax-coated rice paper, each about the size of a sugar cube. I was told it was very potent—one whiff or breath would render you unconscious in seconds and you'd be out for hours.

After Brutus and Golly returned with their checklists, I told them to report to Adventure while I attended to any needed quality control. She set them to sorting crates and boxes according to category: food, tools, weapons, clothing, lamps, oil, maps, charts, and so on and so forth. After meticulous sorting, they labeled each box with black marking wax. Adventure was determined to set sail before dark, and she took a keen interest in keeping us on task. If she heard a word of raillery from either Brutus or Golly she'd scold, "Shut your gobs and get cracking!" We were shipshape in no time.

Together we raised the mainsail. I talked us through the steps, and we each did some hands-on. "First off, we must attach the shackle to the clew. Brutus, loose the mainsheet. All right, Golly, pull the halyard . . . get the luff tight. Looks good, feels good. Adventure, secure the mainsail to the cleat." We backpedaled astern to admire our work. The sail swelled and billowed like a cloud.

Our course was west by southwest on a calm sea. A brisk, salty breeze set Adventure's scarf aflutter. The vast open waters thrilled us to the core. Two miles out, the wind kicked up and the waves rose. The Duchess was asail!

While nautical navigation was second nature to Morningtown's seasoned mariners, our staying on course required conference and consensus. Adventure trusted the sprites, but she was only familiar with the northern constellations. Brutus and Golly knew the landmarks south of the Coverture well, mostly depending on memory, but they had little knowledge of the Cerulean Sea. We all knew the skies were brighter to the east because the air was significantly colder and the sprites glowed in greater numbers, with a greater intensity to generate sufficient warmth.

I squinted as I scanned the sky. "I've noticed irregular line patterns between the sprite groupings, like roads on a map. What are those?"

"Cracks in the sky," said Golly. "So say the greater minds."

Brutus added, "Water from the surface leaks through and the sprites stay clear."

"It builds up and freezes in the winter," said Golly, "then rains down in the spring."

"It's gotten worse over the years," Brutus said. "More and more rain falls, flooding the fields."

Stroking my chin, I muttered, "Melting ice sheets. Par for the course."

Stanislaus had provided us with a standard crystal compass. The magnetically infused quartz stones formed a glowing ring: red for west, amber for south, green for east, and blue for north; unfortunately, when the Coverture shifted and wavered in excess, the crystals flashed and glowed in an unpredictable manner, making the compass totally useless. Nonetheless, we reasoned that a combination of methods and close adherence to the charts would stay our course to the island. And if needed, we could fall back on the words of a salty old seadog, a wizened elf with a long white beard: "Sail with the warmest wind, straight away from shore, follow the dim of the sky till the gull cries fade and die, then watch the crystals as red becomes orange, follow the glow to the devil's hands, the gateway. And may Neptune spare your souls."

As night set in, the sea became an emerald looking glass spangled with spritely glints; the view was panoramic and went on forever. Finalizing strategies and a plan of action was the next order of business. The area below was cramped and stuffy, so we unfolded some wooden chairs on the deck and enjoyed the brisk ocean air. The pole lamps were positioned too high to facilitate the reading of maps and logs, so I brought up a lamp from the lower deck and hung it from a cabin support beam; adjusting the wick to full flame proved adequate. Notebook and lead pencil in hand, I recorded the major points of our brainstorming.

Knowing we'd be facing flying monsters with stone-crushing beaks and scimitar talons, we realized our success would com-

pletely depend on stealth, cunning, and the element of surprise. Because we had no knowledge of the lay of the land or
fortifications, natural or constructed, a recon would have to
precede direct action. And though we'd be extricating a crim-
inal, the mission was inherently a rescue. We talked well into
the wee hours.

Wearily, I said, "Let's give all this some private thought and
put some polish on the plan when we're rested."

"Champion of an idea," said Adventure. "I'll take the wheel
and the first watch."

Golly and Brutus needed no further invitation; they contentedly retired to the forecastle. I shared some final thoughts
with the cat. "I'll be up to take my turn in a couple of hours.
Any problem at all, don't hesitate to ring the bell."

The cat smiled, quoting John Masefield. "'All I ask is a tall
ship—'" "'And a star to steer her by,'" I said with a wink.

# Chapter 11:
## Restin' and Ribbin'

When I relieved Adventure, she yawned and said, "That wasn't much of a rest."

"Couldn't sleep. Too much on my mind."

The cat yawned again. "Weather's clear, sea's calm, and I'm off for a good sleep."

"Golly snores," I warned her.

"No matter. I'm dead on my feet."

"Roll out a mat and sleep in the cabin," I suggested. "Best idea I have heard in days."

Alone with my thoughts, I sought some perspective. Logic and scientific objectivity seemed my best foundation. I considered some basic facts. To the best of my knowledge, I was alive. I was still on the planet Earth. And if so, I had to be beneath the eight to twelve miles of crust, inside a bubble or pocket within the mantle. The primary source of heat was volcanic magma. The light of day was generated by living things called sprites: plant, animal, hybrid, there was no way to know. The Coverture, neither matter nor energy based on observable properties, connected other planets, galaxies, perhaps even dimensions; understanding the phenomenon was of no consequence. It simply existed.

The people of this world came from many worlds. I found it very curious that so many of the natives resembled people mentioned in the legends and fairy tales of the surface world. And then there was the culture, the history, the scientific and technological progress—a parallel, a potpourri, a fusion of earthly and extraterrestrial constructs. Though there was an awareness of surface world (oberlands) advancements, the people of Morningtown and the northlands of Ultrania chose to live in a Dark Ages realm. It was a bizarre socio-cultural stagnation—industrial-strength ethnocentrism. Then again, most scholars consider the term Dark Ages a misnomer; relatively speaking, many parts of Europe and Asia thrived. The developments and achievements of this period rival the flourishing Renaissance. The years between 476 and 1453 AD, gave rise to water wheels and windmills, crop rotation, cannons and mounted armor, gothic architecture, algebra, and musical notation. Advancements in the unterlands seemed arbitrary and incongruent. To me, this seemed maladaptive, but to the natives, this was a preferred aspect of culture.

The crystal compass glowed red orange, south by southwest. According to the maps and charts, we were in direct line with the enigmatic island. They may have been bird people, but I seriously doubted they were bird brains. From what I had gathered, they were more of a civilization than a clan, tribe, or rudimentary pre-society. Another consideration was the abating of their raptorial proclivities. Their attacks on the people of Morningtown had ended suddenly, decades in the past. But it was unlikely their predatory natures had changed.

Why had they stopped crossing the sea and dining on inhabitants of the continent? Perhaps they had been decimated by disease. They may have migrated to a more bountiful hunting ground. Perhaps they all flew into the Coverture in hopes of returning from whence they came.

While I was pondering our inevitable foes, the sky had brightened just enough to note a massing of cumulonimbus in the northeastern sky. Occasionally, a cold gust swept the deck. A fair warning on land or sea.

By the time Brutus and Golly crossed the deck to relieve me, the distant clouds had darkened and spread. At first sight of the impending storm, their jaws dropped. They pointed out the disturbance as though I were oblivious. I nodded and said, "Oh, I noticed, gentlemen. It's kind of a hard thing to miss."

Approaching the wheel, Golly said, "No need for frets and tizzies just yet. It may piddle its puddles right where it sits."

"Might. Might not," said Brutus.

"You both have your talents, but I doubt you'll ever be weathermen."

Brutus sent Golly a perplexed look. Then he offered, "I'm not sure we'd want to be."

"You've weathermen in the oberlands?" said Golly. "Yeah, they're on the news every day," I said.

"I'll bet they're quite interestin'," said Golly.

"Well, they all pretty much say the same thing," I said.

"Any of 'em spin about like them twistin' storms?" asked Golly. "What?!"

"Golly, don't be daft," said Brutus. "Probably the worst they'd do is spit a bit of lightning."

"What are you guys talking—oh, wait. I see. You think our weathermen are human forms of weather, like maybe a happy cloud man."

"Oh, aye, now he'd be a good bloke to meet, an 'appy cloud man," said Golly.

"I'd be all for that!" said Brutus. "But if I were to see a twisting lightning man coming my way, I'd be getting under a bridge, and fast."

"I as well," said Golly. "As would most."

"OK, OK, OK, ummm, yeah—who's on first?" Before either could say another word, I raised the shush finger and held up my hand. "I just can't take listening to any more of this, you guys."

Brutus and Golly appeared clueless.

"A weatherman is not a person made from some form of weather— like a guy who might float around and rain on flowers. There are no people like that. None at all."

Golly pressed. "Then why the 'ell do you call 'em weathermen?"

"It's a nickname," I said. "A synonym. The real word for them is 'meteorologist.' Their job is to gather information and make guesses about what sort of weather lies ahead."

"Sounds like a bloody useless waste o' time to me," said Golly. "If it rains, it bloody well rains."

Brutus said, "Good evening, all. I'm a weatherman, and my job is to make guesses about the weather."

"Oi, weatherman, will we be havin' a storm tonight?" "Might. Might not."

Brutus and Golly had each other in stitches.

"I wasn't joking about the weathermen. They are required to do a lot of studying. And most of them work really hard."

"They call guessing the weather 'ard work? Crivvens galore! Buildin' and raisin' barns—now that's what you call 'ard work.

"Agreed, agreed," said Brutus.

Golly asked, "And you say somebody gives 'em coin and note for just sayin' what the weather might be?"

"Yeah, some of those guys are really well paid."

Golly gave Brutus a knowing look. Brutus smiled and said, "You're having us on, mate." They laughed heartily.

"Weathermen." Golly laughed. "Oi, you really had us, you little wag."

"Go on to bed now, Captain. We can see you're overly tired," said Brutus.

I took a long, discerning look at the eastern sky. Golly said, "Not to worry, lad. The rain'll hold off."

"Right, and Golly knows of what he speaks—he's a weatherman!"

I could still hear them laughing when my head hit the pillow.

***

When I awoke, the clock in the cabin read 10:22. Plenty of light filtered through the curtains, so I knew the storm had moved on. The wheel was tied off. Golly on the starboard side and Brutus on the port were casting fishing lines. Adventure was whittling away at a thick slat of wood. "Looks like an arduous project," I said to the cat.

"I've a point to prove, Captain. Early this morning, I made the claim that betwixt a sword of wood and a sword of steel, the wooden weapon is at times the better."

"I suppose there could be peripheral benefits, but overall, I'd be more confident in a steel blade myself."

"Which is just how Golly felt, and he wouldn't hear a word of reason. So, I've decided to prove my point with a full-on demonstration."

The words prideful, stubborn, obstinate, and cat came to mind, but I didn't utter a single one. She was already more than a bit miffed, and I did not want her hair standing on end.

Sometimes it's best for a captain to just lean against a mast and let things take their course. "Well, I'm always willing to lend an ear to reason," I said.

"Ah, but it's all come down to the element of surprise—this entire enlightening enterprise."

Swiveling on the stool of practicality seemed a good maneuver, as did a change in subject. "When I went to bed, a demon of a storm was brewing."

"It must have drifted north. Sometimes the Coverture draws them in —like it's swallowing them for sustenance. Good for it, good for us." "A classic win-win."

"One way to put it. An outcome seldom seen in life."

Unable to leave well enough alone, I asked, "So, what's the likely outcome with the Golly demonstration?"

"Win-lose, of course. Need you further inquire?"

"Win-lose. I'd say there's good odds you'll prove your point." "Aye."

At the port corner of the stern, Brutus reeled in his line. "Any luck?" I said.

"Oh, I'm getting lots of bites. Every time I cast a sprat, my line gets bitten in two."

"Same thing's been 'appenin' with me," Golly said. He crossed the deck to join Adventure and me.

"I'm surprised. I'd have thought the angling this far out would have been lucrative," I said.

Golly said, "We've caught nowt. In these waters, it's mostly the big lurkers. Too big for our river lines."

"How big of lurkers?" I said.

Overhearing, Brutus looked from stern to bow. "Twice the length of the Duchess," he said.

"Behemoths," said Golly.

"I'll leave those for Captain Ahab," I said.

"Oi, I know that story. Book's in the town library."

"Great book," I said. Looking aside, I rolled my eyes and muttered, "Why does nothing surprise me anymore?" I stepped behind the tied- off wheel and checked the compass. "We've gone a little south," I said.

"We steered away from the thunder last night, a few miles, just to be safe," replied Brutus.

"Shrewd sailing, mates. You're a fine crew."

It was midday. The disagreement between Golly and the cat was about to be settled. Adventure was primed to parry. The sword she had whittled was half-again the size of Golly's broadsword. She had used a soft, flexible wood—ash I believe. Both weapons probably weighed about the same. The cat's design was unorthodox, extra thick around the cross guard and pommel. But the grip was trim and perfectly carved to fit her hand. The cat went to mid-deck and tapped the deck's floor. "Fetch your blade, Golly. Let's have a go."

Golly chuckled good-heartedly and said, "You've asked for it, cat. Just cos you've a toy sword, don't think I'll go easy."

"Go as lively as you like, dog man. I'll have it no other way."

Brutus fetched Golly's broadsword from the rack near the ship's mast. With a strut of pomp and some flash and flare, Golly performed a brief floryshe. Adventure waved his foolishness aside. "I'm not here for a dance, mate," she said.

"Nor I. Do you really aim to spat with that stick? It looks like a piece o' garden gate."

"I'll make do."

Extending their swords tip to tip, they circled slowly, feinting, jabbing, and juking all the while. "One blow'll have your blade in splinters, young lady."

"So, stop the huffing and puffing, you big bad wolf—strike the blow!"

Golly lunged forward. He was surprisingly quick. Instead of springing back, the cat stepped into the blow, and as she came forward, she switched her grip from the hilt to the lower part of the blade. She let the broadsword connect while bending back like a willow in the wind, catching the sharp edge of Golly's weapon in a crook between the forte and cross guard. With a lean for leverage and a twist of her wrist, she wrenched the steel from the dog man's hand. She shuffled sideways and then pulled the broadsword from the wood. While the empty-handed Golly wiped egg from his face, Adventure stood self-satisfied, holding both swords like torches over a lesson well learned.

"Don't feel too badly, Golly," I said. "A few days ago, I saw her use the same trick against a nine-foot wasp. You're in good company."

"Aye, she pulled the wool over a bit, but a lesson learned adds gold to the mind. The young lady got the best o' me this round."

With grace to her manner, Adventure returned Golly's sword. "Golly Gorki of Morningtown, you are grand of body and grander of heart!"

The dog man raised his sword. "And proper grand are we all!"

## Chapter 12:
## From Respite to Rage

Adventure brushed the wood dust from her hands. "Fun's done," she said. "Back to work."

At the water barrel, Golly filled a bucket. He walked the deck with a ladle, offering each of us a drink. Standing near the central hatch, Brutus called, "Should we bring that box of oranges up from the hold? They'll shrivel in the heat."

"Yes, the fruit. Bring it all up, Brutus," said Adventure. "The apples, plums, and pears as well."

Heading for the hold, I said, "How on earth do you folks come by oranges when you live in an evergreen forest?"

"We cart 'em in from the southlands," said Golly. "About halfway between here and the Fever Jungles, there's a stretch along the coast that runs a ways inland. It's covered with orange orchards, easily fifty acres—limes and lemons too. It's mostly gnomes that does the farmin'. I've done cart runs, me an' Arkle, bringing loads up north."

"Bananas, pineapples?" I asked.

"Fever Jungles for those. It's an 'orrible land of 'orrible things," said Golly. "Takes an odd sort to risk his hide for bernaners. A braver man than I."

"Brave?" said Brutus. "Takes a fool is what I say."

"A brave man, a fool—quite often, they're one and the same," I said.

Brutus and Golly nodded and smiled. Golly said, "Every brave fool I know lives under a headstone."

"Aye," said Brutus. "I've seen risk without reason bury many a dunderhead."

"Gems of wisdom, lads," said the wry cat. "Now let's get to the goods."

Along with the fruit, we brought up some essential hardware. Adventure joined me as I rooted through a crate of weapons. I said, "We have five recurve bows and two hundred arrows. These creatures are birds of prey, and we know they'll attack from the sky. We'll need quick access to the bows and strategic positioning."

"How about a set at stern, bow, and mid-gunwale on both sides?" said Adventure. "Keep one set back near the mainsail."

"All right, I'll set them out before dark," I said. I noticed the cat was breathing a little heavily. "You look out of breath."

Adventure brushed a hand over her forearm. "It's a curse—all this fur. But a little panting gives me a quick cool-down."

"Yeah, I've noticed the heat around here kind of sneaks up on a person. It's getting warmer, but the sky gets no brighter."

"All heat in the unterlands comes from the ground, Captain. The sprites supply light only for the land. They keep the heat to themselves."

"That makes sense. And I haven't seen any sign of sunlight penetration. So, I agree, the heat here would have to come entirely from magma flows and the dispersal of steam?"

"Maybe a bit of outer sunlight warms the stone of our sky," said Adventure. "I've never paid it much mind."

"But you do have seasons—the deciduous trees have lost their leaves."

"Oh yes, four distinct seasons in the mid-coastal areas. I'm told the Fever Jungles are always sweltering. Lands well north of the Coverture, and in the far eastlands stay frozen solid."

"Oi," said Golly. "Are you two bein' weathermen, then?" He and Brutus laughed and slapped their legs.

"Enough of that!" said Adventure. "We've already had enough of a laugh about the stupid weather."

Golly was doing some panting of his own. And the little elf had sweat beads dripping from the end of his nose. I asked, "How hot is it likely to get?"

Brutus, Golly, and Adventure shrugged. "None of us have been this far out to sea," said Adventure. "But one thing I noticed in the logbooks—as the years passed, the spells of hot weather mounted, one on top of the other."

"It's got warmer on land as well," said Golly. "I remember the frosts coming early October when I was a lad. These days, it may not frost till mid-November."

"And it's come to rain overland far more often than it snows, even in the dead of winter," said Brutus.

Golly said, "The old dogs say it happens in spurts and bouts. It changes every twenty, thirty years or so."

Brutus added, "And we've all heard the stories of surface factories filling the sky with soot."

"Them people above'll end up killin' us all," said Golly.

I explained, "Ice ages, drought ages, flood ages have come and gone since the dawn of time. There are arguments both ways. Some call it global warming. There's something to it, but I can't say I know how bad it really is."

"The ice caps are melting, Captain," said Adventure. "Ultranian scholars claim to have proof. To me, the days just come and go. Hot, cold, windy, mild—I take it as it comes. But the toad we seek thinks we're caught in a heat trap. He blames it on the surface dwellers. It's why he wants to burn the oberlands to a crisp."

"Oi, what a right loon!" said Golly.

"He's a blind fool!" said Brutus. "Setting fires up top will surely put even more soot in the sky. What happens up there will happen down here . . . sooner or later."

"I don't claim to be a scientist," I said. "But if your toad man were able to use that Orb to set off the super volcanoes, as he's threatened —I think there are twelve—he'd mess things up pretty bad. There'd likely be a volcanic winter."

Adventure, Golly, and Brutus awaited account.

"The sky would fill with ash. Thick black clouds from the deserts to the mountaintops would settle over everything. It would stay that way for many years—twenty, fifty, even longer. A black blanket would block the sun. It would smother and freeze most living things —almost nothing would survive."

"No joshin', lad," said Golly in a faint voice. "No joshing."

Brutus asked, "What would happen to us?"

I said, "The way things work, your volcanoes would probably

all blow up too.”

“Be the end of us,” said Golly. “Be the end of everything.”

Hands on hips, her gaze determined, Adventure said, “And we’re going to put a stop to it! The whole muddled mess.”

“You bet we are!” I said.

“All well and good,” said Golly. He got to his feet and began to pace. “First, we’re gonna cook, then we’re gonna freeze, then a twirlin’ weatherman might come and blow us all to the dark-lands.”

Golly was clearly confused and frustrated. Adventure and I sought to counsel and console. Brutus, however, had heard enough of the doomsaying; he wanted nothing more than to get on with the next task.

“We’re all for helping,” said Brutus. “But Golly and I are just working men. You tell us how, and we’ll help.”

“We’re ’ere to lend a hand, Captain,” said Golly. “We’re ’ere to stay the course. And we’re trustin’ in you and the cat to lead the way.”

“So, what’s next on the list, Captain?” asked Brutus.

I looked at Adventure. The cat’s eyes surveyed the ship, stern to bow, gunwale to gunwale, crow’s nest to cargo hold. She said, "Knapsacks—for the inland trek. Pull just enough from your duffel to get by— water flasks, some hardtack, a spare tunic, matchsticks."

"We'll be there for more than a day, then?" said Brutus.

"We'll be facing jungle terrain, most likely," I said. "We don't know the size of the island or the objective's location, so most of our time will be spent scouting and exploring. In the service, we call it a recon. We could be in and out in a day, or it could take a week."

"We're not strangers to livin' off the land, me and the elf," said Golly. "Once Brutus, me, and me dad lived in the Farthingale Forest more than a month, living on nothin' but our wits and wiles."

"Good to know," I said. "We're going to have to count on each other." "What about weapons?" asked Brutus.

"For the trip inland," said Adventure, "Golly, take your sword. Brutus, a bo staff. Captain, a sling and pellets. I'll take a double-curve bow. And we'll each take a small blade and a pouch of dust."

"A complimentary combination," I said. "Sound strategy." All affirmed with a nod.

Adventure said, "We'll need to put some polish on our three

plans: main, backup, and every man for himself."

I suggested, "Once the heavier work's done, we could tie some of those target bladders to the yardarms and get in a little archery practice."

Brutus and Golly were all for the idea. Adventure said, "Not boasting, but I'm as good with a bow as I'll ever be. Maybe I'll give the captain's sling a go."

"Who's up for festivities tonight?" asked Golly. "We can uncork some ale. I'll find me squeeze box—maybe the elf'll dance the 'ornpipe."

"Gladly," said Brutus.

"It's a date!" I said. I turned to Adventure, but she was nowhere in sight.

"She must have gone below," said Brutus.

"Up here!" The cat waved from the crow's nest. "All's clear, all directions!"

With full sails we knifed through the waves toward a red satin horizon. The daytime sprites turned out their lights, while the nighttime gems shone on. Golly came from the cabin with an iron pot of fish stew; Brutus carried a bowl of fluffy biscuits. Spoons and forks, jars of jelly and jam, plates and mugs and jugs covered the table. I made one last walk around the deck before sitting down with the crew. As I neared the table, I couldn't help but feel they'd been talking about me.

"Goodness, Captain," said Adventure, "with all that strutting around, you put us in mind of a little tin soldier."

"Oh, is that so," I said. "Well, I am little, I am a soldier, but there's nothing tin about me."

"Nor wood, nor stone," said Golly. "But seeing a little lad parade about like a sergeant major does look a comical sight."

"You guys are all full of beans," I said. "Brutus, you haven't taken a jab at me yet."

"No need. Point's been made."

"You all know, I can't help being the innocent victim of an artesian elixir. In the upper world, that water would be worth trillions. You're blessed with a treasure humankind has searched for since the birth of civilization."

"For us, it just protects from the plague," said Golly. "The taking off of the years only happens for outsiders."

"Makes sense," I said. "Nature has to run its course." My first spoonful of the fish stew evoked a fond memory. "Mmm, lobscouse— it's delicious!"

"We call it sailor soup," said Brutus. "You've got to crumble in your biscuits—that's the tradition." Both Brutus and Golly had turned their stew into a thick, fishy mush.

"It's very good just the way it is," said Adventure. "I'll be happy with a biscuit on the side."

"My uncles from the north of England cook the biscuits right on top, like a crust," I said. "I like it both ways, but I wish we had a bottle of HP."

"HP what?" said Golly.

"It's a popular sauce in England," I said. "HP—Houses of Parliament. It's sweet and tangy. There's a bottle on every table."

"The inn makes a good sauce, with tomatoes and brown sugar," said Brutus. "Good with roast rabbit."

"I'll have to try some."

Golly went into the cabin and came back with a concertina and a tub for the plates and cups. "I'll take 'em down after and give 'em a washin'." The big dog sat and downed another ale.

"Look at that crimson sky—it's absolutely lovely," said Adventure. "I'm going to take a look from the stern."

"'Red sky at night is a sailor's delight,'" I said. "On the surface, it's a good sign."

"Here, it's just a red sky," said Brutus dryly. "And the red's going dim; it'll be dark soon."

"When I first came through the Coverture," I said, "it changed colors. Does the Coverture here do that?"

"Sometimes," said Brutus. "Mostly it's just a cloudy wall that wafts and sparkles now and then."

"It does some lively bendin' and flappin' sometimes, like a sheet pegged on a line," said Golly. "Then suddenly, it's a mirror, showing ya you and everything behind."

"Yeah, I saw that happen a couple of times. Quite an anomaly— mighty strange."

"Nobody in Morningtown goes near it," said Golly. "Step inside— most never come back. You could end up anywhere. Stanislaus knows more about it than any of us, but 'e keeps it to himself—to protect us, I suppose. 'E just says keep away, and we do."

"The sprites are sparkly bright tonight," said Brutus. "A sure sign of fall."

Adventure strolled back to the table and gazed up at the twinkling onyx sky. "Will you be playing a tune then, Golly?"

"Right then, the time's come for a tune," said Golly. "Where's me squeeze box?" He pulled the concertina from under the table, leaned back, and began to play a seaworthy tune, one we all knew well— "The Drunken Sailor."

Golly's melodeon introduced the shanty, and we all sang. Brutus and Adventure gathered lanterns and placed them in a circle of sorts. They stepped to the center and danced a dance apparently known in both the north and south. Up on their toes they bounced with hands on their hips, kicking to the front, kicking to the side, tapping their heels, sidling into a promenade, circling, whirling. The cat's finesse and the elf's flying feet were a genuine delight. I clapped and sang high tenor; Golly added some bass. The ale cast its merry spell.

Out of the darkness, like the slap of a demon's hand, a fierce wind howled through to shiver the timbers. The four of us went sprawling. Another blast snuffed the lanterns. Almost blind, we groped for handholds, each of us knowing we had to bring down the sails. I crawled toward the stern, hoping to reach the mizzenmast. As my eyes adjusted to the darkness, I saw the outline of Golly and Adventure at the central mast and the sail coming down. Brutus was nowhere in sight. Jagged bolts tore through the air, lighting up the frothy whitecaps. The waves rolled and churned. The Duchess rocked and bobbed. Thunder rumbled like boulders tumbling down a mountain. Hammers of rain pounded the deck. Onward I crawled, finally reaching the mizzen. Clinging tightly to the pole, I managed to bring the canvas down. Across the deck, the foresail collapsed. With the sails down, we had a good chance of surviving the briny rage.

And rage it did. The waves were monstrous. Clutching a cleat at the base of the mast, all I could do was hang on. Again and again the lightning flashed, and the thunder shook us to the bone. Rain swept the deck in sheets. Enormous waves splashed across the floorboards.

Then I saw Brutus as he ran toward the cabin. Hunkering at the starboard gunwale, Golly and Adventure waved for him to get down. He kept running. Another wave crashed as he reached the cabin door. Caught in the deluge, the elf disappeared over the port side.

Surrendering my grip, I ran full out and dove for the gunwale as the next wave splashed over. Pulling a throw ring from the wall, I waited out the next wave and glanced over the side of the ship. The waves seethed: grabbing, snatching, colliding. I scanned the swirling surface, ready to throw the ring, but the elf was gone. Adventure and Golly joined me near the mizzen. We felt hopeless, helpless, and paralyzed. Our friend was gone, claimed by a merciless sea. The wind whipped the rain. The waves tossed the ship. All we could do was ride the rampaging torrent.

The cat's ears perked; her eyes flashed and fell upon a rigging dangling from the stern. Adventure sprang to the rail. She grabbed the rigging and pulled. Golly told me to hold fast, and then he went to help Adventure. I saw them pulling for all they were worth, eyes fixed on the waves. Their efforts slowed. Sadly, shaking their heads, they loosened their grips on the lifeless ropes. A moment of quiet spoke. Then again, the cat's ears perked. I heard it too: a faint sound eked out between the crashing swells. Big Golly took hold of the rigging and strung it over his shoulder. His feet slipped and slid as he trudged toward the bow. Leaning dangerously over the rail, Adventure reached down. I rushed to the stern and hugged her around the waist. "Pull me back!" said the cat. I braced my feet against the ship and pushed away. The cat tumbled backward on top of me. Brutus was in her arms.

In a few breaths and a heartbeat, the wind hushed, the waves calmed, and the sky cleared. Sprites sparkled in the Neptunian sky. The last of the rain trickled and dripped from the yard-arms, pattering on the deck in restful refrain. Just as quickly as it had appeared, the tyrannical typhoon had vanished.

# Chapter 13:
## Beyond the Forbidden Reef

Below deck, Golly, Brutus, and I huddled around the pot-bellied stove. Adventure insisted on staying above to steer the ship and watch the sky. Fortunately, the storm had not sent us far off course. When daylight allowed, we would inspect the sails and get them billowing again.

"I've seen storms form in as little as an hour," I said, "but that thing absolutely came out of nowhere."

"It's the Coverture," said Brutus, still shivering. "Sometimes it swallows storms, sometimes it spits them out—just like the waves spit me into that torn rigging."

"Praise Heaven," I said. "We thought we'd lost you for sure."

Brutus shrugged coyly and said, "I've never been much of a swimmer."

"Well, I'm gonna give you some lessons," I said. "First chance I get." "I'm game," he said, with a light in his eyes.

Golly stirred the joys and dreads of the night into a somber recounting. "Worst cold and blizzard ever came through the Coverture was over thirty years ago. No warnin'. The wind froze the ponds and rivers in a single breath. It was nighttime and fires were burning, so most of us made out all right. But cows and horses turned to ice, in barns and in the fields. Same for animals in the wild. We found 'em by the dozen in the woods, solid as rocks."

"Almost anything can come through the Coverture," said Brutus. "Any time, and any place."

"I can understand why you all keep your distance from it," I said. "But it brought me here, and it's likely the only way I'll get home."

Golly warned, "No! Don't be thinkin' that way, Captain! You step in at the wrong place and there's no tellin' where you'll end up. In my time, maybe forty or fifty have gone in, and only one's come back."

"Joody Goody Woodenleg," said Brutus. "He's a shoemaker. He said he couldn't stand not knowing what was on the other side, so he stepped in. He said he saw some trees and rocks and hills, turned right around and ended up back where he started."

"That's sort of what happened to me," I said. "Adventure and I came back through at exactly the place I'd gone in. We know the exact spot—the way back to Ultrania."

Golly headed for the cabin stairs. "Not worth chancin' it, lad. Once we're back from the island, you and the cat best stay with us."

"On that I agree," said Brutus. "Stay away from the Coverture."

"I know you both mean well, but I've got to find a way home. I've just got to."

"Easy for us to spout off," said Golly kindly. "It's not so easy to be missin' your 'ome."

With an appreciative nod, I said, "I'll go up and take the wheel. That cat needs some time to dry out."

"Let me go up in your stead, Captain," said Golly. "I'm feelin' me oats."

When the cat entered the cabin, her fur was soaked. Brutus handed her a warm towel, and she vigorously rubbed her head, face, and arms. "No good in changing tops," she said. "With this sopping catskin, a new tunic would be soaked as soon as I put it on."

"We thought the same," I said. "We're getting close to dry."

"Good thing we brought the sails down," said Adventure. "The wind would have ripped them to rags and toppled the whole ship."

"We're a mighty lucky crew," I said. Brutus nodded.

Adventure said, "When you go back up, one of you'd better get to the crow's nest and look for the landmark—the reaching hands that mark the reef."

"I'll get up there," said Brutus. "It'll take my mind off my woes."

As first light seeped through the cabin curtains, Brutus and I went up to the main deck. Golly called out from the wheel, "Right on course, lads! South by southwest all the way!"

On the Duchess, the crow's nest sat above the highest yardarm on the main mast. The elf climbed what was left of the rigging, nimbly negotiating the pegs on the way to the nest. With a pouch of hardtack and a jug full of water, he planned to man his post till dark. I relieved Golly at the wheel, and he went to unravel and inspect the heavy masts. He and Adventure also planned to fix the torn rigging—the one that had saved the elf's life.

The cat, somewhat dry now, stepped out of the cabin, stretched and yawned. None of us had slept in more than a day and would not have a chance to even nod off until night-fall—if then. According to the charts, we were little more than a day's sail from the island; however, without the sails, we were resigned to rolling with the waves, which could easily set us back a day. The older logbooks said the bird monsters cir-cled the skies well out to sea; they watched for ships and dove for fish. And there was always the chance of another storm.

From this point on, we'd be sleeping, dining, and taking care of odds and ends on a rotating basis.

Inspection of the sails was slow going. The massive canvas sheets could weigh more than a ton when wet. On occasion, I would tie off the wheel and scan for tears in the sopping sails, which Golly and Adventure had hefted and spread across the deck. The sea was calm, the wind steady. Once the sails were unfurled, we'd be racing with the wind. It was hot on deck and hotter down below, so we each kept a jug of water nearby. We had three barrels of water, plenty for the journey home, even accounting for our prospective prisoner's share.

Thanks to the efficient though perilous efforts of Golly and Adventure, the sails had been spared the storm's wrath. When we raised them, they were as sound as the day they'd been made. Again, the Duchess ruled the high seas—at least, the Cerulean Sea—and what a beautiful blue it was, alluring all the way to the bank of mist that lay in the distance. Brutus first noticed it from the crow's nest and thought it was merely a low, drifting cloud. As we sailed closer, the cloud thickened, and the humidity climbed rapidly. It was a little like sailing into a health club steam room.

We adjusted the sails and gradually slowed to a near stop. At times, we couldn't see more than a few yards ahead. It was a meandering, fitful mist, at times giving way to patches of azure blue. It was at the periphery of such an opening that we saw the ominous stone hands reaching up through the water. They were stained red-brown from the iron in the rock, but they appeared to be streaked with dried blood.

"I'm taking us through!" I yelled.

"All's clear!" Brutus yelled from the crow's nest. As spry and nimble as a spider monkey, he descended the mast, joining Adventure and Golly at the bow.

Curls of mist floated over the deck like ghosts. The wind blew hollow, like a doleful flute, as it flowed within the cupped palms. Up close, we saw the stone was ancient, cracked, and barnacled. From above came the cries of gulls: screeches of fear, yawps of warning, caws of pity sang out as we cleared the gateway. The milky vapor bathed my hands, beaded on my face, and dripped from my chin. I could no longer see any of the crew. "Are we clear?" I yelled.

Moments passed. "Clear!" called the cat.

Again, the mist thinned. Though dense steam surrounded us, the Duchess drifted 'neath open sky. A weak, feeble breeze helped nudge the ship along.

We met mid-deck to discuss our situation and our next move. "We'll need someone at the wheel from here on. No tying off," I said. "One in the crow's nest. And one to trim the sails. This will allow one of us to get some sleep. We'll rotate posts every four hours, day and night." All agreed.

I took the wheel. Adventure climbed to the crow's nest. Golly headed toward the forward sail. We decided Brutus should be the first to sleep because of his near drowning. The elf had no complaints.

Though we were at full sail, our progress lagged in a timid wind. On the other hand, the steamy mist had gradually cooled. As evening approached, the air was balmy but pleasant. After making a slight adjustment in the angle of the foresail, Golly raised his head and began sniffing.

"What is it?" I said. "Smoke."

I carefully scanned the mist surrounding us, then walked the deck and looked inside the cabin. The smoke was not coming from the ship's stove. But if Golly smelled smoke—there was smoke.

"It was just a whiff," said Golly. "It came and went. Must have been nothing."

"Still, we'll keep an eye out. We may have passed over a magma chamber—deep under the sea floor. That's probably why it got so steamy. Your sensitive olfactory bulbs may have detected something seeping up out of the water."

Golly sniffed. "I've no old smellin' factories in me 'ead, Captain, but there was something." He raised his nose and sniffed. "Nothin' now."

When I glanced at the crow's nest, Adventure was holding a telescope to her eye, focused on a clump of clouds drifting northeast. She leaned forward, then back; she lowered the spyglass and looked toward the wheel. "Mountain peaks!" she yelled and pointed. "Three spires! It must be the island!"

Golly and I couldn't see the peaks. We hurried to the base of the mast. "How far off?" I said.

"Maybe a day's sail. Not half of that if the wind picks up."

Golly's eyes went wide. Now we could see it. Conical crowns poked through the clouds. A wisp of smoke swirled from the middle peak. "We're nearly there, Captain! No more than a stone's throw," said Golly.

"Maybe a wee bit more," I said. "We don't know the size of the island. No matter. Time and distance aside, we can be certain that things are about to get very interesting."

"Aye. And that ruddy sweat of a fog's creepin' in again," said Golly.

A grey plume rose above the mountain, followed by a roar and a rumble. "There's some serious geothermal activity on that island," I said. The smoke continued to pour out, and the rumblings became louder. "I'd say the island's only five or six miles off."

Adventure jumped from the low yardarm, landing lightly on the deck. "My turn for the wheel," she said.

I patted Golly on the arm, "You go get some rest," I said. "And tell Brutus to take the crow's nest."

"I'll sleep like a log," said Golly.

As the big dog man headed toward the forecastle, something struck the ship with a thump on the starboard side. Not much of a thump, but we all heard it. Hurrying to the starboard gunwale, we watched the water's surface. Jaunty after a delicious sleep, Brutus joined us. "What's up with you lot?" he said.

"Something's out there," I said. "Under the water." Adventure said, "We heard something bump into the hull."

"I heard some bumping as well," said Brutus. "Down in the cabin. It's what woke me up."

"There's a good size to it," said Golly. "From the sound o' that thump."

At that moment, we all saw a ripple roll along the hull, directly below us, and then veer off in an S pattern, disappearing into the mist. The ship moved into a clearing. The water was a sky-blue mirror. Again, we saw the disturbance as it circled back toward the ship. Only a few yards away, the ripples vanished; whatever caused them had gone under. From directly beneath, it rammed the hull. The Duchess dipped sideways, then rocked back. We heard a scraping along the keel.

"It's gone to the other side," said Brutus.

We crossed the deck but saw nothing but silky, thin vapor. "A whale?" said Golly.

"Whales don't move like that," I said. "A shark?" said Brutus.

"It was near the surface. We'd have seen a fin," said Adventure.

"Nobody's been past the reef and lived to tell the tale," said Golly. "We've not a clue as to what it is."

Silently, we wrestled our thoughts.

"This thing's playing with us," I said. "It's a thinking creature—much more brain power than a fish."

"Maybe that's it," said Brutus. "It's playing, like the dolphins in Kearn Harbor."

"I'd not count on it," said Golly.

Adventure sighed. "It's time. Let's get our weapons—and be quiet about it. Nothing's been set out; it's all mid-ship, at the back of the cabin."

At the weapons rack, Adventure took a bow and quiver. Golly and Brutus strapped on their broadswords. I lifted a slingshot from a small box. Adventure said, "Golly to the stern. Brutus, the bow. Captain, man the starboard gunwale, and I'll cover the port."

We held our positions and watched like hawks. All was silent, all was still. The steamy vapors formed whiffs and wisps, poofs and puffs that drifted high and low in all directions. Sometimes the Duchess drifted into a clearing, sometimes she was swallowed by clouds of steam. It was in such a whiteout that the creature struck again. Its body and tail slammed into the starboard side, sending me to the deck. I sprang to my feet and got back to my post.

"Did you see it?" Adventure called.

"I saw its shape!" I said. "It has a long, slender body. It lashed the hull with its tail."

"Any damages?" said Golly.

"Could be," I said. "There was a crunch." "Next clearing, I'll take a look," said Golly.

Finally, blue waters returned. But we were still encircled by clouds, sitting in the hole of a swirling donut. "There it is!" I yelled. "We'll all need bows—and plenty of arrows! Hurry!" At the weapons rack, I handed Brutus and Golly each a bow, and they grabbed handfuls of arrows while Adventure kept a lookout. "This thing means to harm us," I said. "Otherwise, it would have swum off."

"It wants us for a luncheon snack, I expect," said Brutus.

"I think it's gone under," said Golly.

"Look!" said the cat, pointing beyond the ship's bow.

Ripples turned to mounting furrows as the unknown beast approached. Faster and faster it came. It meant to take us head on. Adventure rushed to the bow with an arrow nocked. She leaped onto the forecastle and pulled her bow to full draw. As the rest of us scrambled to ready our bows, Adventure lowered her weapon and relaxed her draw. She shook her head with uncertainty and called, "It's gone under again!"

Suddenly, off the port side, a great grey, mottled head burst from the sea. Concentric rings of water formed around the slender neck and body; its head rose higher than the crow's nest. With exophthalmic eyes it surveyed the deck, tipping its head and twisting its neck, scanning the entire ship. The eyes were dark, distant pools. Its serpentine neck swayed like a punji-charmed cobra. Its attack was like the lash of a whip, its head flying as though disembodied, rows of ivory spikes parting and snapping. The head then recoiled and rose to a zenith—all of this in a few beats of the heart.

Adventure had let loose three arrows, but her well-honed skills were foiled by the beast's erratic undulations. "To the cannons!" I yelled, realizing too late my voice would draw the beast's attention. Golly and Brutus, disoriented by the sudden attack, ran into, and fell over each other. Finally, rolling free of their arm-and-leg entanglement, the two reached a cannon. Adventure leaned against a mast to steady her next shot. All the while, the serpent had a bead on me. Had I run for the cabin, I'd have been snatched into the air. So, I backed slowly toward the stern, hoping to stow myself in a rear hatch. The monster reared its head to strike. I ducked behind the wheel. Adventure let her arrow fly, sending it deep into the serpent's neck. It let out a shriek that shivered the bones of sunken pirates; it fitfully tried to shake away the shaft.

All I could do was hug the wheel. Adventure nocked another arrow. Golly rolled a cannon toward the mizzen and locked it in place. Brutus rolled a powder keg through the milky haze.

When I looked up, a cavernous maw descended. Had I not been shielded by the helm, it would have swallowed me whole. The creature snapped and pulled back with a mouthful of wood from the wheel and other chomped-up parts the deck. I was as vulnerable as a naked newborn. As Adventure's next arrow lodged behind the serpent's jaw, another shriek resounded. Meanwhile, Golly fought to pry the lid from the airtight powder keg, and Brutus crouched at the ready with cannon ball and ramrod in hand.

A thick blanket of mist settled down over the ship. With a raging splash, a second serpent erupted from the water. Through diaphanous fumes and vapors, we watched this new horror bite and tear the arrows from its mate's flesh. Adventure was completely hidden in the fog, but I was barely able to discern the outlines of Brutus and Golly.

One of the monsters clenched the main mast in its teeth just below the crow's nest and swung its head, violently rocking the ship from stern to bow. The top of the mast broke off and crashed onto the deck. As the ship trembled, Golly struggled desperately to open the cask of gunpowder. With a powerful tug, he wrenched the lid free, losing his balance in the process. Some of the contents flew into the air, the rest spilled onto the deck. The dust-fine particles floated in the mist and began to spread.

Sightless in the mist, both serpents had attended to the sound of Golly's tumble. He and Brutus were now the prey. I saw the shapes of two long necks stretching out to where Golly lay. Brutus was up and fumbling to load the cannon. Adventure leaped and landed amid the fray, with bow pulled to full draw.

As the sea giants loomed over my friends, I yelled, "Here! Hyah! Hey! Over here!" But the monsters paid no mind. I stamped my feet and clapped my hands. Still, they paid no mind. I needed something to throw. When I reached down for a fragment of the wheel, I felt my eyelids growing heavy. Things seemed to be moving in slow motion. Something very strange was happening.

At first, I thought the water vapor in the air was selectively bending light; it had taken on a greenish tint. The verdant hue deepened. Golly and Brutus appeared to have fainted; they lay still on the deck. Adventure's bow fell from her hands. Her knees wobbled and she too collapsed. The gigantic serpent heads drooped groggily. Their long necks flexed, swayed, and twitched, then melted into the water. Enveloped in emerald vapors, a woozy stir got the best of the last of my lucidity. I held my breath and struggled to stand, dropping in a dizzy spin after just one step. My last thought was a realization: In a panic, lost in the mist, cocooned in confusion, Golly had pulled the lid from the keg of green slumber dust instead of the gunpowder. Now, left to her own devices, the majestic

Duchess strayed through the foggy furls and over the lapping
waves.

# Chapter 14:
## Island of the Valgars

In the middle of a lagoon, surrounded by a tropical jungle, the Duchess rested peacefully—as did her crew. The caws of macaws, toucans, and parrots and the chirps of finches, parakeets, and hummingbirds vexed the rousing Adventure Cat. "Such a clamor!" she said. "Won't you please stop? My head is pounding!" The cacophony intensified. "Very well, let's try this." The cat yowled like a banshee. The flutter of wings rivaled the roar of a waterfall. The remaining birds zipped their beaks.

The cat looked to the sky and all around. "What a lovely day! And what a beautiful place." In a hushed tone, she said, "This must be the island!"

An irregular strip of sand and rock formed the lagoon's perimeter. Grasses, fungus, and shrubbery afforded the jungle a delicate fringe, like the lace of a doily. The trees were tall, dense, and strewn with vines. The leaves of the canopy were a lustrous green, but the jungle's depths looked dark and dank.

Crocodiles basked at the water's edge. A daring heron strolled by. From the undergrowth crept a lime-green dimetrodon with a tiny mammal clenched in its jaws. The fin of a small shark sliced the still water. The mountains rumbled; the jungle roared.

Adventure examined the splintered stump that was now the main mast. She surveyed the fragments of the ship's anatomy scattered over the deck. "The wind's gusting up," she said. "We've got to get the sails down or we'll end up beached." She touched the snoring Golly on the arm, and he woke with a start.

Quickly sitting up, Golly swiveled his head and gazed in wonder. He locked eyes with the cat. "Where's them sea beasts?" he said.

Adventure nodded toward the mouth of the lagoon. "Out that way, I suppose."

Golly stood and rubbed the back of his neck. He walked to a gunwale and took in the view. Adventure joined him. The dog man said, "So this is the famous Valgar Island, then?"

"More infamous than famous, I should think," said Adventure. She scanned the trees and looked up at the smokey peaks. "Finding the toad in all this . . . it's going to be a nightmare."

"Aye," said Golly. "And that's puttin' things in the nicest of ways." Golly glanced at his sleeping friends. "Shall we wake 'em?"

"No need just now. Let's lower the sails and mull things over," said the cat. "I'll take the mizzen, you get the fore."

Standing where the mainsail had been, Golly and Adventure considered options. "You're the barn builder," said Adventure. "Can we replace the mast?"

"Aye, there's lots o' good, straight trees—lookin' round, I can see a dozen. And we've got the tools. We'll just down a tree, skin it, and tip it into the hold." Golly put his hands on his hips as he glanced at the crumpled sails. "We can make it home with a single sail if we must. I've seen it done."

"Sew the two together?"

Looking down into the mast portal, Golly said. "May be the only way o' sortin' things."

Neither the cat nor dog realized they were being watched—in fact, being studied—by two hulking figures lurking in the treetops. Neither the atavistic auricles of the cat or the dog's keen sense of smell provided the slightest clue. Their instincts were obscured by the jungle's atmosphere. Hidden among the fronds, shifting eyes perceived and reasoning minds calculated. Still unseen by the crew, the ornithoids looked for all the world like the Egyptian bird god Horus.

Adventure and Golly listened to the angry mountains rumble and watched them spit black smoke and orange flames. Caught up in the awesome display, they did not hear the near-silent whoosh as the Valgars swooped down. The taloned feet of the bird men hooked deeply into the chest and shoulders of the dog and cat. As the mighty wings of the bird men lifted the two high and away, Adventure yelled, "Leave a sign! Your boots!"

Golly kicked away a boot, then another. As the Valgars banked toward the smokey spires, Adventure pulled at her blue scarf and let the silken shawl drift to the top of the tallest palm. In a matter of seconds, the Valgars and their captives disappeared into the clouds.

***

Moments later, on the deck of the Duchess, Brutus sat up, yawned, and rubbed his eyes. With an expression of wonderment, he stood and surveyed all that was. "What's happened?" he said. "Where is everybody?" Getting his bearings, Brutus hurried around the ship, looking for his friends. He checked the forecastle and the darkness of the hold. On his way to the cabin, he saw me sleeping near the stern. Kneeling, he noticed the green dust on the floorboards. He held his breath and backed away while dragging me by the arms. Arduously, he shuffled along until we were clear of the sominous powder. He listened to my heartbeat and the sound of my breathing. I'll leave him to sleep.

Brutus walked the gunwales, gazing into the jungle. From the starboard rail, he spotted something on the sand. It appeared to be a boot. He picked up the telescope that lay near the cabin's wall and put it to his eye. Quickly adjusting the lens, he said, "It's Golly's for certain!"

Across the deck, the rowboat was well secured to its cleats. The dinghy's not been touched. Why would they have swum to the beach? It doesn't make sense. Then he spotted Golly's other boot near the forecastle. A boot on the boat and one in the sand, fifty yards apart. It's a riddle. And one I could well do without.

Brutus released the rowboat and turned it upright. The elf gathered weapons and supplies; next to the starboard gunwale he placed knapsacks, water jugs, a bow and arrows, a broadsword, a bo staff, and two pouches of slumber dust. From the forward hatch, he pulled a tangle of blocks and tackle. Dragging the rigging alongside the supplies he said, "All's in order. Time to wake the lad, er, gentleman —such that he is."

Once again scanning the jungle, Brutus saw something floating in the water a few feet from the bow. He grabbed a gaffing pole and hustled along gunwale to retrieve the item. Snagging, lifting, and examining, he said, "A waistcoat, and a fancy one at that—brass buttons and lined with satin. Must have been a dandy man about."

Directly below, water bubbled up with a gurgle. A knobby

snout shot straight out of the pond, followed by a long, narrow mouth whose jagged teeth parted and snapped. The massive fin tail of the creature slapped and sloshed up a tub full, drenching the elf. The denizen splashed away and disappeared. Thoroughly insulted, Brutus took an indignant step away from the rail only to feel a blast of air at his back. With a waft, a whoosh, and a snatch, the elf was taken up into the sky. He looked down as the ship became smaller and smaller, while ahead the mountain tops became larger and larger.

***

The Adventure Cat stood on a gritty stone floor looking up at the craggy hole of a volcanic chamber. At the other side of the chamber, Golly tested the integrity of a heavy wooden door that was locked, chained, and barred on the outside. The burly dog man laid a crushing grip on the iron handle, leaned away, and pulled with all his might, but the door did not budge. He took hold of the rusty bars of the small window, yanking and twisting with all his might. The tarnished metal held tight.

In the flickering shadows of an oil-soaked torch, a peculiar figure of a man was chained to the rock wall. He croaked, "I told you it was no use, you stupid oaf. Up top's the only way out." He fixed his goggle eyes on Adventure and said, "You and this fleabag oaf will be meat in a Valgar's belly by morning."

Golly walked toward the toad man and said, "Shut your gabby

little gob, froggie. You're turnin' me stomach."

Rounding the huge pile of hay in the center of the room, Adventure said, "I'd not call the dog man stupid, an oaf, or any other rude names for that matter, Parnie. When time comes to break free of this pit, you can bet Golly will lead the charge."

"Stop your mewing, Katherine," said the toad. "I've told you ninety times—the only way out of here is by me jumping up through that hole."

The cat glanced at the craggy circle above. "Even you can't jump that high, toad," she said. "Not without that stolen chunk of glass."

"Stolen?" retorted the toad. "Sweep the dust off your own stoop, mouser. I've got one good jump left in me. You know perfectly well a body draws substance from the Orb. And I've held two wedges in my hands. I got an extra dosing."

"True," conceded Adventure. "But it soon wears off and you've been without it for days. We've seen it happen to Piranda time and time again. If not for that fact, I'd never have trapped her in the tower."

"No arguing that. Good job I grabbed the slice and ran. I knew that little rabbit wench would set the witch free. And I'm surprised you got out of there with your bonce and scruff adjoined."

"Lay it to rest, toad. And don't pillory our Evelyn. She's just a shaken little waif, imprisoned and enslaved, same as us. You certainly did your share of bowing and scraping."

Parnie made blah-blah-blah croaking sounds. "Rabbit girl?" said Golly.

Adventure replied, "Piranda's other servant, Evelyn. Neither the toad nor I can cook worth tuppence. So, the hateful old thing stole away with a baker's daughter. She placed a rabbit curse on the lass and made her a kitchen maid."

Golly sadly shook his head. "A shame it is—a shame for all."

The toad man was far from finished with his wheedling. He squatted low, rose on his webbed toes, and flexed his chained arms. With a deep croak, he said, "I can still feel the power surging." He looked up. "I know I can make that jump. You've got to let me try before it's too late."

"Do you think us daft?" said Adventure. "You have no power. You look awful—half dead. How long have you been here?"

The listless toad muttered, "Days and nights, nights and days."

Golly asked, "So they knew you were a jumper. Is that why you're chained?"

"Why else?" He added, "They also know I stole their precious piece of Orb."

"And they want the slice back," said Golly. "That's why they 'aven't supped on ya."

"Exactly. But they do have plans for me—once they've lost their patience. They've shown me." The toad's eyes rolled to the left, rolled to the right. "I'll be put on my knees and chained to a flat wheel. As the wheel turns, they'll swoop down and gouge lumps of flesh from my bones. For them, it's a game, quite entertaining. It gives them cause to squawk and crow with the wildest hilarity."

Adventure's eyes narrowed. "You witnessed such a thing?"

"Oh yes, just as I've told you. They chained a monkey—a big, hairy monkey—to a slowly turning wheel. One at a time, they swooped down and tore pieces from it, right before my eyes. All that was left was a head with sheer terror frozen on its face, along with few odd scraps of skin and bone."

Golly and Adventure exchanged glances. Golly said, "He's deceitful and sly—but there could be some truth in it."

The cat folded her arms, then twisted her whiskers.

Parnie warned, "Same's in store for you. You're fools if you don't set me free. On my honor, I give my word—I'll anchor a line and throw down a rig for climbing."

"Liar!" said the cat, pointing at the toad. "You'll go after those Orb bits and have twice the power!"

The toad's googly eyes shifted as he sought to fib again. "If you—" "Shush!" said Adventure.

The dog man wore a smirk. The cat hissed and showed her fangs. The toad had lost his last scrap of credibility. Suddenly, their eyes darted to the hole above. A flapping clatter echoed off the walls. For an instant the opening went dark, and then something plummeted onto the pile of straw and sank out of sight. The straw stirred as the thing peered out. It was Brutus. Stunned, terrified, he drew back into the hay.

Golly said, "It's us, Brutus! Me and the cat."

Brutus peeked out again and then slowly crawled from the straw. He lunged forward and hugged the big dog around the waist.

"It's all right, lad," said Golly, returning the hug. "Poor sausage, I know you've 'ad a time of it."

Rubbing the front of his shoulder, Brutus said, "Their hooks— they've put holes in me."

"We've all got 'em," said Golly. "We've both had worse, you

and me. Nothing to be done."

"If only I'd had my sword," said the elf, fists clenching tighter with each word. "If only I'd had my sword!"

"Don't worry, Brutus," said Adventure, extending her claws. "Any bird man that comes through that door will see his feathers fly."

***

Night had fallen when I awoke. Still drowsy, I sat on the deck holding my head. "My brain is pounding," I mumbled. "I feel like I'm gonna puke. That green dust. It must have poisoned me."

I stood slowly and leaned against the stern. Spritelight sparkled across the lagoon like sequins on black velvet. As my eyes followed the outline of the jungle, I said, "This must be the island. The others—they must still be asleep."

Gaining my sea legs, I walked toward the cabin. Through the jungle seeped the sounds of night: chirps, cackles, caws, growls, roars, chatters, squeaks, and squeals. From the water came tricklings, sloshes, dunks, splashes, and splunks. I hurried to the cabin and looked within. "Anybody there? Hey! Anybody? Adventure?"

Vision adjusting to the dark, I inspected the damage to the

mast and then noticed the rowboat, block and tackle, and supplies. I issued my assessment aloud. "Looks like they were setting up for a morning escapade. They must be in the forecastle." I checked. Empty bunks were all I found. I continued muttering to myself. "They're gone. They left the boat, and they didn't take a single weapon. They wouldn't have swum to shore—not all three . . . I don't get it. It makes no sense at all." Rumbles. An explosion. The jungle went quiet. Blobs and clumps of lava spread across the distant the sky like fireworks. Lost and alone, I returned to the cabin, went inside and closed the door. I fumbled around and found a lantern and matches in the middle of the table. I kept the flame dim, latched and bolted the door, and pulled the curtains over both windows. "Lord knows what might be out there." Above the bookshelf were two crossed cutlasses. Laying one on the table, I gripped the handle of the other, then took a few swings and jabs. "A genuine pirate sword, trusty and true," I said. "Early- eighteenth century."

A thump came from outside. Someone was on the deck. I barred the entrance and lowered the flame. Click, clink, clack. Someone was twisting the handle of the door. The handle rattled and the door creaked as something weighty pushed against it. The hinges squeaked and strained. Pounding, scratching. The lantern flame died; it was pitch dark in the cabin. More pushing and pounding from outside, but the door held. There were bawks, squawks, and clucks. After a brief silence, a laggardly caw sirened high into a spine- tingling screech.

# Chapter 15:
## Enwalled

Gathered around the fettered Parnelius Wermbom were Adventure, Golly, and Brutus. All three folded their arms and stared at the scoundrel. The toad man feebly tugged at his chains; crumbs of mortar fell away, but the bolts held fast.

"Did you see how the mortar gives way? It's ancient. The three of you could easily wrest the shackles from the wall." The toad rattled his chains. "I swear to you. I'll find your ship and bring back a rope ladder. If I—"

"Cor blimey, Parnie! Put a sock in it," said Adventure. She drew close and put a finger in his face. "You claim possession of both Orb pieces. Where are they?"

"Buried," he said. "In the jungle, maybe two miles south. When they found their slice gone, the bird men shrieked out in rage. I could hear them as I moved through the trees. They hunted me on the land and in the air. Circling above, one spied me near a beach as I headed for the waves. When I turned back and leaped to escape, he nearly snatched me from the sky. I landed in the jungle and crouched, without twitch, without a twatch. I held my breath and cringed low until the ponderous louts went tramping by."

Golly pried, "Why couldn't they smell ya? Eh, froggie?"

"Birds aren't able to smell, you oaf!" said the toad. "They have no sense for it. And they don't hear much either. Have you never read a book?"

Golly scowled.

Adventure looked at the dog man. "Aye, Golly, though I hate to say it, he's right about the birds. At least that much is true."

Brutus asked, "Right then, toad—why didn't you use that Orb against them?"

"Learning its powers takes time, you little dullard. One must be very careful. For now, all I can do is jump, jump high as the clouds and glide on the wings of my coat. But I lost the waistcoat in the trees. No more gliding till I find it."

"That must have been the one I found in the lagoon," said Brutus.

"It's mine! I'd hung it to dry after my long swim. It's mine, and I'll have it back!"

"All right, all right, Mr. Parnie, calm down," said Brutus. "It's back on our ship."

Pacing, the cat turned to the toad. "Can you find the spot where you buried those pieces of Orb?"

The toad said, "Easily. I buried them right at the foot of a stone carving. It was all green-teethy and covered with vines."

Adventure pressed, "A carving of what?"

"A skinny little man, with a swollen head and great big eyes."

"There's a stone man like that in the Farthingale," said Brutus. "Odd- looking thing."

Golly asked suspiciously, "If them bird men couldn't smell ya, hear ya, or see ya—how'd ya end up here?"

"When I went to retrieve the crystals, I heard them moving through the trees. I hid again, but they noticed my digging. Their sharp eyes fell on the matted grass where I'd knelt. I tried sneaking away, but they had me penned. One bonked me on the conk with a heavy hand. When my eyes opened, here I was, chained to this wall."

"The toad tells a good story," said Brutus. "At least I'll give him that."

"But there's a huge hole in his yarn," said the leery cat. She looked the toad in the eye. "I don't believe you're as hapless as you claim. With a full half of the almighty Orb in your hands, you should have been able to lay waste to those creatures."

Impatient, Parnie snarled, "You know the Orb can be danger- ous, Katherine! It could easily destroy its holder. We've both burned our hands for the touching of it."

Adventure paused in thought. Begrudgingly, she said, "I'll

grant you that. Piranda took proper care with her trials. She could transform people and things, but only after holding it for a time. As far as—"

"And that's the end of it!" said the toad. "Piranda was a charlatan. Most maddening of all—she cannot reverse her spell! We're trapped in these bodies, Katherine! Forever, unless I learn the ways of the Orb. Think about it! I could return to the mountains and find the tablets and scrolls. I could learn to change us back! You'd be a woman again, a noble knight of the grandest order."

The cat sighed. "Highly doubtful."

"Not doubtful. The Orb has cryptographs, which ascribe to its secrets. I am convinced there are scrolls and tablets hidden in the mountain caves. Once I find them, I'll do the ciphering. Once I've found each of the quarters, I'll fuse the whole and soon master the wonder, the majesty, the glory of the indigo ball. I would know all, I could do all, I would rule all and live on and on forever . . ."

"With such power in your hands, I can think of no greater monster— you horrible, nasty old thing!"

In the wake of Adventure's words, the silence in the chamber was ice cold, the tension tighter than a clam at high tide. Finally, Golly said, "So that's that. The only way out is, we fight! That's all there's left to do."

"I'm for that!" said Brutus. "I'll gladly bloody their bloody beaks."

Parnie's frog-mouthed raspberry scoff resonated. "You can't battle those things! You two are thicker than Swift's porridge. A couple of addle-brained dolts."

Adventure approached Golly and Brutus with sincere reverence. "You're very brave men—among the bravest I've ever known. But we've all seen the size of these monsters, those terrible beaks and talons. Without our weapons, we'd be slaughtered. They'd shred us like lumps of beef." The cat stared at the dungeon door, gazed up at the opening, twisted her whiskers, and said, "I have another idea . . ."

*** 

It was morning. Having spent most of the night with my shoulder glued to the cabin door, I had reached the point of now or never. I took one of the cutlasses from the cabin table and slipped a telescope into the pocket of my trousers. Quietly, I unlatched the door, then burst out onto the deck.

Scattered on the floorboards were feathers, some quite colorful, some of quite a length. I looked at the deep gouges in the cabin door. "Valgars," I said and scanned the jungle. The water's surface was still, and the sky was clear of smoke. To the north, atop the fronds of the tallest palm, was a strange speck of blue. Telescope in hand, I took a closer look. It was the Adventure Cat's royal blue scarf. She left a sign. They've taken her to the mountains.

Using the block and tackle, trial-and-error positioning, and leverage, I managed to lower the rowboat and supplies into the lagoon. Making certain the corks in the water flasks were fully secure, I turned my attention to the weapons: a broadsword, a slingshot, a bo staff, a bow and quiver of arrows. I unlaced a leather pouch and carefully removed a small packet of the slumber dust that Burgomaster Stanislaus had provided. The dust could be dispersed by tearing, squeezing, or on impact. After rowing a few strokes, I threw a packet at the ship's hull. Bursting on contact, it spread quickly and dissipated—a successful field test.

Other than the faint songs of birds, the jungle was relatively quiet. I could hear the oars as I rowed. Perhaps the heat and humidity had consigned the wildlife to repose. Then again, perhaps a visit from the top of the food chain had sent them into hiding. At this thought, my eyes went to my bow and arrows. I brought the oars in and reached for my bow. I nocked an arrow, drew back, and drove it into a cypress stump. Setting down the bow, I pulled the saw-tooth blade from a sheath at my hip; in the jungle, it was an all-purpose tool.

As I rowed closer to shore, I noticed a swampy inlet. Sitting at the mouth of the canal, I gazed up through the canopy at the smokey spires to get an estimate of distance and a feel for direction. I mumbled, "Those peaks could serve as watchtowers." Considering this, I reasoned the only safe approach would be under the cover of trees. At least there was no shortage of those.

Deeper inland, the swamp came alive. Enormous dragonflies chased enormous mosquitos. Crocodiles lazed among the roots and in the mud. Herons, egrets, and storks patrolled the shallows. Milky plumes steamed eerily through tufts of tall grass. Schools of fish brushed alongside the boat. On a slab of stone, a small fin-backed lizard flicked its tongue at flies. From their sanctum among the foliage, huge-eyed lemurs and tarsiers ogled all.

"Dry ground, dry ground, my kingdom for dry ground," I said, laughing at my own nonsense.

Off to the left were some hefty boulders and a few downed, dead trees. When I reached the site, I found the turf to be somewhat mushy; still, it was solid enough to traverse. Pulling the boat onto a firm base, I lashed it to a palm. At this point, the stealth strategy would click up a notch. For my trek: the saw-tooth knife, a coil of rope, and a pouch of slumber dust. Eyeing the flasks of water, I juggled the ups and downs. Carrying water can be an encumbrance, especially if you need to move with quickness and finesse through trees and brush. As per habitual preference, I decided to down a quart and leave the rest. Plenty of fronds and ferns covered the boat nicely.

As I began my jaunt, there was a great flapping of wings. A griffon vulture touched down, perching nearby on a branch jutting from the swamp. Its neck bent into a p-trap. It started bobbing its head and then made a screaming hiss. I muttered, "Are you trying to tell me something, buddy?" The vulture tipped its head and nodded; it squawked, cackled, and spied me with each eye. It seemed to caw, "Take care," before winging away. "Roger Wilco, and out," I said.

Sharp leaves and grasses posed a constant nuisance as I hiked through the rattan and bamboo. After a mile or so, the trees, vines, and grasses thinned out. The avian sound-around was a symphony compared to the screeching of that griffon vulture. Whether by providence or random chance, I finally wandered into a clearing. Glints of spritelight danced among the leaves.

It was all very beautiful until I saw a ten-inch spider crawl into the middle of a twenty-foot web. The arachnid's exoskeleton gleamed like a black pearl. Similar webs entwined the trees in all directions, which meant similar spiders dwelled among the trees in all directions. A huge, hirsute fly buzzed into one of the sticky nets and was instantly pounced upon; its life-surrendering squeal was nauseating. Like it or not, I was in spider land.

When I turned to retrace my steps, eight writhing legs dangled in front of my face. Instinctively, I struck out, the spider went flying, and I hustled back to the head of the trail. I'd prefer sharp grasses to tree tarantulas anytime. A carnivore's roar thundered in the undergrowth, a shrill gnarr pierced the air. I had to get out of the jungle.

Trotting back the way I'd come, I noticed the boscage to the south grew less dense. Weaving in that direction, I found the brush and grass kinder in nature. Eventually, I would curl back and head toward the mountains. Though it was the long way around, it seemed taking the path of least resistance was the most sensible option. At first, I thought I'd come upon a wanderer's dream. Soft light filtering through the canopy bathed a variety of tropical blooms: violets, morning glories, lilies, orchids, torch ginger, orchids, hibiscus, and jasmine. Their unearthly perfume stirred a giddy delight. The soil was soft and moist, and the grasses were tall and supple.

High above, the palm fronds gently swayed. Ahead lay a spacious glade. An inviting windmill palm beckoned me to rest. With my next step, something tapped me on the head. Then something struck me lightly on the calf. When I looked down, there was a nut of some sort inches from my boot. It was large, light green, and kidney shaped, resembling a raw cashew. Hundreds of them littered the ground. Another glanced off my right cheek. Clusters of these nuts hung among the loftiest branches. And there was something else up among those trees. Of course: a perfect paradise must always have a ruinous snake. But these weren't snakes. Curious, and perhaps emboldened by my unthreatening manner, one emerged, lithe and nimble, and traipsed along a bare branch. It was similar to a proboscis monkey. Its nose was enormous, and it had a pot belly and a fur coat of many colors. I chuckled at a memory—the creature looked for all the world like my little league baseball coach clad in his favorite argyle sweater. But there was one disturbing difference . . . this creature had wicked eyes.

And now the trees were alive. The monkeys crept from an umbrage and slunk from the shadows. Their fur mimicked the colors of the glade's flourishing blooms. A cacophony of hoots and howls saturated the air. The cashew-like nuts flew by the handfuls. And they were thrown hard; they stung. I ran. Keeping to the treetops, the simians followed. The nuts kept zinging. Leaping from a lofty roost, one of the beasts landed in the grass in front of me, staring in deliberate opposition. Horns curved from its elbows. It curled back its lip, exposing wicked incisors, fang-like detention for stabbing and tearing. Years ago, I'd learned that woofing like a guard dog could scare animals away. I gave it a try. My intimidator backed off a few steps. The trees went quiet. But these mutant primates weren't fooled for long.

Harlequinesque monkeys dropped from the trees, one after another, and began creeping toward me from all directions. Something heavy landed on my shoulders, toppling me down.

It now stood above me. When it raised its arms and hooted, I gave it a swift kick to the vulnerables. It screamed, somersaulted backward and hobbled away. The others froze, stared, then slowly crept closer.

Subtly, cautiously, I unlaced the slumber dust pouch at my waist. I relaxed, took a deep breath, and held it. Slipping half a dozen packets into my left hand. I transferred one to my right, pinched the packet open, and flicked it into the horde. I flicked another, and another. As the monkeys drooped and dropped, I hopped over bodies and raced away.

Dodging trees, jumping over rocks, brushing vines aside, holding my breath all the while, I put as much distance between myself and variegated varmints as possible. About to pass out, I knelt in the grass and gasped. Starting with shallow breaths, ending with deep breaths, I renewed my strength and sprinted on. Ignoring scrapes from branches and scratches from brush, I made my way northwest through the jungle.

At last, I reached the jungle's edge. Just through the trees, waves rolled onto a rocky shore. White froth topped the incoming tide. My eyes followed the beach to where the waves lapped against a scree of rock, the base of the volcanic spires.

The mountains puffed and grumbled. Somewhere within their chambers, I believed I would find my friends.

A premise, an assumption, a hypothesis, an estimation—I needed a structure on which to base decisions. I tapped my memory files and brainstormed. Militarily, for thousands of years the strategy of taking the high ground has been universal. If I were to set up a fortress on the island, the highest peak would be my watchtower, and my base of operations would be nearby. Prisoners would be held close to the command center in the interest of readily gathering information. I felt certain there were joined chambers—whether excavated, constructed, or formed by nature—within the Valgar compound. The interconnections were likely to be intricate.

My first tactic had to be recon. I would watch the comings and goings, identify entrances, wait until dark, and then scout the perimeter. Optimal positioning would require crossing a sixty-yard stretch of open ground where a patch of jungle crept up to an outset of rocks and shrubs. A sound from above seized my attention. Among the wispy clouds, a human-like form flapped massive wings as it circled the rocky steeples. Staying just out of sight, I followed the jungle's edge, stopping at the sight of a trickle from a narrow ledge. I'd been perspiring heavily, and the humidity of the jungle had kept my body from cooling. As the flyer soared beyond the spires, my thirst demanded I reach the water.

Knife in hand, I made my run. Rocks of all sizes peppered the beach. Out of the sand popped scorpion-like crabs. Dodging them was like playing hopscotch. If not for my boots, they'd have pinched my feet to bloody stumps. The sixty yards seemed like sixty miles. Finally reaching the base of the mountains, I negotiated the nooks and crannies till I reached the water. It was incredibly refreshing. Luxuriating, I let the water drench me to the bone. Opening wide, I swallowed away till I was good for another 50,000 miles.

Again, there was movement in the sky. Six Valgars flew in formation, like a Blue Angel squadron. I ducked beneath some scraggly shrubs. The cursed things were as itchy as heck, but I dared not move. Bird men out of sight, I moved on, rounding a craggy mound, and there it was, sent from heaven—the entrance to a cave. Staring into the caliginous hollow, I heard the squeaking and winging of bats and saw a flickering point of light. As I stepped into the welcoming foyer, my eyes soon adjusted. The light came from a torch; it burned at the end of a long corridor that appeared to branch right. Strewn through the hallway were bones of all sorts; a patrol of sizable rats rattled over them. Halfway to the torch, a hulking form came into view: the shadow of a Valgar. Its scalding scream turned me to ice. A moment later, thawed by sheer terror, I spun and ran. Bursting from darkness, I was slapped to the ground by a giant wing. I pulled my knife, but it was kicked away. Monstrous talons sank into my chest and shoulders. I was launched skyward and dangled like a chicken in a butcher's shop.

***

With folded arms, sour expressions, and frequent eye rolls, Golly, Adventure, and Brutus gave audience to the fettered toad. He cycled through wallowing in self-pity, throwing fits of anger and spite, and pledging the allegiance of his body and soul to the doubting trio. He sniveled and whined, grumbled and growled, humbly groveled, and made promises from his heart of hearts.

"In this confinement, relegated to this ordeal, I've had hours untold to mull over my greedy, wretched life. I've come to understand the virtues of loyalty and honor, generosity, goodwill, and selflessness."

"Enough, enough," said Adventure. "I've been locked in a tower and subject to your drivel for what feels like an eternity. You lie, upon lie, upon lie, upon lie."

"Oh, what a tangled web we weave, when first we practice to deceive," said Brutus.

Golly said, "Oi, this is no time for Shakespeare, mate." "Sir Walter Scott," the elf corrected.

"Please, gentlemen!" said Adventure. "The matter at hand!"

The toad vowed, "Once I'm free of this filthy pit, I'll slip beneath the sea, make my way to the jungle, exhume the Orb chunks, find your ship, and then return with a climbing rope and duffel of weapons."

"No," said the cat caustically. "You'll head straight for the gorge and the third slice of Orb—provided you have all the luck in all the worlds."

"Sounds right," said Golly. "And you won't be jumping far with them bird men 'overin' about."

The toad declaimed, "I'm a toad, oaf. I can breathe through my skin. I can stay beneath the ripples as long as I want. Any time I like, I can spring from the water and hop a dozen times before sinking."

Golly and Brutus narrowed their eyes. "Horse muck!" said Brutus. "Tell them, Katherine!"

The cat huffed, "Yes, I've seen him do such things. Sometimes Piranda would have him fetch sticks she'd thrown into a lake. She found it greatly amusing."

The toad jerked wildly at his chains. "Don't be such fools! We'll all end up on the wheel!" He began to cry. "You need me. I need you. We've no time to waste! You must set me free!"

Brutus said, "Rotten as it is, we're all in the same boat. What choice do we have?"

The dog man tugged at a shackle chain. The bolted plate yielded. Crumbs of mortar fell. He looked to Adventure for approval. "I believe I can pull the binding free o' the wall. Then bash the cuffs off with a stone."

"He can't be trusted," said Adventure. She addressed Brutus and Golly most sincerely. "For the sake of you two, I believe I should listen. But this vile creature will never change. However, and not to give false hope, as I said, I do have an idea." She backed all the way to the dungeon door and gazed at the opening above.

Golly said, "What are ya thinkin', cat?" "Acrobatics," she said. "Can you jump, elf?"

"A circus stunt!" said Brutus. "I jump at the carnival games. I can jump a good foot over my own head—one of the best elf jumpers there is."

"That hole looks to be just over twenty feet up," said Adventure.

Golly focused a trained eye. "I'm supposin' a gable barn o' that height would be close to twenty feet, right enough."

"We've got to have perfect timing, Brutus. Golly will brace against the wall. I'll stand on his shoulders and then bend and lock my fingers, like a stirrup."

"A boost," said Brutus. "Golly's boosted me many a time."

"When your foot hits my hands, Golly will stand up. I'll jump, lift, and throw you high."

"And I'll grab the rocky rim and pull myself out the hole."

"If we miss the first time, you'll fall in the hay, and we'll try again." Golly clapped. "Jolly good idea. Jolly good."

"I'll mark my steps," said Brutus. "The way we do at the carnival. I'll start my run clear back by the door."

A determined Brutus walked to the dungeon door and stretched his legs. Adventure practiced a bend-and-boost exercise. The chamber wall curved inward, so Golly worked out the geometry.

Clearly worried, the toad said, "Acrobatics?! You'll be falling on top of each other like stumblebum clowns. I've been saving my strength. I can get through that hole in one jump without any blundering boost!"

Adventure helped Brutus with the timing of his steps. Standing on the optimal spot, Golly said, "It's now or never, mates."

With his back to the door, Brutus fidgeted. Golly set his stance, and Adventure pounced lightly onto his shoulders. Her tail afforded perfect balance. Brutus stepped to the side and lined up his approach. Not one of them heard the slight rattle of a chain outside the door. In less than a flash, the door popped open, and a taloned hand scooped the elf into the corridor.

Before Adventure and Golly crossed half the chamber, the door slammed shut and the lock clicked. Golly pounded the door with both fists. Adventure hissed like a feral stray; her tail was puffed and the hair on her arms stood up. She paced and twisted her whiskers. The toad gloated, "Now look what you've done. They'll chain that elf to the wheel and tear him to ribbons."

Adventure eyed the crater. "I can manage most of that jump, Golly," she said. "With a good throw, maybe you can boost me just enough."

The toad croaked, "You can't fly, you stupid cat! I'm your only hope."

***

After a last mighty flap, the Valgar carrying me went into a glide. Thickening smoke burned my eyes, and I began to cough. Once over the smokey cones, I believed I could make a successful jump. I reached up and tried twisting the creature's toes. At that moment, the bird man clutching my shoulders let go.

Plummeting in freefall, I had no idea I would soon be in the company of my friends. I dropped into the chamber and landed right in the middle of a haystack. When I rolled down the straw, I surprised only the toad. Adventure and Golly beamed with welcoming smiles. The cat helped me to my feet.

The big dog man tousled my hair.

"Relieved to see you again," said Adventure.

"Me as well," said Golly. "Too bad it 'ad to be down here in this 'ole."

"Who's that little brat?" sneered the toad.

I dusted the straw from my clothing, walked up, looked him in the eye, and said, "That's Captain, to you, frog face. You took a ride on my airplane—without a ticket. Now that we've officially met—it has not been a pleasure to make your acquaintance."

# Chapter 16:
## Chains

"They've taken Brutus," said Adventure. "The toad's told us the bird men have some sort of wheel. It's part of a ritual. The creatures chain a prisoner to a spinning platform and then take turns swooping down, attacking with their beaks and talons . . ."

The toad's face twisted. "Till all that's left is a gaping, hollow-eyed skull." His insane laughter curdled the air.

"Shut yer ruddy gob, froggie!" said Golly. "Or I'll be ringin' the seven bells out!"

"Never mind him, Golly," said Adventure. "There's no time."

"Aye, back to business." Golly hurried beside the haystack and interlocked his hands. "I'll toss ya right the way up through that blinkin' hole, Miss."

My eyes measured the chamber bottom to top. "That's gotta be two stories up. Maybe three."

"Timing is the trick," said the cat. "It'll be close."

Adventure paced her steps to the farthest point in the chamber. She studied the distances and angles. "Should do," she said. She bent at the knees, popped up and bounced on her toes, flexed her neck, and shrugged her shoulders. Golly set a wide stance and formed a secure stirrup. The cat shot me a glance. "Count to three, Captain."

"One . . . two . . ."

In loping strides, Adventure covered the ground in a blink. She hit her mark and Golly gave a mighty heave. High she flew and grabbed the rocky rim. Her lithe body swung up and she hooked the opening with her heel. The stone cracked and crumbled. She shifted her grip, but the rim kept giving way, leaving her to dangle by one arm. Claws piercing the eroding ore, she swayed like a pendulum, gained a new grip, and again hooked a heel. With a bouncing rhythm, Adventure nudged a knee and elbow over the ridge. As she crawled out, chunks of rock broke away from the rim. She froze. With utmost delicacy she inched a little further. Crrrrrrack! The cat, a slab of stone, and thousands of gritty crumbs tumbled into the straw. "It's no use," said Adventure as she bounded from the hay. "The stone's too weathered. It won't hold."

Golly gnashed his teeth. "Then we fight!"

The cat pulled the penknife from her pocket and handed it to me. She raised her hand and extended her claws. "We fight."

"We fight," I said.

"And you'll be slaughtered like lambs," said the toad. A silence loomed. "Free me. As I've been telling you—we must work together. Free me. It's our only chance."

The cat paced and twisted her whiskers. Golly and I stood ready. She nodded toward the toad and approached us. She whispered, "To my great dismay, we must free the toad."

"I'm up for the fight," said Golly.

"Fighting's fine with me," I said.

"Brave men. You are both knights as much as I. Misgivings aside; we must share words with the scoundrel."

The three of us crossed the chamber and confronted the toad. Reluctantly, resentfully, Adventure set forth the agenda. With a firm voice and steady gaze, she said, "So it's come to this, Parnelius Wermbom, you sniveling cur. We free you. You find our ship in the lagoon, bring back a rigging, secure it, and drop it to us. We find Brutus and we'll all sail home together."

"All well and good," was the toad's sly reply. "And you'll surrender the Orb, of course."

"Of course. I regret the day I set eyes on the ghastly thing."

Adventure cleared her throat. "Betray us, and you betray yourself. You need us. You need our ship. We leave together or not at all."

The toad's eyes filled with innocence, his words with resignation. "Together . . . it's the only way."

On our honor, we nodded in agreement. The dog man grasped one chain with both hands and easily pulled a fetter from the wall. The second shackle proved stubborn, and Golly gnashed his teeth, grimacing as he strained. The sides of the mounting plate buckled, but the corroded bolts held. Golly gripped closer to the mount and put his shoulder against the wall. Meanwhile, Adventure had taken her penknife back from me and used it to release the first cuff. With a torque and a tug, Golly finally freed the other chain. He pried the cuff open with his fingers alone.

Before anyone could say a word, the toad leaped toward a chamber wall, reversed his position in midair, planted his webbed feet against the side of the chamber, and then kicked. Performing the same maneuver from the opposite wall, he leveled a final kick and shot up and out of the shaft. Looking down from the rocky rim, he leered and taunted, "What fools you are and ever will be. In minutes, I'll have the crystals and be swimming deep beneath the waves. It may take a week, it may take two, and I may be dodging toothy fishes the entire trip, but I'll reach the coast. Then it's on to the gorge and the next wedge!" The laughter of madness followed. The toad looked up, down and all around. "Enjoy the wheel!" he gibed, then hopped out of sight.

Our aspirations had fallen deeper than the darkest of chasms in the land. In the flickering torchlight, among forsaken shadows, Adventure, Golly, and I contemplated our fate, which would almost certainly be a merciless death. Being in the company of warriors at the time of my demise was the only saving grace. Getting piqued for battle was second nature for the three of us. In one way or another, we'd been fighting our entire lives. Golly armed himself with shackle chains. Adventure had her teeth and claws. And I again had possession of the cat's penknife. Though we would succumb to a greater force, we would not be easy prey.

Golly gazed up through the crater at the winking nighttime sprites. "By my reckonin', them bird men have probably caught the toad by now. I'd not be surprised to see him drop through that 'ole anytime."

"That could be the way of it," said Adventure. "But if he can get to the water, he could very well make it home."

"That's a mighty long swim," I said.

Adventure replied, "An impossible swim—for a cat, a dog, or a young man. But for a toad, it's just a long, wet journey . . . If he stays beneath the waves, he'll escape the bird men."

"He'll have to dodge them big fishes," said Golly.

"Agreed," said the cat. "He'll have to mind his p's and q's till he gets past the reef. Then he can hop across the water to his heart's delight."

Golly said, "Worst thing is, he might learn some fancy tricks with them Orb bits."

"Always a possibility," said Adventure. "Piranda had no easy time of it, but she was very careful, very patient."

"That could be his undoing right there," I said. "Parnie Wermbom didn't strike me as having a whole lot of patience."

"No patience at all!" said Golly. "Messin' with that black magic mumbo jumbo! He's likely to bung 'imself up in two ticks o' the clock."

I walked up to the imposing dungeon door, grabbed the bars of the small window, and pulled myself up. "A long, dark tunnel, both directions . . . that's all I can see."

"Hard to see anything," said Golly. "Them torches out there are nearin' their last."

"When do you think they'll come?" I said.

"'Ard to say," said Golly. "No way o' knowin' how bird men think."

Adventure joined me at the door; she looked out the window, opened her palm, and said, "Hand me the knife." She took the blade and began working the archaic latch mechanism. "Whoever made off with Brutus forgot to bar the door. And the outer chain is hanging loose."

"We may be able to sneak away without a fight," I said.

"I'll not leave without the elf," said Golly.

"Indeed not," said Adventure. "But now we'll be able to find him on our terms."

"I know the way back to the lagoon," I said. "We can move through the jungle much faster than those huge birds."

As she probed the keyhole with finesse and precision, a knowing look came over the cat's face. With a quick twitch of the wrist came a click within the lock. Quietly gripping the handle, Adventure slowly cracked the door and peered out. She pulled it open just far enough to slip into the hall. Golly and I followed. I replaced the outer chain and locked the padlock.

Adventure pointed to the torch at the darker end of the tunnel. She handed me her penknife and whispered, "Take the darker path, Captain—not likely as many birds. Golly and I will head into the brighter tunnel, then branch off. Tonight, tomorrow night, we search for the elf. Then, elf or no elf, we must return to the ship." We exchanged glances and nodded in agreement. But neither Adventure nor I believed Golly would leave without his friend. Though it would be tragic to leave the little fellow behind, he had the heart of a giant and the courage of a lion. He'd have wanted us to press on.

As I walked the dark corridor, I pondered our decision to take different paths. There's strength in numbers. I had heard that adage many times. But we were on a search-and-rescue mission, so splitting up made the most sense—we could cover more ground. If the Valgars were going to harm Brutus, chain him to the wheel, it was likely they would do it soon, so a two-party search also made sense. Meeting back at the ship provided a familiar location for a rendezvous.

We had to assume the worst: The toad would reach Morningtown, then move on to the east to search for the third slice of Orb in the Gorge of the Gargoyle. Just as with this island, little was known about the gorge, but I'd heard it described as desolate and volcanic. Supposedly there was a temple, perhaps a ziggurat, which was a gateway to the surface. But it was guarded by a gargoyle, a demonic statue that came to life at the approach of man or beast. The third slice of Orb was lodged in the demon's forehead, a third eye, from which the creature could draw life. Though winged and taloned like the Valgars, it was more bat than bird, and more man than bat. Like a Gila monster, it could exude poison through grooves in its jagged teeth. And the creature was much larger than the bird men, two or three times their size. No one knew for certain. Regardless, for me, there was no decision to be made. If taking on that monster would help me get back home, so be it.

Lost in my thoughts, I was unaware of the confrontation a quarter mile back, at the brighter end of the dungeon corridor.

***

Golly, chains in hand, and Adventure, hair on end, claws extended, stood face-to-face with a Valgar. The bird man stood over seven feet in height and had the featherless chest and torso of a powerful man. His upper arms were bare, but his forearms were covered with plumate. He had the top notch of a sea eagle, and orange, hybrid hands. His thighs were bare skin, but his shins and calves were feathery. At the end of his legs were taloned feet, having only four toes. His eyes were keen, quick, and intelligent. His aquiline beak came to a skull-piercing point. He needed no weapon; he was a weapon. He was clad in an Egyptian-style cuirass and kilt. The creature tipped his head curiously, showing no sign of threat or malice. But he clearly meant to block the path of the dog and cat.

"We've come to get our friend," Adventure said calmly.

"Where's me mate? What 'ave you done with 'im?" said Golly, staving off his proclivity to fight.

"We'll stay our hands, dog man," said Adventure. "The bird

stands placid. There must be a reason."

"Stand placid? He'd better bloody well stand aside."

Adventure's eyes caught the bird's. "Let us pass, and there'll be no trouble. We only want our friend—the little elf." The cat extended her hand, palm down, about four feet from the ground. "He's a small man—about so high."

The Valgar chirped softly and then cawed slowly and quietly. Both Golly and Adventure considered this the warning before a strike. "Stand aside, bird," said Golly. "We mean to pass." They waited politely. The bird simply tipped his head.

"No use, lass. The budgie'll not budge."

"Not likely. I see him as a guard. He's simply standing his post. He'll not let us pass."

"Right then. You go left, I'll go right."

"Take a step, Golly, a step to distract. I'll leg him down and we'll bind him with a chain."

With his right foot, Golly dramatically stepped forward. Instantly, Adventure dove at the bird's legs, digging her claws deep. Her lean, steely muscles came to full strength as she wrestled the creature to the stone floor. With a flap of his mighty wings, the Valgar shot upright. Adventure was thrown ten feet. Golly whirled a chain. The creature kicked out with a taloned heel, sending Golly into the wall. Adventure pounced. Feathers flew. The pointed beak came down on her head, and she lay still. As Golly rose, a snare circled his neck. He was yanked off his feet and dragged along the floor by a second bird. A third Valgar rushed in and slipped a snare around the cat's neck. She too was dragged. After a short distance, the Valgars used their snare sticks to pull Golly and Adventure to their feet. The two were marched down the corridor. Meanwhile, the first guard looked down at the feathers from his cat-scratched wing. He squawked in annoyance and maintained his post.

# Chapter 17:
# The Wheel

The tunnel I walked was somewhat drafty and a little cooler than the dungeon chamber. Many of the torches had gone out, but there was enough light for me to see rats scurry past and spiders crawl the walls. The corridor curved left. Up ahead, it widened and opened into a cavern: a solutional cave filled with stalactites and stalagmites. Pools of oil burned here and there. Bats darted erratically, chasing bugs that I could not see. The whole place smelled like heating fuel, which triggered vivid memories of oil stoves and ice fishing in Michigan, spawning a bittersweet longing for home, to be sitting with my buddies in a shack on the lake, eating 'roni sticks and drinking Canadian beer. As always, for me, reminiscing calmed fears and eased tension. Sometimes a look back sharpens the mind for what lies ahead.

As I looked around, I found myself at the bottom of a limestone bowl with only one way out—the way I'd come in. About to turn back, I noticed a light faintly flickering on a high ledge. A dying torch had been hidden by stalactites hanging over the mouth of another cave. There wasn't much of a climb involved, but the ledge was narrow and fragile in places. Walking the mineral tightrope proved precarious; avoiding the fiery pools below added a strong incentive. I hugged the wall and tiptoed like a ballerina.

The mouth of the next cave opened to a foyer of striated rock. There was a large hole in the side of the foyer—the entrance to a chute. At the bottom of the chute was a wavering light. Down I went, as if I were on an amusement park slide. I popped out of the tube like a champagne cork and landed on my feet.

What surrounded me was astonishing. I was in a treasure vault. It was full of wooden pirate chests full of pillaged booty: Spanish doubloons, pieces of eight, Roman coins, British crowns, jewels, pearls, goblets of silver and gold. There were casks and kegs, crates and boxes, sacks and bags—no doubt all filled with wealth and riches. And there were artifacts from eras and places both known and unknown: a conquistador's helmet, a Spartan's shield, a Ming vase, an Egyptian scroll, works of Renaissance art, a German Luger, a Zulu spear, a fielder's glove sporting a Tom Tresh autograph, and books stacked to the ceiling. Pulling the lid from a crate, I found magazines and comic books. I carefully lifted out a copy of The Saturday Evening Post dated June 1, 1968. There was a picture of Robert F. Kennedy on the cover with the article title: "How Bobby Kennedy Plans to Win It." On the back was an ad for Winston cigarettes.

At that moment, I was overcome by a feeling of shame. Here I was, indulging in folly while I had friends out there in need of help. The door of the treasure vault creaked when I went out. I made certain to close it tight and could not help but wonder whether the treasure room had been dangled as a lure.

Oil lamp wall sconces lit a carpeted, wood-paneled hallway. At the end of the hall was a landing and the banister of a staircase. On the wall was a framed photo of actress Lillie Langtry, circa 1880—shades of the Old West. On my way down the stairs, I expected to see an elegant hotel parlor; what I saw was a stark stone chamber and the opening to another tunnel. Logic and reason told me the Valgars would not have taken Brutus into these recesses. My choices: double back to the dungeon, or press ahead hoping to find a tunnel or outlet that would lead me to my friends. By my reckoning, that would require two right turns.

At this point, I had every reason to believe this area of the mountain fortress had either been deserted or was considered so insignificant that it did not warrant permanent sentries. The torches along the wall had long gone out, but a hazy glow at the end of the tunnel supplied enough light for safe travel. Gusty little drafts came and went; I thought that might be due to a breeze coming from outside the mountain compound. Stealth abandoned, I hurried in the direction of the draft and the light at the end of the tunnel. I ended up in a spacious chamber with a domed ceiling. At the other side of the room was a stage-like aperture to the outside world. In the center of the room was a windowed booth: perhaps a visitor exhibit. As I approached, I noticed broken glass on the floor. The front windowpane had been shattered.

Up close, the display appeared designed to show reverence; it was a shrine. But it had been vandalized. The contents were missing. An engraving was fastened to a marble plinth, but the light was too dim for decoding. At the side of the box was a handle, the crank of a dynamo. After a few rotations, globed lights appeared in each corner of the case. Electricity! Glass bottles had been converted to crude light bulbs. The engraving was written in English:

The Andean Orb

Before you lies a segment of crystalline sphere discovered in the Andes mountains of Peru. It dates back more than twenty million years to the time of a civilization long lost beneath the sea. The finder, knowing of the Orb's infernal origin and its potential for destruction, severed it into quarters and cast it to the four winds. Entrusted to the care of the Valgar race, the Crystal of the West may be viewed but never touched. Justly quake, weary traveler, as you stand at the precipice of all that is and all that will ever be.

A perilous and disconcerting thought: An allegorical emissary of Heaven and Hell had fallen into the hands of an amphibious maniac.

Glancing around, I noted three entrances with doors much like the one securing the dungeon. Prior to choosing one, I could not surrender the chance to get a breath of fresh air. Stone-scultped stairs led to the threshold of the open-air amphitheater. When I reached the top, I found myself in an arena, where I gazed with inquisitive awe at the captivating device in the center ring—the infamous wheel.

It was just as described—adorned with chains, stained by blood. Stadium-like chairs of wicker circled the domain. On the level above was a seatless balcony. With the wheel's gruesome image burned into my brain, I decided I'd had enough fresh air.

Turning to leave, I beheld two feathered giants who blatantly took exception to my presence. They stood in silence, eyeing me, not twenty feet away. Getting past them was not an option, running the other way would have been futile. High in the distance, a flock of the bird people winged toward the arena. Early arrivals circled, hovered, and descended. The show had obviously been sold out. And I was apparently the headliner.

As the two confronting Valgars stepped forward, I stepped backward. This quickstep tango continued all the way to the wheel. The bird men tipped their heads and twittered through their huge, acoustic nebs. To my ears, they sounded happy; to my eyes, they looked quite hungry. The amphitheater now brimmed to the rafters with raptors. And for all the world, it sounded like they had begun warbling the national anthem of

Canada.

One of the Valgars underhooked my arms and sat me on the edge of the wheel. Then I gasped! I could hardly believe my eyes when a quaint little man stepped from behind the other feathered giant. He wore corduroy pants, Benjamin Franklin spectacles, and a saggy,

mohair sweater. The man smiled through a walrus mustache and spoke with an Australian accent. He lifted his arms and pretended to conduct the Valgars in song. "They're celebrating you!" he said.

"I've always liked the melody, but I'm not Canadian. My home's on the other side of the border."

"Never mind that. Stand on the wheel and wave to them."

I was hesitant to comply, but the little man seemed so genuinely cordial that I got to my feet and waved. The birds chirped and hooted wildly. Some of their shrieks nearly pierced my eardrums. One of the bird men helped the old gent onto the wheel, and he waved alongside me. Could things get any weirder? In a place like this—of course. But I hoped against hope, not too much and not too soon.

The little man signaled, palms down, and the accolades faded. He extended his hand. "I'm Professor Otto Winkleheimer from Sydney."

I took his hand and said, "Captain John William Newman from Detroit."

He raised an eyebrow.

"I know, I know," I said. "There was this water from—I guess, a magical fountain—a fountain of youth. It's kind of a long story."

He winked. "No worries. All in time."

The Valgars gently lifted us from the wheel, and we walked toward the farthest door. "First things first," said Professor Winkleheimer. "We must reunite you with your associates."

"What?! How many?"

"All, I hope. There's a beautiful tabby cat, an affable dog man, and a charming little elf."

"Yeah, that's all of them. And they're all right?"

"To be perfectly honest, there was a minor misunderstanding between Adventure, Golly, and one of our passageway guards. The two were determined to have their way. They proved to be valiant and full of fight—an attitude the Valgars greatly admire. Ultimately, they were no match for my ornithoid friends. They were briefly restrained."

Dreading the answer, I asked, "But they were not injured?"

"Other than a slight to their pride, they are perfectly content—save for being exceedingly worried about you."

After a lengthy exhale, I said, "Man oh man." I glanced toward the wheel. "I thought they'd all ended up—"

"No, no, no," the professor assured me. "That barbarism ended long, long ago. And I'm proud to say I had a hand in it."

"What about the toad?" I said.

The professor shrugged. "Don't know. Really don't care. Good riddance to him—he was a surly rodent of a chap."

"Believe me, none of us like him either. But I'm afraid he may have stolen something—that piece of Orb from the display."

"I suspect so. The Valgars are aware, and they're out searching. If he can be found, they'll find him and throw him in a lock-up."

As we passed the Orb exhibit, I said, "Why did the Valgars leave something so valuable unguarded?

"Are you a fisherman, Captain?" asked Professor Winkleheimer.

Wondering which waters he may have been testing, I said, "Uhhh, yeah, I love all kinds of fishing."

"So do the Valgars. They fish for all sorts of things." After a moment's pause, I said, "The Orb slice was bait." "A test of trust."

I said, "That's twice that good ol' Parnie Wermbom has been baited by the Orb. He's obsessed with it. We've been told the crystals could be very dangerous in the wrong hands. Now that creepy nutcase has two pieces."

"And he's playing with fire, young man. If he mucks about, he'll soon be shovelin' Old Nick's coal."

"You don't seem at all concerned."

"Livin' in the down under, you take things as they come."

"I understand completely. The Australian outback can be one of the harshest terrains on earth."

"In certain spots," he said. "But I was talking about this down under, mate. You do realize we're trapped in a bubble, deep in the mantle of the earth."

"I'm glad you were the one to say it."

Our chuckles drew the attention of the largest of the bird men. As he approached, the professor said, "Captain Newman, this is Eka Laka, Chief of the Valgars." The creature extended a hand the color and texture of a corncob. His fingers were long and slender, and his nails were like hooks. Eka Laka's hand surrounded my own like a tent.

"How are you?" I said.

He blinked his wide-set eyes and made the sound "Grrawwwgok," which I'm pretty sure meant "Very well, thank you."

"Good to hear," I said.

Eka Laka walked ahead, opened a door of roughly hewn wood, and then followed us down a candle-lit hallway. He seemed to understand our conversation and occasionally made a strange little squawk or chirp. The professor chuckled after each of the bird man's quip's. It seemed the fearsome Chief of the Valgars was quite a comedian.

Briefly, I recounted my unterland escapades. When I told Professor Winkleheimer about the witch, the trolls, the sea monsters, spider land, and the flower monkeys, he didn't bat an eye. However, I was somewhat surprised I hadn't sullied my credibility when I tried to describe the Coverture. It turned out he was already aware of the displacing paradox. "Well, Professor, now that you know the crux of my story—how did you end up here?"

"I may as well get it over with," he said. "Prepare yourself and don't think me mad."

I looked up at the giant bird man and raised my eyebrows.

"Ah, point well taken." After a long pause, he said, "You've no doubt heard of the Bermuda Triangle.”

“Yeah, sure.”

With an agreeable nod, he tipped down his eyeglasses, peeked over the top, and pretended to share a secret. “That’s how I got here.”

# Chapter 18:
# Ornithology

Considering I was in the holiday guest residence section of the "Valgar Hotel," I had to admit the amenities were seriously lacking— as in nonexistent. But then, I wasn't exactly a paying customer. Even though I was reasonably confident my Australian host was on the level, I reserved at least the shadow of a doubt. As Professor Winkleheimer, Eka Laka, and I walked through the corridor, a large brown bat weaved toward us, headed for parts unknown. The Valgar snatched it from the air. After a crunch and a gulp, the mammal's new destination was the big bird's gizzard.

"Bats and rats," said the professor. "Valgar candy bars."

"Uh . . . I guess," I said. "He sure didn't spend much time savoring it."

"A certain sign he's hungry. But we'll be having our dinners soon."

Suspicion arose. The professor saw it in my expression. "Oh, my goodness, Captain! I was not referring to you."

"No offense, Professor. It's just that I've been through an awful lot lately."

Professor Winkleheimer cleared his throat and raised an index finger. "Now to further address your question about my arrival, I'm an ornithologist, which, as you may know, is a scientist specializing in the study of birds. For three months, I'd been in Brazil observing species along the Amazon. Since the times of the earliest sailing ships, certain tropical birds have been observed heading north for the winter, even as far as the polar region. My intentions were to explore this phenomenon. On my way back to America's Atlantic coast, to make good on a series of lectures, my ship passed through the waters of the Triangle. On that fateful day, the sky was deep blue, the sea was lime green, the sun was luxurious gold, and a calm breeze brushed the sails."

"Positively sensual," I said. "I feel like I'm actually there."

"Well, unfortunately, that's where sensuality ends. As in your situation, a seemingly endless curtain rose from the sea. It shimmered and wavered, sometimes going transparent, sometimes reflecting like a mirror. A mirage was my first thought. Mirages at sea are rare, but they do occur. One example that comes to mind is the fata morgana, named after sorceress of legend, Morgan le Fay, who used witchcraft to lure sailors into her ungodly traps."

"Yes," I said. "I've done a little reading in the area. The sirens of Greek mythology were said to do such things. Bird women. They seduced sailors with their beautiful songs. They could also control the winds."

Eka Laka chirped excitedly.

I looked at the professor for an explanation. He smiled. "When you mentioned bird women, you piqued the chief's interest."

"I guess boys will be boys, no matter the species."

The professor raised his eyebrows, shrugged, and then continued his story. "When I ran below deck to find a camera, there was a sensation of being swallowed by liquid light. Then I felt I was drowning in thick syrup—dreams and nightmares flashed in the back of my brain. Quick as a snap, I was back in the cabin searching for the camera. When I stepped back onto the deck, this very island was on the horizon."

"An experience very similar to my own," I said. "But I also saw vibrant colors, swirling and blending—I thought it was the northern lights."

"I saw no colors. However, I was below deck, enclosed, and you were looking through the windshield of a cockpit. Neither of us have much information to go on. You said your electronic systems were unreliable, so all either of us had to rely on were our senses and our thoughts."

"I agree. And both can be easily fooled." "There you have it."

By the time we rounded the next corner, Eka Laka had eaten a rat and another bat. A gust of wind breezed through the tunnel, extinguishing a few candles. The professor stopped to re-ignite them with an old grinding wheel lighter; it sported a Chesterfield cigarettes ad. He told me it had belonged to his father.

"The northerly winds must be picking up," said the professor. "It would be a good day for a sail."

"You still have your ship?"

"It's as sound as it was forty years ago, Captain. That's when I arrived here. It was the end of October, almost Halloween. Gracious me, come to think of it, it's coming close to my forty-first anniversary."

"You were a very young man."

"All of thirty-one. In the prime of my life."

My heart filled with empathy. "Trapped here for forty years. I'm sorry that happened to you, Professor."

"Nothing to be done."

Like in a cartoon, a glowing light bulb appeared in my brain. "The fountain of youth! Return with us to Morningtown and you can try a glass of the water. It no longer works for the natives in terms of reducing age, but they keep a supply for medicinal purposes. It's pretty close to a cure-all."

The professor nodded and stroked his chin. "Hmmm, tempting . . . very tempting."

"So how much more of a walk do we have?"

"I suspect, in the neighborhoods of Detroit, it would amount to about one city block."

"In that case, I feel right at home."

***

At last, we arrived at the dining hall. Valgar sentries stood on either side of the massive double door. Adventure, Golly, and Brutus sat together at the end of a long, cloth-covered dining table, lost deep in conversation. On our arrival, they cheered merrily. Big Golly sprang from his chair, ran forth, and hugged me like a brother. "There's our lad!" he said. The dignified cat and happy-go-lucky elf stood and nodded a greeting.

"Where in the dickens have you been, Captain?" Adventure asked.

"Where you told me to go—into the darker tunnels." "Are ya all right, then?" asked Golly.

"Now that I'm through with all the wandering around and feeling lost, I suppose I'm OK. It was nerve-racking at times, and I saw some peculiar sights, but all in all I'm no worse for wear."

"Any news about the toad?" asked Adventure.

"Nothing yet," said Professor Winkleheimer. "The Valgars are aware of your concerns. I assure you they'll notify us of any pertinent developments with all due haste."

Valgar servers, male and female, delivered dish after dish of the feast they had prepared. The cuisine was aromatic and exquisite: filets of halibut and cod, steamed clams, grilled shrimp, a crisp crab salad with a close approximation of Thousand Island dressing, cucumber slices in vinegar and onion brine. And there were heavenly loaves of fresh French bread with an olive-based spread. Crystal pitchers of tropical punch were placed within easy reach; the stuff had quite a kick!

A Dutch brick fireplace, at least ten feet wide, was set in the center of the wall behind me. On one side stood the carved figure of an Aztec warrior dressed in full regalia. On the other side was the figure of a World War I doughboy. Next to them was an incurvated stairway that wound high and out of sight.

"I must ask, Professor," I said. "Why on earth would anyone need such a huge hearth on a sweltering tropical island?"

"The island is on the same latitude as the lands to the east. The lava beneath us ebbs and flows like the tides. We have a winter here—at least we did when I arrived forty years ago. Significant snowfall usually began in late November . . . though now that I think about it, I haven't seen snow in ten, perhaps a dozen years. But, as I recall, the jungle would be fully recovered from the cold weather by May. Basically, we had two seasons. Now we have only one. I wistfully admit the cooler weather made a nice change."

"So, it's clearly been getting warmer on the island?" I asked.

"Oh yes, the change was gradual at first, hardly noticeable. But these past few years we've seen some extreme changes. Heat waves. Terrible typhoons. And the lagoon where your ship sits—two years ago, it was dry land."

"Similar things are happening in Ultrania," said Adventure. "Floods and windstorms. It's rare for a summer's day to drop below 90 degrees on the Fahrenheit scale. Some of the mountain glaciers and snowcaps have melted completely away."

"Morningtown too," said Golly. "Summer before last we had days so hot the corn couldn't grow. Field after field just shriveled away. "

Brutus said, "Winters past, we'd have snowdrifts high as rooftops. Now, it's just wet week after wet week."

"Burgomaster Stanislaus says it's from the molten rock under us. The flows have been movin' in funny ways," said Golly. "Always shiftin' from high to low, fast to slow. But Brutus and me, we've been thinkin' it's summat to do with the upper world. People buildin' and makin' things—always blowin' poison in the air. They're cookin' themselves; they're cookin' us. And nobody even cares."

"I suspect Stanislaus is right about the magma flows," I said. "And up top, I know we all could do a lot more. But I believe people do care— most everybody does. Usually when people don't act, it's because they're afraid."

"Afraid of cooking themselves?" said Brutus. "Then why don't they quit doin' it?"

"Hard to say what's holding us back. I'll admit I haven't done much to help. Maybe we're afraid that if we change the way things are, we'll lose the things we have."

The professor offered, "As the mavens say, 'We can't have our cakes and eat them too.'"

"If you ask me, all that cake makin' is what's bakin' us all," said Golly. "Gadflies and gumpfries! Can nothin' be done?!"

The professor said, "Little steps—tried and true."

"I agree, Professor," I said. "Small steps can lead to quantum leaps." "Well, them quantums had better start leapin' then!" said Golly.

Brutus implored, "Get them to leaping, Captain! When you get back up top, get the quantums leaping!"

"Sounds like a good plan: Take small steps and get the quantums leaping. When I get home, I'll make that my mission," I said. "But right now—we do have a toad to catch."

"Right-o!" said the professor. "And if you'll have an old Aussie along, I'll stand right at your side."

Adventure said, "Your help would be most welcome, Professor Winkleheimer—most welcome."

"It's a date, mate! Let's start loading my boat."

"We'll need to get a few things from the Duchess before heading out," I said.

Elation at a peak, the professor said, "We'll sail 'round to the lagoon, do some plinkin' and plonkin', then set sail for Morningtown!"

"Three cheers for plinking and plonking!" spouted the elf. "Hey yo, off and away!" said Adventure.

***

The Albatross was anchored at the end of a T-shaped dock. The boat, tightly fastened to the walkway, was in immaculate condition. And there was plenty of room for the five of us.

When I stepped onto the deck, I set down a box of dried melon and pineapple chunks. "Looks like a twenty-five-footer," I said.

"Twenty-eight," said the professor, joining me onboard.

"Well, Professor, all the three of us have to our names are the clothes on our backs. Have the Valgars finished loading the last of your supplies?"

"I believe I have everything I'll need—along with a few luxuries . . . So, we'll find your things at the lagoon then, eh?"

"Yeah, we started our voyage well prepared," I said. "We did lose some boxes of fruit during the storm. But the basket of oranges still below deck and the dried goods should easily keep us fed."

Adventure hopped aboard and said, "I'm looking forward to another song bash on deck and a bit of a dance."

Golly said, "And that smoked salmon the professor's stowed away ought to go down well with a big mug o' ale."

"That'll be good and well," said Brutus. "Once we get past the seeschlange."

"Seeschlange?" said the professor.

"Sea serpents, if you like," I said. "We were attacked inside the reef. Elasmosaurus would be my guess. Their necks stretched higher than the main mast. Slumber dust did the trick, and we've still got a full barrel of it."

The professor said, "That doesn't completely set my mind at ease, but I'll trust your judgement. I've never sailed our eastern waters—looks like a good thing I steered clear."

As we uncoiled the docking ropes, the Valgars gathered. Along the shore and from the mountain tops, they waved their hands and wings to say good-bye. Eka Laka and two of his soldiers flew ahead to the Duchess to clear the deck of unwanted guests: snakes, lizards, buzzards, bugs, and rats. No doubt they were looking forward to the smorgasbord. The Valgar chief had offered to sail with us—primarily to protect the professor, I suspect. But the professor insisted Eka Laka stay and watch his flock. Nonetheless, he and his two associates followed us to the reef and perched atop the sinister hands. Teardrops welled in the eyes of the feathered giants—as they did in ours.

***

Sleek and slim, the Albatross all but flew over the lapping waves. Though the fuel tanks were filled to the cap with ethanol from corn grown on the island, the plan was to let the wind take us most of the way. We'd save the gas for outrunning sea monsters and storms.

On the first night of the voyage, the professor told us of his terrifying first encounter with the Valgars.

"My approach to the island was from the northeast. The sky

was cloudless, and I was perplexed by the sunless sky. In those days, the mountains lay in a deep sleep, no smoke and fire, no rumbles and trembles. Downing the sails, a quarter mile off, I drifted with the tide and dropped anchor about fifty yards from shore. It took me nearly an hour of working a hand pump to fill my pontoon dinghy. We're not likely to need it, but it's still aboard and it still holds air."

"Ah, so you rowed the dinghy to the beach," I said.

"Almost. I wanted to do a little exploring, so I loaded a few supplies onto the little boat and made certain to tuck a pistol under my belt. The warmth of the breeze and beauty of the island had lulled me into a swoon. Out of nowhere, a Valgar snatched me into the air. I'd no idea there were such creatures. I believed I was in the clutches of a giant condor. I reached for my gun, but it had fallen loose. Just like yourselves, I was dropped inside a dormant crater. Lost and alone, I believed the end was near."

Golly, Adventure, Brutus, and I sat cross-legged on the deck, hanging on the professor's every word. At times, there was genuine fear on his face, as though he were reliving every detail. His arms would reach and flail, his hands would clasp together, his fists would clench. Understandable—this was the first time he had ever shared the tale with another living soul.

He continued. "They watched me from opening above, and

they watched me through the window of the dungeon door. All the while, they chirped and twittered, clucked and cawed, cackled and squawked. And all the while, I listened, day and night, hour after hour. I'd studied the sounds and songs of all sorts of birds my entire life and soon realized these were not just bird sounds—it was a structured language.

"One morning, at early light, I awoke to find the loop of a snare around my neck. I was marched to the sacrificial wheel and chained to the planks. It was then I began to talk, and they began to listen— because I had learned and was now speaking their native tongue. A few of the leaders conferred. They freed me of the chains and bid I address the entire congregation. For hours I professed, preached, and performed. The Valgars sat in silence, blinked their eyes, and tipped their heads. I spoke until my lips were cracked and my voice was in shreds. With my final word, I bowed. In standing ovation, they shrieked and screamed and flapped their wings. Following the fervor, Naka Laka, father of Eka, lifted me down from the wheel and then lifted his voice to the flock. He proclaimed, 'Sorka lopin gwoker nhee' meaning, 'This living thing is an honored friend.' I returned the sentiment in those very same words."

"A friendship that's lasted forty years," said Adventure. "Rod-stvennya dusha."

"Sorry, dear cat," said the professor. "I'm at a loss."

"Russian words adopted by the Ultranians. The closest translation: soul mates."

"Spot on! You've nailed it on the nose!"

"Rodzaven dooska!" said Golly. "That's Brutus and me." The dog man and elf reached out and interlocked curling fingers—their private handshake.

"Now you know the most of it," said Professor Winkleheimer. "Over the years, the Valgars and I have learned a great deal from each other. These ornithoids are highly intelligent. Their limited technology owes to the position of the thumb, which is more toward the middle of the palm, not as manageable as an opposable thumb. Great for strength but lacking finesse. We've made tremendous advancements in fishing and farming, food preparation and storage. We've learned to use the loom and perfected pottery making. We've developed medicines and healing potions. We've exchanged histories, cultures, traditions. No more sacrifices on the wheel, no more drought and famine, no more freezing in the winter wind."

"Rodstvennya dusha!" said Adventure. "Rodstvennya dusha!" said we all.

# Chapter 19:
# Carnival of the Sprites

On the second day of our journey back to Morningtown, I noticed something strange about the sky. It was mid-autumn and the sprites had begun turning the colors of fall: shades of green, gold, orange, red, and copper. I was told all the colors of the rainbow would splash across the sky by early December. From New Year's Day until the first day of spring, a soft, white-grey dome would loom over the land. The nights would be dark save a few bright sprites in the north and in the east.

Our voyage was like a marvelous holiday cruise. The Albatross handled beautifully. Cool were the nights, warm were the days. By day, we enjoyed the brisk ocean air and bright blue of the sea. And there was time to practice the traditional events of the Carnival of Sprites: archery, fencing, boxing, a game like lacrosse, track and field, and tree-limb gymnastics. By night, when we weren't planning our search for the Orb-stealing toad, we'd sing, dine, dance, and be merry.

If Parnelius Wermbom had reached the coast, we expected he would continue to the Gorge of the Gargoyle in hopes of finding the eastern Orb wedge. The legend kept running through my mind: The crystal was guarded by an immortal, bat-like demon. Though never witnessed, it was believed this grotesque stone form came to life whenever a living creature drew near. Professor Winkleheimer said our accounts of the gorge matched up with the books and scrolls he had found on the island. The demon sat upon a crypt-like pedestal amid the battlements of a watchtower. At the base, was a drawbridge that descended over a moat of molten lava, and a doorway that opened to a tunnel leading to the surface world.

Our mission was to capture the toad, take possession of the pieces of Orb, then go our separate ways. Adventure, Golly, and Brutus would return to Morningtown with Parnie the toad under arrest; the professor and I would make the uncharted trek to the surface world and home. If our quest meant we must battle a bastion of Hell, then engage in mortal combat we would. Throughout history, many a myth has shown to be more fact than fancy. The Valgars were real, the oogs turned out to be real, and I had every reason to believe this vile, satanic gargoyle was the genuine article.

From the crow's nest, Brutus yelled, "We're home! We're home!"

We all ran to the bow. Kearn Harbor's lighthouse was a thrice-blessed sight. And to be sure, the watchers had sighted us. When we arrived in Morningtown, the Carnival of Sprites had just begun. With our arrival, the jubilee became even more buoyant. A stage was quickly set for us. I was the last to speak, and I ended my presentation with the sentiment that Morningtown would forever remain "indivisible, with liberty and justice for all." A standing ovation ensued. I heard someone shout, "Liberty and justice for all." Another bellowed, "Words most inspiring—we'll add them to our Magna Carta!"

Raising my palms to the sky, I shouted, "Those words were claimed a long time ago, but you are certainly welcome to borrow them!"

As the crowd dispersed, we rode in coaches to the Morningtown Inn. Again, we gathered in the capacious dining parlor, around the knight-worthy table. We shared our stories, expressed our intentions, and listened to advice. We learned that the toad had passed through on his way to the gorge; he'd been seen slinking and squirming around town under the cloak of night. Other than stealing a waistcoat from the tailor's shop, he had skulked away without incident.

Golly said, "Why in thunder would the bloke 'ave stolen nowt but a coat?"

"Use your loaf, Golly," said Brutus. "A frog eats naught but bugs and flies and he loves to travel light." The words brought a laugh.

"Remember," said Adventure, "he uses the tails of the coat to glide. He floats through the air in the manner of a flying squirrel."

"Aye, agreed on all counts," said Golly. "But he must be 'eaded for the Farthingale. The north wind puts a chill in those woods roundabout this time. 'E'll need more than a servant's wrap."

"Just as well," said Adventure. "And if he froze his froggy legs off, he'd be doing us all a favor." None could disagree.

Burgomaster Stanislaus offered some advice along with a farthing of wisdom. "There is great truth in the jest but take heed—if you're bound for the gorge, you'll all need warm jackets. For such a pilgrimage, your load must be shrewdly devised. We'll have you all fit and fitted. And you'll need the best of land maps, treated for the damp, but be warned, for beyond the Tundra of the Oogs, the maps read scant. And the Farthingale Forest thrusts more thorns than a beach has sand. The black clouds will soon roll in and it may well rain enough to float a barge among the trees. The eyes of troll scouts may be on you from the first patch of ferns to the last. And keep in mind, the Farthingales are much larger and better armed than the Twarvians. There'll be prairie, desert, and ice lands. The gorge itself is unforgiving—nothing but tumbling rock, scalding spouts, and bubbling pools. And it bears repeating, if there's any truth to the legend, the gargoyle will be crouched upon a tomb with the eastern Orb slice lodged in his skull. As for the pathway to the surface, my misgivings are grave. A few borrowed words: 'All chivalrous take heed, for giants be windmills and windmills be giants.'"

"Don Quixote," said Golly. "It was a favorite of the 'eroic ober-lander George Washington. Classic tale. Read it five times my-self."

Adventure nodded. "Nice bit of history, dog man. And your thoughts are most welcome, Burgomaster. Strong words, fair warning. Come the fire, come the ice—naught deters a stub-born knight."

"How well I know," sighed Stanislaus. "How very well I know."

So back to business: We penned our lists, read of myths, stud-ied maps, and honed our course of action. No matter whether the toad was dead or had already pilfered the gargoyle's eye, we'd be on his trail by morning. But now, we would take res-pite at the Carnival of Sprites. We feasted and sang, danced and played, met challenges and sought rewards. Golly won the anchor throw. Brutus proved to be the best five-stone boxer in the land. Adventure outfenced one and all. I gave the slingshot competition a try and earned a conciliatory ribbon. Had pop-corn eating been an event, I'd have likely won. Professor Win-kleheimer spent the entire afternoon providing the Land Down Under Society with the lowdown on the Australian out-back.

In Morningtown, archery was the event of the elite and had been so since the carnival's inception. At the center of the car-nival grounds stood a bronze statue dedicated to the late Peter

Grunwald, a dog man, and the only archer ever to strike within three cubits (about 50 inches) of the tenth target, which rested against a hillside a thousand feet away. The final contest of the final day featured the Adventure Cat and Morningtown's twelve finest archers. The hometown archers were all members of the Morningtown Guard, each with their own hand-crafted bow. Adventure was allowed to select from a fine choice of bows; she finally found a recurve fashioned from yew wood like the one she had used in Ultrania.

Brutus and I accompanied the cat as she walked the range. At each target, she would glance back at the firing line with an expression of satisfaction. At target nine, she placed her hands on her hips and said, "Gentlemen, I assure you I can strike the bull's-eye of each of these targets on my first attempt. However, not one of the bows I examined has the strength to send an arrow to the hillside target. There would be no point in trying. I must conclude the final target was contrived for pure entertainment. We've a severe and perilous task ahead. This is not a time for such fancy and folly."

"But I must ask you, dear cat," said Brutus, "how did our champion, Peter Grunwald, send an arrow within two strides of the target?"

"With the bow of a Morningtown Guard, he'd have had no chance. The story must be tongue in cheek, a tale for the kiddies."

Brutus said, "I assure you, Grunwald's feat is a matter of historic record. Great-grandfather elves will readily attest."

As we stood near the hillside target, Adventure again scanned the distance. She surveyed the field from several angles. She looked at every tree, every flower, every blade of grass. She removed her blue scarf and held it high to test the wind. For a moment, she seemed mesmerized by the beauty of the kaleidoscope sky. She said, "Hmm, the autumn colors are more vivid south of the Coverture. A curiosity. But we've no time for pondering."

"One more thing to consider, Adventure," I said. "As you know, we are the talk of the town, which is especially true for you. This archery match is the grand finale, the spectacular spectacle of the entire games. Everyone under the spritely sky expects you to battle the best of the Morningtown Guard down to the last launch of an arrow."

"Yes, yes, I know. I'm no stick-in-the-mud fuddy. We'll have our show. But in response to the adulation, I feel we should provide the crowd with something worthy of memory, something for the history books." Again, she scanned the grass, the sky, the flowers, and trees.

At the bandstand, near Grunwald's statue, a full orchestra struck up the Russian folk song "Stenka Razin," penned in honor of the Cossack leader who had led a rebellion against a draconian aristocracy. All musicians wore traditional long coats, and papakha hats made of dark sheepskin. The melody was bittersweet yet spoke of a noble strength; the trumpeters did the song justice.

"Look!" said Brutus. "They're waving the blue flag. The practice rounds are starting."

On our way back to the firing line, a group of children ran toward us giggling. A little girl with milkmaid braids and sparkling eyes asked, "Lady Adventure—are you a princess?" The gaggle giggled.

"Ha," said the cat with a jovial grin. "Alas, I am a mere knight, but indeed, a princess in spirit! The children laughed and ran away. Quietly, Adventure posed, "Why must all intrepid women be accused of having blue blood in their veins?"

"You're certainly in a mood," said Brutus.

Adventure glanced toward the statue of the heroic Peter Grunwald. She employed a calculating squint. "Aye, but I should think that mood is soon to change."

Brutus and I exchanged looks and raised our eyebrows. Golly joined us and said, "What's up with you two?"

I said, "I think we're due for some early fireworks." While Brutus and I laughed, Golly appeared perplexed, and rightly so.

Before we could explain, Golly raised an eyebrow and said, "Inside joke, eh? Well, 'ere's a joke—I'm goin' for an ale, and I'll not bring one back for thee." He walked off with mild indignance.

"The stakes are high for all this night," said Brutus. "I'll go raise a pint with the big dog. We'll soon be back."

After an hour or so, Golly and Brutus had not returned. One of the guardsmen told Adventure and me they'd gone to a pub called the Scotch Egg. So, we went looking. As it turned out, a pint of ale had led to two pints, which had led to two more. When Adventure and I got to the pub, most everyone was roaring drunk. Though the crowd was rowdy, it was a frolicking, good-hearted rowdiness. Brutus and Golly were quite full of themselves. Brutus leaped upon the bar for some fancy footwork. Considering he'd had more than a few, his caper roused a clamor.

Golly shouted, "Where's me squeeze box." A patron fetched him a concertina and he called to Brutus, "'The Black Velvet Band,' eh, elf?"

"Start me out," said Brutus. He snapped his fingers in rhythm and sang like an Irish tenor. We all joined in the chorus:

Her eyes they shone like the diamonds You'd think she was queen of the land And her hair hung over her shoulders Tied up with a black velvet band At song's end, Adventure grabbed

Golly, and I grabbed Brutus. "One number's enough for now, lads," said the cat. We hurried through the swinging doors and made a sobering trek back to the contest grounds.

Prior to the flight of the first official arrow, I saw Adventure speaking to Stanislaus at the foot of a naked apple tree. A carpet of leaves, red, gold, and green, surrounded the sturdy trunk. More animated than usual, Adventure presented her case with an abundance of hand gestures. Stanislaus appeared surprised at times, but he also seemed agreeable. I felt certain the two were cooking up a carnival delight.

Because the spritelight was growing dim, torches were lit at the sides of each target. Signal flags were used to confirm the accuracy of each arrow strike: red for a bull's-eye and five points, white for the inner circle and three points, and black for the outer circle and a single point. When the first archer released his shaft, Brutus and Golly were at my side.

Golly said, "That cat can shoot the eyes out of a gnat. But that bow of hers will never reach a thousand feet."

"She knows," I said. "But she's got something up her sleeve. And I think it has something to do with that apple tree."

Brutus said, "Even from the top of that tree, she'll never send an arrow a thousand feet."

"Well, she's looking to please the crowd. And we all know how stubborn she can be."

"She's full of tricks, that cat," said Golly. "She's foxed me more than once."

Twenty excellent archers, male and female, had entered the contest. Four, including Adventure, had struck the bull's-eye of the first nine targets. Night had fallen. Weary sprites of violet, orange, pink, blue, and silver tried in earnest to twinkle and gleam. More torches were placed around the tenth target. From a thousand feet away, it looked like a spot of ink.

As the first archer nocked an arrow, Stanislaus approached. "Golly," he said. "I need a strong arm." He and Golly walked toward the statue of the bronze archer. Golly returned, hefting a bronze bow— the bow of Peter Grunwald.

The weapon was nearly as long, as Golly was tall. It looked like a leaf spring from the bottom of a truck. "May I hold it?" I asked.

"It's a bit 'eavy, lad," said Golly. He raised the bow and drew back on the string. Pulling with all his strength, he was only able to draw back the cord a few inches. "Sorry, lads, but I think the cat may have gone a bit daft. She wants to use this bow for her final shot."

Brutus exclaimed, "If you can't manage it, neither can she!"

"All right, Captain. Take hold," Golly said, as he placed the bow in my outstretched hands.

The thing must have weighed twenty pounds, maybe twenty-five. Immediately handing it back, I said, "I'll tell you one thing, that bow is not made of bronze. It's layered steel, and it's strong enough to support a couple of thousand pounds."

Golly shrugged and headed toward the tree where Adventure stood. Meanwhile, another archer stood at the firing line. The best shot to that point had been about five hundred feet, barely halfway to the target. The third archer didn't fare much better, but a six-hundred- and-seventy-foot shot had placed him in the lead.

Adventure leaped into the tree. Golly passed her the bow. Near the hillside target, Stanislaus stood with a bullhorn. He announced, "Ladies and gentlemen, good people of all means and manner, our visiting guest, the Adventure Cat of Ultrania, will now attempt to best the distance record of Morningtown's greatest archer, Peter Grunwald!"

The crowd roared.

"And she will honor his memory by using the bow created by his own mighty hands."

There came another roar, followed by whistles, shouts, and a long applause.

Adventure busied herself securing and aligning the mighty

bow in a bifurcation of the tree. Next, she twisted a carpenter's nail into the limb straight ahead to use as a sight. She leaned back against the trunk, closed one eye, then adjusted the angle of the bow. She repeated this rite several times. Satisfied, she reached down, and Golly handed her an arrow. The world was silent. The torches burned brightly. Adventure crouched and braced her feet against two thick limbs. She nocked the arrow, pushed with her legs, and pulled the bow string with both hands. Tugging slightly downward on the string, she held her breath, adjusted down an inch, then back up a half. A loud twang and thump rang out when she let the arrow fly. The shaft disappeared into the night sky. Finally, it caught the light of the flames as it arced downward, heading directly for the target.

For a long moment we stood frozen. The arrow struck. No flag was raised. A judge bent down for a closer look. Adventure jumped from the tree and ran toward the hill. Taking the bullhorn from Stanislaus, the judge announced, "Three cubits, one span distant . . . A very narrow margin, but Peter Grunwald remains our champion!" Another thunderous roar: it went on and on. As the cheers faded, Adventure took the megaphone and announced, "Scarf off to the champion!" She waved her blue silk in the air. "Let a year come and go. Then I'd like another try!" The crowd's roar surged anew.

As we strolled back to the inn, Golly said, "Just as well . . . but

I'm still a bit disappointed the cat fell short."

All truth known, Brutus, the burgomaster, and I believed the cat could have hit that target dead center had she wanted. What a lovely and curious creature she was. The Carnival of Sprites would never be the same.

# Chapter 20:
## To the Farthingale

The lamp-lit streets of the marketplace bustled. At a long oaken table, Golly wolfed down an entire pan of apple strudel. Brutus filled up on pretzels and beer. Dozens of others enjoyed bowls of lentil stew and bread just out of the oven. Jugglers, mimes, and harlequin clowns wandered the walkways. Adventure, the professor, and I took Burgomaster Stanislaus up on an offer to tour Morningtown's Conundral Museum.

Our perusal of the museum's curiosities and treasures started out in the historical library. The books were arranged chronologically based on publication year, except for books that had arrived through the Coverture, which had most often been found like shells upon a shore by scavengers, within a few yards of the portal's wavering wall. The library council would usually provide a handsome reward in credits, coins, or goods for each book, relic, oddity, or conversation piece.

Stanislaus guided the professor to the Legacy of Morningtown nook, where the bookshelves held sixty-four constantly updated volumes detailing the history of the southern unterlands. Bona fide archaeological evidence indicated civilization began with the Sumerians six to seven thousand years ago, but the professor told us there were transcribed accounts alluding to Earth civilizations dating back millions of years. Evidence of these civilizations was said to be buried deep beneath the earth's crust and miles beneath the ocean floor.

Meanwhile, Adventure and I eagerly walked toward the technology center. Few things about Morningtown bewildered me at this point, but when I saw a laptop computer on a display table labeled Upper World 21st Century, my jaw literally dropped. I tried explaining the device to Adventure, who pretended to be enthralled. When I realized my presentation was deader than the machine's battery, I mercifully excused the cat to investigate on her own. She went directly to the tools and weapons annex. As for my interests, I'd have given my two front teeth for a viable Wi-Fi connection.

Our final meeting with Burgomaster Stanislaus, the elders, and the town council was in the archives in the basement of the museum. We reviewed the maps, rechecked the checklists, posed questions, and provided answers when possible. Passing through the Farthingale Forest would be the first test of our mettle. The forest was dense and entwined with needle-sharp thorns varying in size from slivers to spearheads. For the most part, the heart of the forest was uninhabitable. The Farthingale trolls lived in the grasslands to the northeast, and they only went into the forest to hunt tough-skinned boar and slinkers (armored aardvark-ish things). As a people, these trolls mostly kept to themselves. They were basically Stone Age people with the heavy brow ridges and stocky frames of

Neanderthals.

Beyond the forest was an open prairie and a low rise of mountains known as the Crookeds; this was as far as the people of Morningtown dared venture. East of this range was the Tundra of the Oogs, populated by creatures primarily described as nightmarish. They fed on the antelope and reindeer herds, which risked leaving the mountains for the plentiful lichens and ground fruits of the tundra. Stanislaus availed us of his limited knowledge of the region.

"The elders advise you to make a tight loop to the south, avoiding the mountains and hopefully the oogs. Age-old journals say these creatures are globular, voracious, and move like lightning. The longer route will cost you a day, maybe two. However, in truth, I know of no one to have to have journeyed to the tundra and return."

"Oi," said Golly. "We got to the Island of Valgars and back right enough."

"A feat that warms the cockles of my heart," said the burgomaster. "But roll the die once too often, and a snake eye is bound to pop up."

Adventure quipped, "These oogs sound similar to the mythical pwerdoks that Ultranian parents still invoke to frighten impudent children."

In half-jest, Golly said, "Brutus and me, we may not be kiddies, but them oog stories put a right scare in us two."

Brutus forced a little smile but remained silent.

"We Aussies are tough as they come," said the professor. "But I'm all for the longer trek. Not worth chancing it."

"If it means losing some shoe leather to save my hide," I said, "I'll pack an extra pair of boots."

"My goodness, haven't we a room full of whingers this night," said Adventure. "Tells me it's time we all went to bed."

Golly snipped, "So says the wag of a cat. Willie Winkie's creepin' about. We'd best be off then, mates."

Adventure blinked her long eyelashes and shrugged. "Any other clouts?"

Brutus and I yawned, and that was the end of it. We headed for the coaches, the inn, and the beds.

***

Wainwright Arkle Ware assisted us in loading our supplies and gear into the back of his lumber wagon. We each had our personal shoulder bags, tools, and weapons. It was decided that Adventure would carry Golly's knapsack along with her own, and the dog man would carry the rolled-up tents. The light canvas shelters were coated with a milky sap from rubber plants, making them entirely waterproof. Draping these over a frame of branches would provide adequate protection from wind and moisture. Each of us had a warm jacket, durable overalls, and thick-soled hiking boots made of soft, polished leather. And Professor Winkelheimer proudly donned his bushman's hat.

Though confident we'd be able to live off the land, Brutus and I carried a supplement of jerky, corn dodgers, and rice. The professor insisted on bringing along wax boxes of buckwheat flour and powdered eggs. We had a bottled chlorine mixture and some cheesecloth to purify and filter water. Our plan was to transport our supplies by wagon along Jack-O'-Lantern Road to the edge of the Farthingale Forest. From there on, all would be riding on our backs. A crowd had gathered, and a hero's sendoff waved us on our way. For Adventure, Golly, and Brutus, it would be a brief jaunt away from home; for the professor and me, it was a sentimental and final good- bye.

As we passed the farms and fields, the planters and plowmen waved. It was strange to see gigantic pumpkin houses spread out among the homes of wood and brick. As the cart lumbered on, the barns, silos, wells, and windmills became few and far between. The moos, whinnies, brays, and lows of the livestock faded with each roll of the wheel.

Golly looked back from the shotgun seat and said, "Not to be boastin', mates, but nearly 'alf o' them barns out there were the work of these two 'ands." He held out his big dog man mitts, spread his fingers, and smiled.

"Sounds like a lot of boasting to me!" said Brutus, spreading out his own fingers. "These little hands had a hand in most of them—the windmills too!"

"Aye, aye—I'm 'avin' ya on, dafty."

"Well, daffy-down-dilly, I'm having you on back!"

The cat rolled her eyes. "Enough, you two! Just because your mum's not here doesn't mean you can row over mince pie."

"Crikey, cat!" said the professor. "That's telling them."

I intervened. "If no one minds, I'll offer a little gem from my pilot training. Relaxation exercises were critical in preparing for dangerous missions. We were taught to free our minds by freeing our faces. We trained all forty-three of our facial muscles to calm ourselves and even fall asleep. It can work wonders, especially for the muscles around our mouths."

After a moment of silence, there was laughter. It was a lesson well learned.

At the forest's fringe, we unloaded the wagon and made final decisions about what tools and weapons to carry. Adventure kept her bow and arrows in her bedroll, but she carried a bo staff. The professor had a .38 revolver tucked under his belt.

Golly and Brutus had Roman broadswords at their sides, along with pouches of slumber dust. Like the cat, I carried a bo staff, and I had a slingshot tucked away in the pocket of my jacket. As Arkle's wagon turned back toward town, we made the first of many turns on our way to the Farthingale. Contentedly we marched along the leafy trail, covering nearly five miles in two hours. Professor Winkleheimer belted out the first verse of "Waltzing Matilda," and the rest of us joined in the chorus.

"After all the talk about the brush and brambles," I said, "I thought it would be a little tougher going."

"Not to worry," said Golly. "We'll need the big knives soon enough."

"Should be a clear and open road for another three or four miles," said Brutus.

None of us made mention of it, but Adventure, Golly, Brutus, and I believed the professor, all of seventy, might slow the journey considerably. But the "rugged old mucker," as he called himself, was keeping pace just fine. He claimed to have walked over ten thousand miles during his ornithological expeditions—across deserts, through jungles, around the outback, through deep Siberian snows.

"The dark's not long off," said Adventure. "I'll scout ahead a ways— look for a place to bivouac."

"Aye," said Golly. "No 'arm in that." The cat jogged ahead.

"There's no denying the fact, lads," said the professor. "I'll welcome a sit-down come the dark."

To my mind, that was the professor's way of saying he already needed a sit-down. So, I slowed to a stop near a fallen log and said, "Hold up. I need to adjust these straps." I set down my satchel and lowered my ruck. The others followed my lead. We swigged from our water flasks till they were half-empty.

"Considering the load on our backs, we're sure puttin' the yards behind us," said Golly.

"That's true enough," I said. "In the military, we train many hours for a hump like this. Fifteen minutes per mile, a ten-minute break every three miles."

"We've bested that, I should think," said Brutus.

"I agree," I said. "But we started out riled and full of fight. We'd better slow our pace. We'll be sore enough in the morning as it is."

"You're right," said Professor Winkleheimer. "The cat knows it too. That's why she's gone lookin' for a place to stop over."

"Thinking with our hearts instead of our heads," said Brutus. "We all know better, but we do it all too often."

"Wise words, elf," said Golly. "Wise words."

Adventure appeared from around a distant bend. She broke into a slow run. A little out of breath, she said, "Stopping for a rest, that's using your nods." She took a long drink of water. "The vines get pretty thick up ahead. And the thorns are proper nasty. But I did some hacking and found a clearing—a good place for a camp. If anyone wants a wash-up, a creek cuts to the far side of the glade."

"Best thing—it'll be a dry night," said Golly. "No need for the tents."

"Let's hope our luck holds," said Brutus. "There's a bite in the air now and then."

Golly nodded. "Aye, I've felt it. A little nip o' winter."

After one last sip from her flask, Adventure said, "So much for the rest. The spot's not far, a bit more than a mile. We'll make it before dark."

Although the autumn sky had been a panoramic sunset throughout the day, to our good fortune, modest sprites of gold welcomed the evening, which still left us plenty of light to make camp by. Broadswords drawn, Golly and Brutus made short work of the inhospitable Farthingale and blazed a trail into the glade within minutes. Unloading our supplies along the creek's bank provided an ideal access to water. We rolled small boulders into a sitting circle, built a small fire, and boiled a pot of coffee. Our night's meal was sweetened jerky and roasted corn. In the interest of conserving lamp oil, we assembled small hearths at each end of the camp. The green wood did a lot of spitting and crackling, and it cast a poor flame, but at least the smoke had a pleasant hickory scent.

Holding a small map, Adventure said, "The creek splits off from a river to the north. We can follow it southeast for ten miles or so before it curls behind us."

"We'll run across lots of small streams and ground springs," said Golly. "Fresh water'll be plentiful all the way to the tundra. After that . . . I don't know."

"Reindeer do their share of drinking," said Brutus. "There'll be water. And we can always melt some snow."

Looking up through the branches, the professor said, "The night sprites are brightening a bit. Lots of purple ones, though. Back on the island, that usually means rain."

"'Ere too," said Golly. "Could 'old off. Maybe we'll get lucky."

Sitting on a log, stirring the fire with a stick, Adventure became philosophical. "I may say the word from time to time, but I don't really believe in luck. Things happen. We make choices—some good, some bad."

Clearly feeling playful, the professor teased, "No luck, so you say. Well, wouldn't you call running across that witch, Piranda, a stroke of bad luck?"

"I've come to accept my feline condition, Professor. Butting heads with Piranda was inevitable. No luck involved, good or bad."

"Witchery aside, how about science—any luck involved?"

Dryly, Adventure said, "Add, subtract, multiply, divide—there's the magic in science."

"Oi!" said Golly. "All o' them maths don't sound very magical to me."

I said, "With all those barns you built, Golly, I'd think you'd be pretty good at the magic of math."

"I'm good at usin' a tape measure. I'll grant you that."

Adventure stood and said, "I offer that any form of magic is simply science pending further investigation."

I clapped. "Now that's a statement I can stand alongside. And today's science fiction is tomorrow's science fact."

"So often said and so often seen," said the professor. "Once I get home, I'll have a whole lot of to say about science fictioning and science factioning."

"Makes two of us," I said.

Brutus made the rounds, handing each of us a piece of saltwater taffy. "In the name of fictioning, factioning, science, and black magic, let's have a chew on some candy."

Chirping crickets, jolly banter, and a few tall tales rounded out the evening. Before pulling out the bedrolls, we gathered sticks and branches to keep the fires going. Golly said, "I'll take the first watch if nobody minds." The moment the words left his lips, he tilted his head and harkened to a rustling in the trees. "Did anybody else hear it?"

"I did," said Adventure, reaching for her bo staff. "Could be trolls," said Brutus, drawing his sword.

Gun in hand, the professor said, "Could be. Could be a boar or a bear or the toad man. If the blighter pokes his head out, I swear I'll draw a bead."

Quickly wrapping cheesecloth around the end of a stick, I added a few drops of lamp oil and lit a bright torch. I joined Adventure and Golly at the camp's entrance. "Give me the light," said Adventure. "If there is something out there, I'll either chase it off or flush it out—so be ready."

The cat went into the thorny vines. Golly and I stepped back and followed the torch's flame as the cat weaved her way. "Yeoww! Ouch! Ummm." Shirking brambles and stepping away from the trees, she said, "Well, that settles that. No use trying to search in the dark."

Golly lifted his nose and sniffed. "No smell of anything, but the camp smoke could be hidin' it."

Adventure rubbed her arm and picked briars from her fur. She said, "Nothing with skin on it will roam around out there for long. These woods are a better protection than spears and arrows."

"Aye," said Golly. "Them briar vines are laced right the way through these trees like the 'oops in a farthingale gown—the name fits."

"It's a good name, no denying that," said Adventure, still picking bits of thorn from her fur.

In the light of the flickering torch, I noticed something dangling from a thorn: a rectangular strip of woven cloth. I handed it to Golly.

"It's from a jacket—tore straight along the seam. Same twill used in Morningtown's tailor shop. Not from our coats, though—none of us 'as walked out this way."

"Good quality to it," said Adventure, as she felt the texture. "Unweathered. Someone else passed through . . . and not long ago."

Scratching his head and yawning, Brutus said, "Maybe it's the someone we heard creeping around." Collectively, our eyes swept the area.

"Never mind that now," said Golly, taking the torch from Adventure. "You all go on to bed. I'll keep the watch."

"I'll spell you in two hours," I said. "Using my facial exercises, I can fall asleep in seconds. I've also got an alarm clock in my head." As an afterthought, I shot quick glances at Brutus and Golly. "And don't ask me how a clock got inside my head."

"Ah, you're a right jester, Captain," Brutus said wearily. "We're learning your gab, and you're learning ours."

"Yes, I admit, I have found myself using Morningtown-speak," I said. "And on this nippy night, it's a fine sleep I'll be havin' here in the tangly ol' Farthingale."

"Oi, sod off," said the dog man.

"Ta. I'll not sod off, but I will nod off." And that left me with the last word of the night.

Two hours later, my brain buzzer sounded, and I was wide awake. Golly was standing beside the creek, eyes fixed on the opposite bank. I pulled on my boots and hurried over. "Is there something over there?" I asked.

"Not likely," said Golly. "Mostly just keepin' me eyes open . . . but I'll show you somethin' else."

I followed Golly down the rocky bank to a narrow sand bar,

where he pointed out a pair of what might have been foot-prints. Might have. "What do you think?" he said.

Bending down close, looking from several angles, I had to admit the evidence was inconclusive. "There's something there. I just can't make anything out of it. Maybe when the sky brightens a little."

"We'll 'ave the cat take a look when she wakes," said Golly, as he yawned. "I'm needin' a sleep."

For me, the rest of the night passed slowly. I simply walked the camp in random patterns. Sometimes I hoped I would see something, but usually I was glad I hadn't. When the morning sprites finally woke, it was as though a swirling sunrise had filled the sky. Adventure had roused before the others; she went for a walk and returned with a nest full of bird eggs.

"I'll give them a light scramble," she said. "Wet enough to dip a hard roll."

"Sounds good to me," I said. "But first, maybe I should show you the tracks Golly found."

When Adventure looked at the prints in the sand, she said, "Much bigger than Parnie's feet, but all tracks swell over time. It's possible the toad could have made these. Along with that piece of cloth you found, there's a good chance he's passed through."

"How much ground can he cover in a day?"

"Loads. Miles. Jumping and gliding, using the Orb—and now he's got two pieces. Heaven help us if he gets them sorted."

"So, at this point," I said, "it looks like all he can do is jump really high. Now if he could shapeshift, he'd have a tremendous chance of stealing the Orb. He could turn himself into a griffin and tear that gargoyle thing a new one."

"Indeed, Captain!" said Adventure. "If that means what I think it does, we may be in for a doozy of a fight."

"Doozy," I said and chuckled. "Odd you would know that word." "Doozy? Ultranians say it quite often."

"So do Americans. It's a reference to the Duesenberg automobile— stylish, elegant, extraordinary. It came out around 1915, 1920, somewhere around there."

"I think not, Captain. To my recollection, the word daisy, the flower, lies at the root."

"I like my story better." "And I like mine."

When we reached the top of the creek bank, the others were up and mulling around.

"I hope you two'll be sharin' those eggs," said Golly.

"Put on some coffee, dog," said Adventure. "I'll slice that block of cheese and we'll have omelets."

Cheers in the morning make for a cheery day. We all knew the journey ahead would be long, arduous, and offer its share of peril, so we needed all the cheer we could muster.

After a delicious breakfast, we packed up and headed out. Getting through the next five miles of forest was murderous. The vines were extremely thick and fibrous. Some of the thorns were barbed like fishhooks. For hours, it felt like we were struggling with both the physical and the mental elements. Golly and Brutus hacked away with their swords until their arms ached. When Adventure and I took over we gave it our best, but molasses on a cold day would have moved faster. Professor Winkleheimer insisted on taking on extra baggage while we did the chopping, but as he trailed farther and farther behind, we gradually slowed to a stop. We sat on our backpacks and swigged from our flasks.

"How far's the next water?" the professor asked.

"Not far," said Adventure. "Happily, drink your fill. If the maps are right, we'll not want for water."

"Wonderful!" said the professor, swallowing away.

Golly used his sword to push aside some heavy branches. "Doesn't thin out at all up ahead. Is there no way at all around this lot?"

"It's gotten much worse from when we were lads," said Brutus. "Nobody comes this far east anymore."

Golly pulled some vines and thwacked some branches. He peered curiously through the trees and jabbed at something.

Each time he made contact, we heard a thudding sound. The dog man turned and said, "I think it's a wall—there might be a building behind this clump."

Adventure jumped up, and they both started chopping away.

"Yes, it's a structure," said the cat. "A little house! I'm looking through a window."

Brutus and I pulled at vines and uprooted ferns. Brutus said, "It's a trapper's cabin, Golly!" The elf squeezed his way in through the broken door. "It's like the one where we found that treasure!"

"Treasure?" said the professor, finding new life. "Let's have a look." He strained to lift his stiff old bones.

Golly slipped a brawny arm around the older man. "'Ere, let me 'elp ya, codger. We'll get ya through that door."

Brutus said, "We once found a pirate's chest, years ago. It was mostly empty save for a few coins and sparkles, but we were kiddies and thrilled beyond words!"

"True, all true," said Golly. "Me dad would take me and the elf huntin' and campin' in these woods, summer and winter. Used to be lots of town folk would 'unt the Farthingale."

"What happened?" I asked.

"Trolls," said Golly. "Over time they moved farther and farther south. Wasn't worth fightin' 'em. Any road, we're a people of the sea."

An intense flash lit up the forest. Thunder boomed. Wind shook the leaves. A brighter flash, and the thunder boomed again. We dragged our supplies inside and huddled under the leaky roof. For the rest of the day, the rain pounded and poured. It pounded and poured all night long, while we sat in the wet and shivered in the dark.

# Chapter 21:
# On the Prairie

At first light, drenched, cold, and miserable, we pushed on through the dripping woods. Gradually, the thorny branches thinned, revealing more and more of the spacious autumn sky. The final mile was relatively tolerable. After a brief pause to gorge on hickory nuts and blackberries, we gratefully left the bristly Farthingale behind.

Ahead lay miles of tumbleweed, prairie dog holes, and low rolling hills, but compared to the near-impenetrable forest, we were gliding along like performers in the Ice Capades. A tarantula here, a scorpion there, a hawk diving for a jackrabbit, coyotes yipping near and far— all were common sounds and sights along the way. About five hours into the hike, we saw the first antelope skeleton. Not long after, more reindeer and antelope carcasses lay before us. Wherever we saw the bones, we saw the tracks. Imagine horses wearing stiletto heels: a rounded toe, a long space, followed by the puncture of a spike, with strides of ten to twenty feet. There were thousands of such prints.

"If the tracks look this scary," I said, "I would really hate to see the things that made them."

"They could be from the oog things the burgomaster mentioned, but his description was a bit vague," said Brutus.

"I've seen drawin's in books," said Golly. "But nobody puts much stock in 'em. There's nobody left alive that's ever seen one."

"The legs bend back and forth a couple of times," said Brutus. "Like one of those green bugs with the helmet heads."

"A praying mantis?" I said.

"We call 'em crusader bugs," said Golly. "It's probably the same thing."

"But it's the bodies of the things," said Brutus. "It makes me sick to think about them. Sort of like huge, boiled eggs, but wobbildy- gobbildy, like thick jelly, with a thick hide that holds it all together. And they have mouths—"

"Now then, Brutus," said Golly. "They're only stories—pictures in books."

"If you don't mind," said the elf. "Their mouths can pucker up, reach out and grab things, then drag them inside their gluttonous holes."

"And they've no snouts either," Golly said. "I've seen the same barmy drawin's."

"Something made those tracks, Golly," said Brutus. "Barmy as it all is, there's got to be something to it."

"Aye, granted. Them books might be spot on. Maybe I'm

turnin' a blind eye."

Adventure asked, "Why didn't Stanislaus and the elders present some of this kind of information when we met?"

"'Cause they probably think there's no truth in it," said Golly. "Mostly nonsense—campfire tales. Same as we thought, before we saw them bones and hoofprints."

"They do very much sound like the pwerdoks of the steppe," said Adventure. "Just stories and fairy tales in the minds of most. But all of these strange tracks were definitely made by some type of creature."

"Maybe the pwerdoks crossed over," said Brutus, "came south through the Coverture."

"Based on the spacing between these tracks, these oogs are a pretty good size," I said.

"Forty 'ands high's what we've heard," said Golly.

"Hmm, that's about—thirteen, maybe fourteen feet . . . so I'm picturing a thirteen-foot boiled egg, running on spider legs, with a mouth that can reach out and grab you, sort of like, like a—I don't even know what."

"And whip arms," said Brutus. "They can curl around, lift you, throw you fifty yards, so some say."

"Sounds like a video game monster," I said.

"What?" said Brutus, Golly, and Adventure in unison.

"Computer, TV stuff—kind of like your imagination coming outside of your brain and into a box."

"Well, after my time up top," said the professor, "from the look of those antelope bones, these oog things aren't a part of any telly game. But, as a man of science, I've got to maintain some empirical reserve."

"Let's assume for a moment the things are real," I said. "If they follow the reindeer herds, the oogs most likely stay on the other side of that little mountain range. The maps say it's all tundra over there—deer and antelope by the hundreds. Prime hunting grounds."

"Aye, that'd likely be the way of it," said Golly. "There'd only be strays on this side—mostly."

"Consider this," said Adventure. "The pwerdoks of Ultrania are known to hibernate. They dig holes and bury themselves for six weeks, then crawl out and eat everything in sight. As a child, the stories had me terrified."

"That being so, we could be standing on top of an oog right now," I said.

Adventure shrugged. "I suppose—if there's truth to the tales."

"Crikey, you lot!" said the professor. "I've seen some mighty strange animals in my time. Lots of odd beasts live on the island, but these oog stories are turning us into looney tunes. Such an animal would be biologically maladaptive. No genetic lineage. Any number or combination of things could have made those marks on the ground. Weather and erosion can change the look of spoor. And the only bite marks on those bones were made by weasels and rats."

"He's right about the bones," said Brutus. "They weren't broken up. Nothing big has crunched on them."

"Aye, true about the bones," said Golly. "But the tracks—hard tellin' about them."

Hoping a distraction might clear the slate, I said, "Who's got a good hiking song?"

"Crackerjack of an idea, lad!" said the professor. "We all could all stand a change of pace. "How about the 'The Happy Wanderer'? Anybody know the German words?"

"Mein Vater war ein Wandersmann," said Golly. "We sang it in school."

I didn't know the German words, but my traveling companions knew them well. They sang away, taking turns with the verses. At least I was able to join in the chorus. The tune put a bounce in our step, and before long, thoughts of the hideous oogs faded, as did the lights in the psychedelic sky.

We set up camp near a pond likely fed by an underground spring. Considering its perimeter, the pond was more like a small lake; and based on the lay of the land, it was probably quite deep. We constructed four campfires along the water-front. The scrub brush was plentiful; it burned hot and reached high into the night air. The jellybean-colored sprites twinkled, and coyotes wailed among the rolling hills. We lugged some flat rock slabs close to the fires and built some Flintstone couches. We listened as the professor pointed out key positions on a map. "We're about four days from the gorge if we pass through the mountains. We're at least six days away if we take the safer southern route."

"We haven't seen a single deer or antelope," said Adventure. "Maybe there's no game left here on the prairie."

"Them deer could be in 'idin' in the mountains," said Golly. "Or maybe they're the 'ibernatin' kind."

"Around here, only mountain bears hibernate in the winter," said Adventure. "The deer and antelope herds search for food year-round. They must have gone east—to roam the tundra."

"A good bet they've gone into the Coverture," said Brutus.

"As good a bet as any, elf," said the professor.

"If all those weird tracks were baked deeply into the ground, I'd be inclined to cross the mountains," I said. "But some of those tracks— they're pretty recent. And considering the stories, the bones, the tracks, the presence of a food source—I'd bank on those oog things being a real threat."

"Might be, might not," said Brutus.

Adventure said, "Brutus could be spot on about the Coverture. The whole lot of them—reindeer, oogs, antelopes and all—may have migrated north. Southern Ultrania is quite nice this time of year. The conditions and terrain would be inviting."

"That waverin' wall could swallow 'em up and spit 'em out any place," said Golly.

"If the captain and I know a way through the curtain," said Adventure, "then there's a good chance that over hundreds, even thousands of years, these animals have found a safe way to get back and forth."

The professor folded his arms and offered a summation. "Whatever the reason, whatever the situation—we've got a decision to make. Cross the Crooked Mountains or take the long way around."

I said, "At our final gathering, I got the feeling Stanislaus and the council strongly suggested we take the southern route."

"It would be the best bet for avoiding a fight," said Brutus.

"Agreed," said the professor. "But we all knew from the start this trip would have its dangers. We're bound to end up in a brouhaha before we're done."

"Not so bad so far," said Golly. "And savin' three days walkin'—that's mighty invitin'."

Adventure said, "If the toad gets his webby fingers on that third slice of the Orb and gains the smallest insights into its use, we could be at the mercy of a monster far more horrible than oogs or pwerdoks."

Stymied like everyone else, I offered, "Why don't we sleep on it? Face it fresh in the morning. That's what my dad would have told me." The faces of the other four told me their dads would have said the same. The discussion was tabled till morning.

A pestering nip in the air prompted the gathering of more branches and brush for the fires. The tents were set up on either side of the central hearth. The shelters could comfortably sleep two. We took turns keeping watch at three-hour intervals. At least a million points of light twinkled above; the specks reminded me of the colored glitter we used for grade school art projects.

Near the pond, Golly and Brutus were making a fuss. As they wandered through the yarrow, sage, bluestem, and milkweed, they pointed, gabbed, and grumbled. Finally, Golly put his hands on his hips and called out to the rest of us. "Oi, you lot.

Come 'ave a look!"

Most of what they'd found amounted to splotches of disturbed prairie dust. But near the water were two webbed footprints, smaller and more defined than the ones we'd seen near the forest creek.

Adventure measured the tracks using the span distance between her thumb to her little fingertip. She said, "Nearly two spans. Those are almost certainly Parnie's web prints."

"Definitely sharper impressions than those at the creek," I said.

"Less moisture here," said the cat. "The creek bed was wet, muddy in places, and the tracks were several days old—these prints are fairly

new. They haven't expanded yet. I'd say they're no more than a day old."

"So, what's done all the muddlin' and churnin' back there in the dust?" said Golly.

"The toad wanders about when he searches for bugs," said Adventure. "I've seen him do it many times. He walks, hops, jumps, kneels, and shuffles around when he chases grasshoppers, dragonflies, and such."

"Does he know we're on his trail?" said Brutus.

"Absolutely," said Adventure. "And he's quite clever—at least he thinks he is. He'll leave signs to throw us off, sometimes just as a tease."

"That makes sense," I said. "With the energy he gets from the Orb, he could jump way out ahead, leaving us completely in the dust. He's staying close for a reason.'"

"It might be that the Orb's power is draining down or he's losing his connection with it," said the professor. "We've still no idea how the crystal works."

"From what I've seen," said Adventure, "if you lose contact with the Orb, the power within you drains away. I saw that happen often with Piranda. But on one occasion, she held the slice too long. The crystal burned her hand and left blisters. She noted every incident in her Book of Spells. And she learned to be very careful."

"If the tracks end here," I said, "he either went into the pond or jumped clear over it."

"Bein' part frog, he could stay under the water for days," said Golly. "He could still be down there."

"Possibly," said Adventure. "But my guess is he's moved on. I've no doubt he does have a plan, I'm sure of that. And that plan must have something to do with us."

"Even so, there is a bright side to all of it," said the professor.

"Him hanging about means he hasn't seen those oogies. Otherwise, he'd have jumped from here to Hell's breakfast."

"Very astute, Professor," said Adventure. "He's a proper coward. Any glimpse of such a thing would have sent him packing."

Golly stretched and rubbed his eyes. "It's somebody else's turn to stand guard. I'm off to bed."

The professor said, "My turn. I haven't stood watch even once yet. And don't any of you get to thinking I'm too old for the job."

In unison, we assured Professor Winkleheimer we were totally confident in his resolve and ability to pull his weight. And also in unison, we noticed something on a distant hilltop, silhouetted against the glow of the eastern sky. We had seen it earlier: an eerie- looking shape, unmoving, tall as a tree. At first, we hadn't paid it much mind; it was just some stable, innocuous structure. Perhaps because we'd been so busy gathering firewood, making plans, and idly gabbing, it hadn't made an impression. But it did seem oddly out of place, and it was certainly worth keeping an eye on.

"Might be pyre poles," said Golly. "A sign of trolls." "How so?" said the professor.

"They like to build tall fires," said Brutus. "Ones that reach high as a bird's nest."

"Sounds like a rite of some kind," I said. "Celebrating a successful hunt, summoning spirits—"

"Hush!" whispered Adventure . . . "I just saw it move." We froze. We watched. Our world went silent.

# Chapter 22:
## Oogs

As the thing on the hill turned, the spritelight revealed its full profile: near giraffe tall, rotund, basically a cephalopod with slender legs jutting from its bulging gut. Its silhouette moved again, this time waving tentacle arms. This was no legend; this was no myth—this was an oog. It appeared to be watching our fire, our camp, and especially . . . us.

Adventure quietly said, "Move very quietly . . . find your weapons . . . no sudden moves."

We walked on feathers, heel to toe, across the dusty scrubland, shifting our eyes from the hill to the ground, gingerly avoiding bone- dry grass and brittle weeds; the silent prairie soil was amiable. The creature lingered without a twitch, no doubt attending to our every move, perhaps unaware that we were aware. It lay in wait. Considering the conglomeration of spoor we'd found, we could guess that oogs were not lone hunters. One oog would push our limits, two would spell our doom.

While the others slinked toward their weapons, I touched a torch to the fire. Keeping my eye on the monster, I knelt and remained perfectly still. Adventure had found her recurve bow and a handful of arrows. Brutus and Golly crept from the tents, swords in hand. The professor was nowhere in sight. I suspected he was rummaging for his handgun.

Holding our weapons and our positions, we waited for the creature's approach. After studying us, it finally made its move. With a loping stride, the oog galloped down the hill, directly in line with the camp, and stopped on the other side of the pond. The sprites in the eastern sky supplied just enough light for us to get a good look.

The monster was pear-shaped. The top of its head was about five feet higher than a basketball hoop. Four drumstick legs clung to the corners of its cube-like pelvic bone. The creature's knee joints flexed backwards like those of an ostrich.

On the opposite side of the pond, the oog began to pace, as though uncertain how to cross. As it reluctantly stepped into the water, the top of its body inflated as it kicked its way toward us. When it stepped onto land, it towered tall as a tree. We didn't move; it didn't move. While we hoped it was only curious, we knew we were in for a fight.

The firelight illuminated its massive form and gave it a burnt orange tint. Blubbery, puckered lips bulged low on its abdomen. Its body appeared to be filled with viscous fluid. Through its translucent skin, two large lima-bean structures were visible, tethered inside the head. Perhaps, together, they formed a brain. The monster had no facial features and there was no discernable neck. Its legs were covered with thick, coarse hair. On its knobby feet were fang-like claws. For arms, two ropey tendrils dangled from just below its head.

Judging from its reaction to light, the entire ventral side of the monster appeared to function as an eye. Walking toward the closest tent, it turned its attention to my backpack.

Reaching out, the snaggly fingers of its tentacle grabbed the bag. The oog pulled the pack to its lips and swallowed it whole. I could see my belongings floating inside its stomach. Slowly, the items dissolved; they were being digested. Next, it reached for the tent. Its torso expanded as its mouth stretched wide. It downed the tent in two gulps. In a loud whisper, Adventure said, "We've got to drive it off or we'll have nothing left."

The oog continued to devour our camp, occasionally hoicking out things it found disagreeable, primarily items comprised of metal. When I approached with a torch, the creature responded with a step in my direction. I stood perfectly still and lowered the torch, but I had clearly caught its attention. In a flash, it lashed me with a tentacle, sending me into a backward roll. The torch went flying. Adventure fired an arrow deep into the monster's belly, where it floated in a thick, cytoplasmic soup. Emerging from the second tent, the professor opened up with his pistol, firing bullets at the creature's brain. Awkwardly, it teetered and stumbled, but it did not fall. With the dexterous fingers of its tentacle, it plucked the lead slugs from its rubbery forehead, examined each, ate them, then disgustedly spit them onto the ground.

Adventure charged the monster, knelt, and let loose another arrow, then another. They seemed only to tickle the creature with delight. It whipped a tentacle around the cat and flung her high into the air. She went flying over the prairie and splashed into the pond.

Brutus and Golly rushed in with their swords, heading for the oog's hairy legs. The monster kicked out with a lower limb and sent them rolling like soccer balls. They bounced against the rocks and lay lost in a daze. At the top of his lungs, the professor hollered, "Hyah, hyah, get away, ya damnable beast!" He hurried with all the speed he could muster and with all his might he hurled a full pouch of slumber dust. The monster's lips puckered, extended several feet, and glommed on to the sedative. A deafening sound— "Grak! Grak!"—burst from the sides of its head. Its great glob of a body trembled. It smacked its slavering lips and waved its tentacles.

Still woozy, Golly staggered forward, waving his sword, yelling incredulously, "A whole purse o' dust and it bloody well wants more!"

As the professor backed away, the oog slapped him down; it raised its foot and held a sharp, bony heel over his prone body. Brutus had not moved since his fall. Adventure ran to his side.

"Rest easy, elf. I'm taking your sword." She streaked toward the monster, pounced like a panther, dug the claws of her foot into its belly, and propelled herself to the top of its head. As she raised the sword and plunged it down, a hole opened, and the cat dropped down into the creature's gut. She thrashed around in the oog's fishbowl belly; her panicking plight was clearly visible through the creature's translucent skin. She kicked and pushed and scratched at the inner lining of what must have been its stomach. She flailed wildly as her oxygen waned. Clearly, the cat was suffocating.

The professor rolled away from the oog's feet and reached into the pocket of his coat. Suddenly, the monster began to retch and heave as though it were sick. It gagged, coughed, and puked out the cat, along with a flood of syrupy goo. Swinging his sword at the monster's leg, Golly was slapped by a tentacle, curled up, and lifted twenty feet in the air. The dog man kicked with wild futility. He groaned, "It's crushin' me ribs!"

The oog reared back its whip of an arm as though it were going to heave a ball from left field. The professor yelled, "Hey, hey, over here, ya gobbly wanker!" With his back toward the others, obscuring their view, the Aussie fished something from his pocket and pointed it toward the oog. From the professor's glowing hand bolted a tiny ball of energy. It struck the monster near its brain, and the creature collapsed in a cloud of prairie dust. Golly wrestled himself free of the tentacle; he wheezed and held his side as limped toward a dying campfire. The oog lay on the scrubland, silent and unmoving.

Beneath a brightening sky, four of us scrambled to break down what was left of our camp, while the cat had a quick wash in the pond. We worked frantically, not speaking a word. It didn't take very long, for the monster had eaten a pastel of our supplies. After salvaging the best of the rest, we hotfooted south. The professor glanced back and said, "Crikey, it's gone." We all looked in all directions as we trotted along.

"Maybe it's run off into the mountains," said Brutus.

"Might 'ave dug itself under the ground like them pwerdoks," said Golly.

"I'm thinking it won't be back, mates," said the professor.

Slowing to a stop, I did a scrutinizing 360 sweep of the terrain. "So, what the heck happened back there?" I said.

"I seen a fireball," said Golly.

"Yes," said Brutus. "It was a huge, silvery spark. It hit the blighter dead center."

"Could have been ball lightning," I said. "Ball lightning is pretty rare in the upper world, but it does happen. Here inside the mantle, things could be different."

"I've never seen such a thing, not in all my years," said Golly.

"Nor I," said Brutus.

"A divine stroke 'o luck, it was," Golly muttered.

I offered, "The oog's anatomy, its physiology was unique to say the least; so, its body chemistry and nervous system would be foreign in nature as well. Maybe extreme stress stirs electrical surges within the species. Maybe it had some sort of epileptic seizure . . . Or maybe the slumber dust had a delayed effect."

"Brainy posits, Captain Newman," said the professor. "You're a man in search of a mystery. We all love a mystery, but we've no time for Holmesian postulates."

"Whatever it was," said Golly, "it saved us. And it won't be likely to save us again."

Brutus said, "Thinking about one of those oog things coming at us again gives me a right case of the shivers."

"Outside of chuckin' a wobbly, the wretched beast seemed to be a thinker," said the professor. "It might put two and two together and figure we're the ones that knocked it on its gobbling bum. So, it may well stay clear of us from here on."

"Associative conditioning," I said.

"Well, well," said the professor. "We've a psychologist in our midst." "Far from that," I said.

"If associatin' means addin' two and two, let's 'ope the thing can do bit o' math," said Golly.

Sword in hand, Adventure stopped and cleared her throat. "Never being the most trusting soul, I'm not convinced the thing is gone. I'll hang back a little. I think I'm quick enough to elude it and buy us some time."

"No need, I should think," said the professor. "We'd best stick together, cover some ground, and count our blessings."

"Yes sir, united we stand," I said. "Looks like that's the only way we're going to get through this."

Adventure relented and joined the professor and I as we walked in step. "It's a shame we have to be so quiet," said the cat. "I'd love to sing a madrigal. It would soothe my heart and soul."

"A madrigal," I said. "We sang a madrigal the day we met."

"I remember it well," she said. "'Early One Morning'—one of my favorites."

"A lovely song," said the professor. "But we'd best keep our voices down for another mile or two—we'll have a song first chance."

Adventure rubbed her hands and arms. "That quick splash in the pond didn't nearly get that stinkard's vomit off me! It's far more viscid than Piranda's gloppy web."

"Fret not, dear cat," said the professor. "There's a bubbling spring a mile ahead."

"Thank goodness!"

"Let's sidle up to Golly and the elf," said the professor.

We heeded the old Aussie's advice and clomped along in a cluster. "I've got a confession," he said as he took something from his pocket. It was an indigo crystal. He handed it to Adventure and said, "Take a look, pass it around. If it gets warm or you feel a buzzing, drop it right away."

"It's a slice of the Orb!" I said. "You've been holding out on us, man. What's the story?"

"The toad man stole a worthless piece of glass. I melted it with sand, sulfide, and plant extracts, then shaped it inside a forged mold. It took a few tries, but I finally managed a passable falsity."

"Very sly, me old mucker," said Golly with a wry smile.

Holding the slice, Brutus asked, "If it gets warm, what will it do?"

"And there's the rub, elf. I've no idea. When I pointed it at the monster, I was filled with fear—terror's more the truth. It just went off, shooting out that sparkly little ball."

"You'd never used it before?" I said.

"Never had a reason to. The first time I read the engraving, back on the island, I paid all due reverence, made the switch, and locked the real slice away—safe and sound."

"Would you like me to carry it?" asked Adventure. "Please. I'm well rid of it. But you must take great care."

"I'll look after it. We'll put it in the Morningtown vault once we get home. By then, we should have three of the four wedges."

"So, where might we find the fourth piece?" I asked.

"Somewhere south of the Coverture," said Golly. "So says the lore. But there's nothin' to point the way."

Brutus said, "It could be anywhere from the Coverture to the Darklands, from the coast to the Farthingale."

"The Farthingale for my money," said Golly. "Buried under all o' them thorns."

"I say it's in the Fever Jungles," said Brutus. "Blood-draining flies down that way. Nobody would go looking for a lump of glass in those foul swamps."

"Blood-draining flies?" Adventure said repulsively. "Land's sake—at least the north doesn't have any of those snakes in their boots."

"Snakes in their boots," I said. "Now there's a new one. I'll ad it to my thesaurus. And land's sake? My grandmother used to say that—it's anachronistic."

"Oi," said Golly. "You're usin' some pretty big words today, lad."

"I guess I am." I laughed. "Fifty-cent words they used to call 'em in the old pulp fiction days."

"Fifty-cent words?" said Brutus.

"It's a long story for another time," I said. "I'm just blabbin' because I'm tired."

"Well, there's nothing fancy about 'land's sake,'" said Adventure. "A fairly common term in Ultrania."

"Morningtown as well," added Golly.

I sighed and said, "That does not surprise me at all."

The professor unfurled a small map and gave it a discerning eye. He said, "The hot spring should be just ahead, near that peaked outcropping."

"Not to offend," said Adventure. "But I simply cannot stand this nasty fur. I'm running ahead. If that bubbling pool's inviting enough, I'll dive right in."

By the time Adventure reached the spring, the sky above blazed with reds, golds, and greens. Warm mist swirled over the ebullient spring. She tested it with her toes. "It's positively summery," she said. With a branch from a long-dead tree, she tested the depth. "Well over my head." The cat tossed aside her tunic and complacently traipsed about in her modest linens. She contemplated her water entry and ended up climbing to the top of the highest rock. We arrived in time to see her graceful swan dive. She burst up through the bubbles, exclaiming, 'It's wonderful!"

Brutus wasted no time shedding his boots and togs. Wearing only a loincloth, he sat at the pool's edge, dangled his legs, and then daintily slipped into the water. "Come on, Gollywog! Have a soak!"

Wearing long woolen underwear, the dog man jumped from a rock slab and landed like a cannonball. The red-brown rocks circling the pool formed a little theater. Professor Winkleheimer knelt, filled his bushman hat, then splashed it on his head. Like Adventure, I climbed to the top rock, "Clear the middle!" I said and dove deep. When I popped up, I called, "Come on in, Professor!"

"Another hat dunk'll do me," he said.

We splashed about for a while, then spread out around the perimeter and relaxed. "I'll start a little fire and scramble some powdered eggs," said the professor. "Maybe peel an orange or two."

"And we'll be grateful as can be," said Golly. "I'm hungry as a Farthingale bear," said Brutus. "There are no Farthingale bears," said Golly.

"I know," said the elf. "They all died of hunger." Everyone groaned as we climbed from the water.

We dripped dry and devoured our eggs. The oranges were as tangy as they were sweet; we savored them because they were the last. We basked in a sunny glow of familial warmth while inhaling the pool's intoxicating steam. For one full hour we luxuriated, free from past tribulations, escaping, for a moment, the fears of things that lay ahead.

"Time's come," said Adventure. "Let's have a song."

I started singing the old-time favorite "Bye, Bye Blackbird," to which the professor harmonized. The others leaned back, gaily clapping to the beat. It truly was a magical moment, a page from a fairy tale.

## Chapter 23:
## Sand Blizzard

With each step, the prairie dust gave way to desert sand. Wild rye, buttercups, and milkweed gave way to feather grass, ghost plants, and cactus. The cold winds east of the mountains and the intense heat of distant canyons trapped an arid column of air over a strip of naked terrain; fortunately, the desert trek would take no more than a day. Up ahead, a Joshua tree waved a welcome. Beyond was a sea of sand.

Golly complained, "Some o' the deepest sand I ever trod."

"On the map," said the professor, "this desert's a fairly short span of terrain, but for the leg's it'll be the longest stretch in the journey."

Adventure eyed the eastern sky. "Four hours of good light at best."

"Coldest desert I've ever crossed," I said. "And I've crossed my share."

"One o' them old books said it can get well below freezin' out here," said Golly. "The wind's kickin' up, and it's got a bite."

"'The wind's like a whetted knife,'" I said. "Eh?" said Golly.

"From a poem—John Masefield," said the professor. "That's something we learned in school."

"My mother used to recite it—Sea Fever," I said. "Late November, when the wind swept over the lakes, she'd quote the 'whetted knife' line."

"Poems is me favorite," said Golly. "I'll 'ave to give it a read."

"My favorite's a good true-to-life thriller tale," said Brutus. "Sometimes there's dwarves and elves in them—like Rumplestiltskin. A story doesn't get more real than that one."

He labored to hop and skip over the sand and spoke in a creaky voice:

Today do I bake, Tomorrow I brew. The very next day, Her child I'll win! For her own sake, If she only knew,

The name she must say, Is Rumplestiltskin!

Brutus laughed with hammy wickedness.

Golly said, "Oi, elf. You're soundin' a bit touched, mate." "Having a little fun," said Brutus. "As I am oft wont to do."

"Do much more of that," said the professor, "and your legs'll be lead —as mine are already wont to do."

Adventure said, "You let us know, Professor, anytime you need a rest."

"Ta," he said. "I can plod along another mile or two." "Will we reach the oasis before dark?" Adventure asked.

"Not at this rate, lass. We'd have to pick up the pace, and it's not in the cards for my old gams."

"Two miles it'll be then," I said. "Two miles to bivouac."

We trudged on. In the deep, shifting sand, each mile seemed like ten. The gusts of cold wind cooled us, but they also drained us. We'd been rubbing the grit from our eyes for hours. A sideways glance convinced me the professor was failing. To lighten the mood, I humped ahead a few yards, spun, brought my trailing foot smartly around like a leftenant and said, "Compan-eee, halt!"

"We're stoppin'?" said Golly.

"This spot'll do fine for the night," I said. "No posts for the tent," said Golly.

"We'll unroll the canvas and use it to shield the wind," I said.

Adventure foraged through the packs. She handed out raisins, corn dodgers, and jerky. "This is the last of the food we packed. We'll have to hunt and gather from here on."

As we sat in the sand, sipped from our flasks, and downed our meager fare, Brutus said, "Funny how the air's so cold and the ground's still warm as a bun."

"Enjoy it while you can, elf," said Golly. "Another hour of this wind, and the sand'll be cold as a gravestone."

"What's up ahead, Professor?" I asked.

"That blinkin' map's branded on my brain," he replied. "We'll reach the oasis tomorrow afternoon—a touch of the best before a clout of the worst. From there, it's on to the rocklands and canyons: a geothermal jumble of geysers, hot springs, tar pits, boiling oil, lava flows. There'll be crevasses and trenches, likely bottomless. Also, brimstone, charcoal, and saltpeter deposits, which we may as well call holes full of gunpowder."

"Good to know. I won't be lighting any matches," I jested.

"Ha-ha," said the cat playfully. "We could all have a good laugh over things if the odds and outlook weren't so dreadfully bleak."

"Grotty as it gets," said Brutus. "Grotty?" I said.

"Grotesque," said Golly. "And speakin' of grotty, where, in all this, do we find that grotty gargoyle?"

The professor pulled a note from his pocket and read. "This is from the most credible account I came across when I searched the museum archives. I scribbled it down." He read the verse aloud.

In the eastmost canyon lies a gorge Gouged deep in the skull of Hinnom Atop does squat a great horned bat With tongue and teeth of venom It guards the door forever more All seen with eye of night Stand not before, ignore its lore Twill smite thee down in spite

"A middlin' verse," said Golly. "Quite nasty, but a good rhyme to it."

The professor cleared his throat. "These words are the basis for the legend. No mystery to the meaning. Anyone trying to pass through the door to the surface world will be seen by the eye of night—the slice of indigo orb. This will bring the gargoyle to life, and it will attack any intruder with its poisonous bite."

Adventure said, "If it comes alive, the monster's just as vulnerable as the rest of us. I still have my bow and seven fine arrows. As well as that chunk of Orb—for what it's worth."

"I have a solid oak staff," I said.

"My sword's as sharp as ever," said Golly.

"I've still got a small pouch of slumber dust," said Brutus. "And I've got my trusty tooth-edge Bowie," said the professor.

"Most important of all," said Adventure, "we've got each other!" A spontaneous cheer erupted!

I looked in the eyes of each of my friends and said, "This is the first time I've truly felt I might find my way home."

"Me as well," said the professor.

Adventure offered, "And I've come upon the premonition that we will find the toad and retrieve his ill-gotten gain." She stood and reached out her hand, as did we in kind. Embraces, vows, and well-wishes followed. The cat said, "Determination and valor can lay low a thousand swords." We nodded in deference to the wisdom.

From the south, the wind wafted at the back of our heads and added a thimbleful of chill. Like ducks in a row, we sat back down to wait out the rising wind, pulling the tent canvas up like a community hood. New layers of sand blanketed the dunes. Our tent started flapping like hung linen on a blustery day. We gave each other clueless looks.

"The storm's been nibblin' at us," said Golly. "Now it's comin' full on."

"We're in a wind alley," said the professor. "We'd better move to high ground."

The rest of us gave affirming nods. At that exact moment, I noticed something peeking over one of Golly's boots. It was a cobra, an Indian cobra. The hood around its head flared as it swayed in the wind. I whispered into Golly's ear, "Don't move. Look at your right boot." The dog man's eyes went wide.

Slowly, I extended my bo staff, out and away, keeping the stick within the snake's striking distance. With quick little movements, I wiggled the end of the staff. The cobra struck, but its fangs failed to penetrate the oak. It wound away, in search of a softer touch, vanishing, and reappearing as it crossed the blowing sand. We all jumped up, each holding tight to our billowing shelter. Blinking and squinting against the billions of grains, we noticed something flowing over the sand and through the silica clouds. Snakes. Cobras. Hundreds. We kept our flasks and weapons and abandoned all else. The tent canvas flew off like it had wings. Running all-out, we reached the base of a massive dune. The snakes closed in.

"Get to the top!" said the professor. "Stay on the windward side!" he yelled as we climbed. "Get down and dig in!"

From the top of the dune, we winced and huddled against the wind. We watched through slits of eyes as the snakes neared the base of the dune. "They're a species from India!" I yelled. "Poisonous!"

"Pound and kick!" said the professor. "The vibrations may drive them around us."

The cobras kept coming, straight up the side of the dune. Thousands of snakes, thousands of fangs filled with poison. But farther off, something else was coming, rolling across the horizon: a blur, roughly cylindrical, nearly a quarter mile long. It grew in height as it gathered more sand. It was a tornado, twisting on its side rather than upright—a sand-packed steamroller.

"Stay low, dig in, lock arms!" yelled Adventure. "It's our only chance."

The snakes that didn't go around the dune were blown over our heads. Though the twister was a half mile away, it seemed within spitting distance. Earlier, we had soaked our tunics with water to use as breathing masks, but the fabric was getting clogged, and the air was getting thin. Then, most bizarrely, the wind-blasted sand started to turn white—and it was wet. A heavy snow, a blizzard as fierce as I'd ever seen descended over the dunes. Buried, blind, battered by ice, we huddled as a whiteout smothered everything. It had gotten so cold that our breath froze and crackled like bacon in a pan. Then, like the bottom falling out of a full basket, the sky was empty. When we wiped the drenched grit from our eyes, the view was clear all the way to the painted horizon. A blizzard of salvation had saved us from a savage desert storm. Faith, fate, physics, chaos—the cause meant nothing, the result meant life.

Our food, supplies, and shelter had been buried or blown away. With the soggy clothes on our backs, our weapons, and near-empty water flasks, we sauntered through the melting snow. We were numb from the trauma, body and mind. But according to the maps, we would soon encounter a fertile oasis. A place to get dry, seek sanity, and lay our heads. This shining promise of sanctuary gave us the strength to carry on.

# Chapter 24:
## Date with Insanity

Approaching the rocklands was like opening the door of an oven. We'd been drenched by the snowstorm, but our clothes had dried against our skin long before our first sight of the oasis. Along with the heat, the first signs of dehydration had set in.

"Me mouth keeps sealin' shut," said Golly.

"In the outback," said Professor Winkleheimer, "we use the pebble- in-the-mouth trick."

"That works?" said Adventure. "Most times."

"But not for the reason you might think," I said. "It doesn't stimulate saliva production. Keeping the pebble closed in your mouth preserves the moisture that's already there."

"Makes sense," said the professor. "I suppose we ought to stop yapping then."

"Aye," said Golly. We all agreed. Trudging along in silence, we mulled our thoughts and weighed our options.

Bands of pink, yellow, orange, and blue filled the sky with dazzling swirls. Despite our dizziness and dire need for water, we gazed up in awe. "Look!" yelled Brutus, pointing at similar colors hovering over the distant sand. "The oasis!" His impulsive nature sent him trotting ahead toward the life-sustaining refuge. Atop the next rise, he threw his arms wide believing he had reached the spring-fed waters. Then his arms dropped in dejection; he turned in circles of confusion and then fainted onto the parched desert floor. We hurried to his side only to find the oasis had been a mirage. No water, no palm trees, no fig trees, no sprawling vines of grapes.

Slowly rousing, Brutus said, "It's gone." He scooped up a handful of sand. "It was here, and it—it just disappeared."

Golly knelt beside his friend. "Never mind, mate. We'll find the real thing—the one that's on the map."

Speaking softly, the professor confided in Adventure and me, "The oasis was on the map, near this very spot. But these maps are more than one hundred years old. The water source, an underground river or stream, may have dried up long ago."

"I've seen mirages on deserts, seas, and from the air," I said. "They're usually reflections of real things. So, there's still a good chance there's water up ahead."

Golly said, "If not, what's the next water then, Professor?"

"Maybe the hot springs in the canyons. But there's no guarantee. There was a side note in a margin on the map, but no exact locations had been marked."

Golly sighed, "If the bubblin' pools are there, we'll find 'em.

'Ot water's better than no water."

Adventure said, "Without water, in this heat, we're good for a day's walk at best."

I took another look at the chart. "The map gets pretty sketchy from here on. Let's just hope the note about the canyons . . . holds water. Sorry, I'm not making light of it. My brain's stalling out. I just couldn't think of any other words."

The professor's raspy voice offered, "Quite all right, mate. It would be quite funny if our lives weren't in the balance."

Humble and ashamed, Brutus said, "I was foolish to run ahead like that. Sometimes I'm my own worst enemy."

"Not to worry, me ol' china. Can you get along then?" asked Golly.

Brutus said, "My wits are about me, my legs are under me. Let's be off."

We slogged along, up a slight grade, more and more doubtful of the map's reliability. If the oasis were no more than a mirage, our journey would end in this parched gulch of sand. Legs heavy, throats dry, we labored along; each step seemed a step toward death. My vision was blurry, a sure sign of desiccation. Up ahead were rolling dunes and arduous climbs. Reaching the top of the first dune before the rest of us, Adventure stopped as though dumbstruck. She rubbed her eyes and gazed intently. She waved us forward, "Hurry," she called. "Come look!" She disappeared over the rise. With the Grim Reaper at our heels, we struggled up the cruel hill of shifting sand.

There it was—a luscious green paradise! When we started for the water, Adventure ordered, "Stop!" She waved us back and approached the pool. "I've a sense about water." She reached down and sloshed her hand. She took a tiny taste and flicked a few drops on her nose. Joyously, her parched voice shouted, "It's pure!"

Like a herd of mad cows, we rushed past the cat to splash within the liquid haven. All five of us, including the professor, ducked under the water and stayed there. We slurped and sloshed and guzzled till we gasped for breath. Blessed with new life, I reclined in a back float, looked straight up, and watched the swirling sky. The others did the same.

Surrounding the spring pool were desert grasses and palm, fig, date, and olive trees. The black olives were rock solid and far too bitter to eat. Though the figs were few, they proved delicious. Our saving grace was the date trees, which bore plenty of sweet, chewy, nut- flavored fruit.

As we sat near the water, dining on dates, the professor and I discussed the prospects of making our way to the surface world. "If we do find a route at the gorge," said the professor, "we'll have no provisions, no supplies for the journey. A sticky wicket to say the least."

"As near as I can figure," I said, "we're somewhere beneath Greenland. The Earth's crust ranges from eight to twelve miles in depth. So, we're at least eight miles down. Most of Greenland is a glacial trough covered by ice. That means a viable passageway would likely lead to a stretch of coast."

The professor thought things through. "As I said before, I believe passing through the Coverture, Triangle in my case, placed us within the Earth's mantle. The question is—how deep?"

I reasoned, "The heat at the Earth's core is estimated to be 10,000 degrees Fahrenheit. Since the volcanic activity at our present level is relatively mild, not that much greater than on the surface, we must not be all that far beneath the crust."

The professor's eyes blinked like the digits on a calculator as he swallowed the last of a fig. "Let's allow twelve miles for the crust and a half-dozen more for the mantle. That's eighteen miles. It'll not be a straight shot from here to there, so we'll have to add some distance for curves, as well as ups and downs."

"OK," I said. "Let's double the distance and round up. We'll round thirty-six miles up to forty."

The professor said, "If we're able to travel two miles an hour, a conservative guess, we can cover forty miles in twenty hours. If we push hard, put in a ten-hour hike each day, we'll make it to the surface in two days."

Finding no flaw in Professor Winkleheimer's logic, I concurred, "I'd say that's the best-case scenario. With a few figs in our pockets and a flask full of water—it's definitely doable."

"Then we're going to do it, me old mucker!" the professor said. We both laughed a hearty laugh.

Adventure offered, "Even if it were four or five days, a flask of water could get you there if you ration well."

"It's not often I've explored a rock tunnel without findin' water drippin' and poolin'," said Golly. "Twenty-mile trip—you'll find water somewhere."

"And it always seems there's mushrooms in caves," said Brutus. "You can eat most types of mushrooms."

With a voice of hopeful confidence, I said, "Unless the path has become obstructed somehow, we're gonna make it home. There's not a doubt in my mind."

The professor said, "It'll be just like a fanciful frolic in the outback, Captain."

With sincerity in both my voice and eyes, I addressed Golly,

Brutus, and Adventure. "But I'm not taking a single step toward home until we secure those Orb slices."

"No one's safe until we do," said Adventure.

"All fine and well," said Brutus. "As long as the toad doesn't outdo us. Might be by now he's figured out how to use the slice he's already got."

Adventure said, "Not likely. Signs along the way show he's staying close to our route. He must think he still needs us."

"Hedging his bet," said the professor.

"That froggy couldn't steal the prize if a bunny rabbit was guardin' it," said Golly. "A right pantywaist he is. 'E'd likely faint at the sight of a flyin' devil."

"Aye," said Brutus. "That's the bloke we've all come to know."

The cat surveyed the little paradise and said, "While there's still enough light, let's check the area for snakes and pests. We'll want a peaceful night's sleep."

"And it's my turn to take first watch," said Brutus. "I'll watch this oasis like a hungry hawk."

"I'll spell you at the stroke o' midnight, elf," said Golly. "Midnight at the oasis," I said and chuckled.

"What about it?" said Golly.

"Oh, don't mind me," I said. "The words just popped into my head."

"Change o' the guard at midnight," said the professor. "Then it's me, next in line."

"You need your beauty rest, Professor," I said. "Adventure and I can finish off the watch."

The professor jovially furrowed his brow. "I don't suppose there's any use in arguing."

"No use at all," said Adventure, still scanning the sand. She cupped her palm to the side of her head. "I've seen a few bugs about, but we're not too bad off. Just remember to cover your groundward ear while you sleep. Knights have been using that simple trick to keep bugs out of ears for centuries."

A pleasant breeze flowed through the oasis. Occasionally it kicked up a little cloud of dust, so I found a windbreak at the base of a palm tree, which also afforded a nice view of the glowing sprites. Sitting cross-legged in the sand, I rolled my jacket into a pillow and then settled back to enjoy the winking specks. Tonight, they were mostly warm hues of orange, yellow, and red.

Adventure was curled up near the pond, looking much more like a cat than she realized. Golly slept sitting up, with his back to a fig tree. The professor was flat on his back, sound asleep, under the open sky. Brutus was dutifully on patrol. As a precaution, he had borrowed my bo staff to complement his pouch of slumber dust. True to habit, he moved around the camp like a key-wound mechanical man. I wish I could have pinned a badge on him.

The chirps of a single cricket soothed our weary souls. Tomorrow's goal was to reach the rocklands by late afternoon. For now, we would simply enjoy the beautiful desert night.

When I awoke, there was something inches from my face. A spear with a chiseled stone point tapped me on the forehead. Looming above me was the stubbly, bearded face of a Farthingale troll. "Up," he grunted.

When I stood, Brutus was nowhere to be seen. Adventure, Golly, and the professor lay perfectly still in the middle of camp. Nearby, lying on the sand, was Brutus's pouch of slumber dust. From behind a palm came the gloating, croaky laugh of Parnielius Wermbom. "Bind them," he ordered. Four shaggy brutes, dressed in bearskin vests and kilts, tied our hands behind our backs. Another troll splashed a pot of water onto my dust-drugged friends.

Delivering harsh jabs with their spearheads, the trolls prodded Adventure and Golly to their feet. When the professor struggled to stand, a troll snatched him up and shook him until his head rattled. Adventure and Golly were jabbed in the ribs and held back when they protested. The troll carried the professor to a slatted cart and tossed him in along with our flasks, weapons, and the sleeping elf.

Gleefully, the toad approached Adventure and said, "Goodness, Katherine, you're looking a bit mussed."

"Shut your green gob, Parnie. And don't think for a squinch any one of us will lift a finger to help with that gorge monster—if he even exists!"

"Oh, he exists—I've seen him," said the toad. "And he is quite horrible. Calling him a monster is far too polite. 'Putrid abomination' would be much more fitting."

"Watch your step, froggy," said Golly. "Or he might putridly abominate you." Golly laughed and received a spear poke to the chest for his trouble.

"You'll soon lose that cheek, dog man," said Parnie. "A long plod through a rock oven should dry up your vinegar."

Adventure said, "We will not help you, Parnie. Not one of us. And I strongly suspect the gorge creature could easily destroy you and all your trolls. You may as well return the Orb slices and stand aside."

"I'll not stand aside," said the toad. "The Orb tells me things." He held the Orb pieces to his ears.

"The Orb speaks to you?" said the cat. "He's psychotic," I said.

"He's gone completely mad," said Golly.

"Mad?" said the toad. "The Orb cries out for rebirth. It wants all its pieces joined—to become one again. And it knows that I, and I alone, can make it so." He smiled wickedly. "It trusts in me."

"Ha!" said Adventure. "Now I know you've gone mad."

"Bah to your insolence, Katherine. Know your place and hear the prophecy. Once joined, once whole, the Orb will cleanse all existence, all eternity. It will draw all within itself, pounding it, grinding it, mashing it, smashing it, till it's smaller than a speck on the head of a pin. It will then explode into the finest of sparkling dust. Existence and eternity will be reborn. And the Orb will rule in the form of my being. But not as an ugly, warty toad; rather, I shall command as a dashing, daring, handsome prince. All will obey, and my kingdom shall extend to the edges of forever."

Caustic and biting was the cat's reply. "My goodness, Parnie. Your noble ambitions know no bounds."

"An inspiring goal, indeed," I said. "And gosh—I had no idea we were in pursuit of a Big Bang Boomerang."

"Blasphemy! Know your place, child!" the toad scolded. I felt the prod of a troll's spear.

Golly said, "Oi, froggy, you're off your soggy nut!"

The toad clapped his webbed hands and shouted to the trolls, "On to the canyons, you filthy beggars!"

Adventure whispered to Golly and me, "The barmy bloke's forgotten my razors. I've nearly clawed my way through these laces."

"No words in the ranks," ordered the toad. "Get between them, you dolts!"

As he hopped along, the toad swallowed handfuls of oasis fruit. "Ah, what delightful dates!" he said. "Succulent as well as satisfying."

# Chapter 25:
## Upside Downfall

Hexagonal spaces on a gameboard came to mind as we walked the parched ground between the desert and the rocklands. Walking ahead of me was Adventure, the professor, Golly, and then Brutus. Between us were short-legged, barrel-chested Farthingale trolls. I had been placed at the end of the line for being unfairly deemed a blasphemer. Adventure was at the front so the toad could mercilessly torment her. The professor was positioned between the dog man and cat so they could provide support when he faltered. Brutus was basically an also-ran; little did the toad know the elf had an authentic slice of Orb buttoned in the pocket of his tunic. And only Golly and I knew the cat's bindings hung by frays and threads.

As they swept through the igneous ridges, riled waves of calidity sought to fry our faces. The same heat blasted us again as it rose from the cordovan stone. Bypassing the gulley's yap, we pressed on toward meaner pastures. The toad led the way in a rickshaw-like contrivance drawn by troglodyte drudges. The yawning mouth of the next canyon revealed natural formations resembling stalagmites; they were ornate and reminded me of slender Thai temples. Some of the structures towered to skyscraper heights. The thought of skyscrapers had me longing for home, but with each trudging step, I feared more and more I'd never see home again.

Over the rattling wheels of the carts, the professor shouted, "Toad! You'd better give us a drink, or we'll not be around to help with that damn bunyip!"

The rickshaw slowed. The toad looked back and waved the command. "Give them a swallow!" He then downed an entire flask.

Adventure swallowed the trickle she'd been given and asked, "How far to the gorge?"

Parnie croaked, "We'll be there soon enough." He waved the procession forward.

"More than a day, at this rate," the professor injected. "And we're off course." The old man groaned after a spear jab to the ribs.

"Where are you taking us, Parnie?" asked Adventure. She turned to hiss at the trailing troll and was spared the spear.

"Patience, Katherine. As you know, curiosity killed the cat." "Ah, words of ignorance from the toad who would be prince." "A sharp tongue and a dull wit, and neither is the better." "Oi, give it a rest, you two. Let us enjoy our stroll," said Golly.

"Dull wit can be contagious," said the toad. "Trolls, clasp your ears."

Another few miles. Another sip of water. It went on and on.

Above, the eggshell glow of an early winter sky faded to grey. The toad led our group up a final grade and onto the destined plateau, where dwelled only rubble, wide slabs of stone, and tufts of scraggly grass. As darkness eased upon the scene, the trolls lit torches and wedged them between the rocks. The toad hopped here and there, surveying all with his googly eyes. He slapped his webbed hands together twice and gestured. The trolls led us to the escarpment's edge. As the toad came forward, the brutes stepped back. We took in the dim-lit panorama of a canyon rivaling the Grand.

Parnie declaimed, "Behold a molten canyon. A cauldron of lava, tar, and liquid iron. An immeasurable crater of steam, ash, and sulfur. A wasteland of crevices, fissures, and chasms. At the end lies the gorge and the gargoyle with its indigo eye— the third Orb slice, soon to be my prize. Tomorrow will be the battle."

"You're no fighter, Parnie," said Adventure. "Nor a knight, nor a soldier, nor a warrior. You lie and connive; you cheat and steal. You have the heart of a coward and the soul of a—" She sighed, "You haven't any soul."

"But you have a weakness, you stupid cat! One that gives me the strength of an army."

"Shades of Titan, Zeus, and Neptune! More lunacy. You're mad, Parnie. You've gone completely mad!" she exclaimed.

"I've not yet told you your weakness: The wretched, pitiful notions about things you call loyalty, honor, and love."

"To be pitied is how those gaping, balloonish eyes of yours can see absolutely nothing—no matter how glaringly obvious it may be."

The toad clapped. "Back to the rock pile! All but the lad."

At spearpoint, Adventure, the professor, Golly, and Brutus were driven back and pushed to the ground at the foot of a rubble heap. I was left alone, at the brink of a fathomless drop. An armed troll stood at my back.

Adventure got to her feet, her back to the rocks, her hands free but well hidden. "A final life's lesson for you toad: Loyalty conveys trust, honor towers above courage, and love is the greatest strength of all."

"All so much gibberish and rubbish," sneered the toad. "Lock it in a box and dump it in the bay." He strolled arrogantly to center stage with a torch-bearing troll on either side. Parnie nodded and the troll at my back prodded me one step closer to the ledge. "At morning's light, you will go to the gorge and bring back the indigo eye. Your pledge now—or the lad falls."

Golly, Brutus, and the professor rose and shouted in protest. Even with hands bound, they tried to fight. After a brief tussle, the trolls' spears forced them back. But this distraction had given Adventure the instant she needed to rush the toad. She pounced. Her claws brushed his webbed feet as he leaped into the air. Troll spears kept the others pinned to the ground. Landing lightly atop the rocks, the toad pointed at my keeper. "Over he goes!"

"Stop!" said Adventure. "I'll get your damned Orb."

A smile, smug and sinister, writhed up the toad's face.

As the guard marched me toward the others, one of the trolls jabbered wildly, "Rock, rock, shining eye, shining, shining eye!" He held up a slice of Orb. During the struggle, it had fallen from Brutus's pocket. The toad now truly possessed half of the mystical sphere, though to his mind he owned three-quarters.

"Wrap those claws!" called the toad from his high mound. "Use heavy straps."

Adventure, true to her vow, did not fight as the trolls tied her hands. Once the cat was securely bound, the toad jumped down to take the "shiny rock." At the top of his lungs, he exclaimed. "It's the Orb! The southern slice!" He hopped and danced in the firelight. "Tomorrow I'll have the last. I'll have the whole of it. The Orb of the Andes shall be mine, and mine alone!"

As he gazed at the Orb wedges cupped in his hands, two of the pieces began to glow; their dark indigo turned to violet. The crystals brightened, quivered, and quaked; the toad's eyes grew wide. His huge mouth dropped open. Clutching the stones tightly, he pointed them at a troll. A halo formed around the brute. The toad lifted the glowing stones, and the troll rose high into the night. As Parnie moved his hand in a figure eight, the sky-bound troll swung helplessly in the same manner. The toad laughed wildly as he moved the troll in a huge circle, and then zig-zagged him across the sky. When the Parnie finally lowered his hands, his tortured toy plummeted. The brute struck the rocks hard and hobbled into hiding.

Bringing the Orb crystals to his ears, the toad listened intently. His wiggly lips dribbled as he muttered, "The Orb's power throbs in my hands." He glanced toward us; his eyes narrowed in disdain. "I don't need them. They're worth nothing to me now . . . I can take the gargoyle's eye. And I'll keep the cat. She's mine, she's mine, she's mine!"

The toad swaggered toward us as we sat bound at the foot of the rock pile. "Rise, disloyal subjects." We refused to stand. "Rise!" He pointed at the guards, then toward us. With spears pointed at our heads, we stood. The toad approached and displayed the three Orb slices. "As you've seen, the Orb's power lies in my hands." He placed the Orb pieces in his waistcoat. "In the morning, I will destroy the gargoyle and take its indigo eye." He tapped and stroked his warty chin. "You, Katherine,

I shall keep—as my servant. I shall feed you table scraps and soured milk.”

“Never!” hissed the cat.

“Very well.” He wafted his hand and barked, “To the ledge! All of them!”

Hands tightly bound, spears at our backs, we shuffled toward the ledge. Toes touching the rim, we stared into the black, fire-speckled depths of a bottomless ravine. The trolls grunted as they prodded us. Looking down the line, I saw Golly raise his nose and sniff. Adventure’s ears perked, and her yellow-green eyes grew wide. Odd; perhaps, they were simply taking in the last of the world they knew. Brutus appeared oblivious, the professor stoic. Me, I wanted to fight. I tugged and twisted at the twine around my wrists. I don’t think I’d ever felt more helpless.

“You’ve one chance. Serve me, Katherine, as you did Piranda. You will be my pet. You will learn how to please, and you will be taught to obey. Serve me and perhaps . . . I will spare your friends.”

“We’ll die first!” growled Golly.

“Right, toad, go ahead, shove us over!” said Brutus. “A thrilling way to go,” said the professor.

“I’ll be flying an F-16 all the way,” I said.

After a brief silence, Adventure said, "My friends have stated their piece, Parnie. I share their thoughts. Do what you will."

"You stubborn, stupid, fool of a cat!" He let out a long, wailing cry—a cry full of anguish, anger, and spite. "Over with them!"

The spearpoint between my shoulder blades sent me off balance and then pushed me over the edge. A gust of wind brushed past my face and a huge shadow flashed before my eyes. Freefall from a thousand feet takes about ten seconds. I had seven seconds left. Another gust and another shadow. Five seconds left. Four. Three. Something slammed into me. It felt like a professional wrestler had me in a bearhug. Then came the familiar lifting tug of a pair of mighty wings. A Valgar had me wrapped in his powerful arms. He flew in a circle, went into a hover, and then slowly descended and set me down—right next to Adventure. Golly, Brutus, and Professor Winkleheimer were also standing safely on the burning canyon floor. With a pinch or two of their talons, the bird men severed our bindings.

One last Valgar landed, clutching the toad by his amphibious ankles. Suspended upside-down, Parnie flailed away as the Orb slices dropped from his waistcoat, bouncing in all directions. "My beauties!" he cried. "My beauties!" His Valgar captor screeched and swung him like a pendulum. He croaked and hollered, bellowed and balled. One of the Valgars gathered the indigo pieces and handed them to Adventure. Professor Winkleheimer picked out the fake slice and tossed it into a simmering pool of tar.

While Adventure, Golly, Brutus, and I made the rounds, thanking each Valgar for our lives, the professor spoke with Chief Eka Laka. What started as a vociferous disagreement soon changed into a mutual understanding. Eka Laka and the professor engaged in an arm-wrestling handshake and each squawked twice. The professor's expression was solemn and a little sad as he approached us.

"The Valgars have come to take me home," said the professor. "It wasn't until now I realized my home was here now, on that tropical island with the bird people. My one regret is I won't be at your side for the final leg, Captain. But the chief won't hear of it. He said that from here on, this is none of the Valgars' affair."

Eka Laka now spoke. Some of what he said we understood. The professor explained the rest. The Family of the Feather had adopted Professor Winkleheimer as one of their own. The old Aussie was no longer an honored guest; he was an ornithoid brother. They had brought along a flight basket, woven from stout jungle grass, to transport him safely home. Eka Laka bid us good fortune, farewell, and sharp talons in battle. After hugs from the men and a kiss from the cat, the professor boarded his basket. As he lifted off, he waved and shouted,

"Get that weather up top sorted, Captain. We've got our lives and our futures on ya!" We cheered and watched them wing majestically out of sight.

***

Morning had broken. The Gorge of the Gargoyle lay five miles to the east. We'd had no food and had taken only occasional sips of water over the past three days. Before darkness fell, we would stare into the face of evil and most likely succumb to a ghastly demise. With no other choice, we summoned the essence that lies deep within every living thing—the instinct to survive. Without reservation, we cast our fate to the wind. We were about to step from earth to firmament—to trawl the pools of purgatory. 'Twould be a frantic grasp at hope; a pitch to save our mortal souls.

The Valgars had placed the toad on a leash, which Golly now held with warranted glee. Parnie ranted, "The Orb is mine! Mine! When morning comes, when evening goes, I'll have it in my hand. I will. I will. I'll have it in my hand."

"What shall we do with him?" said Brutus.

"The Valgars left us some spears and waterskins from the trolls' carts and wagons," I said. "Let's fill a flask at a hot spring and then send him on his way."

Golly glanced around and said, "Where've the trolls gone?"

Brutus said, "The bird men scattered them. They're likely headed back to the Farthingale."

"My trolls!" blathered the toad. "I promised them all of the reindeer herds and every sprite in the sky. And they believed! The numpty- dumps believed!" He laughed hysterically.

Adventure looked at the toad and sighed. "I suppose we'll have to look after him."

"Kindest thing to do," I said. "He can't hop far without those crystals. If he's left alone, he won't last long."

"Hear that, froggy?" said Golly. "We're savin' your sorry green bum." "Even though you did shove us off a cliff!" said Brutus.

"It's all about love and having love for others," said Adventure. "It's a joy and a blessing the godforsaken croaker will never know."

The toad began to ramble. "There was a king and a cake and a cake and a king, a king and a cake and a cake and a king, a king and a cake and a cake and a king . . ."

As we gathered our few accoutrements—water flasks, troll spears, and the indigo crystals—we looked upon the toad with pity and compassion. I said, "If all goes well, Mr. Wermbom, my friends will be back for you."

The toad prattled on. "There was a king and a cake, and a cake and a king, a king and a cake, and a cake and a king . . ."

# Chapter 26:
## Gorge of the Gargoyle

The deeper into the canyon we went, the darker red the sky: pink, rose, scarlet, burgundy, and finally, a brackish blood. The babblings of the toad still echoed. And I'd come to terms with my lot. My journey through the looking glass had reached the end of the rabbit hole.

Adventure, Golly, Brutus, and I stood at the threshold of a gateway to Hell. I pictured myself in the cockpit of an F-16. I activated the battery and flipped the switch to Main Power. I engaged the fuel pumps and set the air source knob to NORM. "Well, folks," I said, "this could be my last dogfight."

"Aye," said Golly. "A fight's likely, but I shouldn't think there'll be dogs about."

"Dogs? Around here? Not a chance," said Brutus. "No dog in his right mind would come to a place like this." He looked up at his broad- shouldered friend. "Well . . . excepting you, Golly."

After a pause, Golly nodded amiably. "And I'll be accepting that as 'omage, elf."

Adventure and I exchanged glances and smiled.

Spears in hand, spirits strong, we ventured toward a blazing arena of doom. Smoke and steam rolled in swells, ash drifted like feathers and snow. Sometimes the ground blasted sulfur fumes, and sometimes it spewed scalding water. Pools of tar and oil bubbled. Lava oozed from zigzagging cracks and trickled down the scarps. Our eyes burned, our feet baked, and our skin was near aflame.

Scores of skeletons, of many species, framed the entrance to a lightless corridor gouged into the face of subterranean rock. We lingered at the doorstep of a descending pathway and gazed at a design of unholy fabrication a quarter-mile distant. The crypt-like structure stood three stories high. It was surrounded by refracted light due to heat waves rising from a molten moat. We four stuck close to the stygian walls, Golly and Brutus on the left, Adventure and I on the right. Dissipating soot unveiled the complex battlements atop the crypt's rounded bailey. In the center stood a colossus, a gargoyle of stone. Its strapping, masculine form was capped by a bullet-shaped head. Ribbed horns curled back over its skull. From its scapula jutted pennons, barbed and batlike. Covering the doorway was a wooden platform, the smaller portion of a drawbridge, sized to abut its land-held counterpart. Pylons crowned by chiseled boar heads four-cornered the moat.

Adventure's quick wave beckoned Golly and Brutus to join us behind a steeple of rock. The cat said, "Once we're close enough, I'll circle to the far pylon, take a run, and jump the moat."

"That trench is full of lava," I said. "Like a lake, all the way around. Miss by an inch and you'll disintegrate."

"No fears. I'll make the jump. That's the least of our worries." She pointed to the drawbridge. "Those long handles on either side— they'll need pulling to release the bridge."

"Which will probably wake the creature," I said.

She nodded. "If the legend holds truth." "Might be just a scarecrow," said Golly. "Perhaps. Perhaps not," said Brutus. "Profound assessment, gentlemen," I said.

Adventure faced me, took me by the arms, and squeezed tightly. "Once the bridge is down, run for all you're worth, Captain. Don't stop, don't look back. You'll have just one chance. That beast is much too large to get through the door, so you'll be home free."

"But the gargoyle's Orb, the indigo eye—you'll need my help."

Adventure fumed, "Be damned the Orb! Let the bloody monster keep it!"

"We'll be ready with the spears," said Golly. "Right up to the end of the bridge."

Adventure unlaced her tunic pocket and removed the Orb slices. She handed one to Golly and the other to Brutus. "There's always the chance I'll be caught," she said. "If it comes to it, try the crystals."

"If it comes to it, we'll light 'em up good," said Golly. Brutus nodded.

A rumbling sound from the canyon was followed by a slight trembling beneath our feet. Our eyes shot to the gargoyle, but it did not move. Staying in the shadows, behind the rocks, beside the steep gully wall, we reached an outcropping about thirty yards from the drawbridge.

Adventure put her hand on my shoulder. "Once the bridge moves, start your run. I'll sprint back to join these two." She reached in her pocket, took out her penknife, and handed it to me. "A farewell gift."

"But you might—"

She extended her claws. "I've always got my razors." She purred as she hugged me. After all the hours we'd spent together, she still treated me like a little boy. Tears glistened in my eyes and there was a lump in my throat as the cat slipped into the darkness.

If I could get through the door, my plan was to keep moving, as fast and as far as possible, to put the maximum distance behind me and this outer ring of damnation. For the journey, I would have only my tunic, tights, boots, and the penknife.

Believing a waterskin would slow my run, I guzzled the contents and set it on the ground. Golly frowned. Brutus rolled his eyes.

"Oi, lad, you should 'ave kept a few swigs," said Golly.

"It could get hot as a kiln in some of those tunnels, Captain. No telling how long before you find as much as a trickle."

Brutus removed his tunic and began tearing it into strips. From this cloth he fashioned a strap and attached his full flask. "You'll be able to carry it easily now. I'll not let you go without water."

"Take mine too," said Golly. He attached another waterskin.

"Thanks. I wasn't thinking straight. Super-hydrating's an old habit of mine. I should've known better." I looped the strap around my neck and shoulder. Brutus took another strip of tunic cloth and bound the flasks snugly against my youthful frame.

"We'll follow with the spears," said Golly. "All you need to do is run like the wind."

"You're good friends. A couple of the best men I've ever known. I'll never forget you guys."

"And we'll never forget you," said Golly. "Eh, Brutus?"

"We'll never forget, Captain." There was a tremble in the elf's voice. "You run and keep on running. Don't mind us. Keep your eyes straight ahead. You'll be home in no time."

I stared at the gargoyle. "Maybe it's just a hunk of stone . . . nothing but a carved-up chunk of rock."

"We'll know soon enough," said Golly.

Adventure crouched behind the closest pylon, well hidden. Satisfied the gargoyle had not moved, she hurried to the next pedestal. She eyed the moat and judged the distance. From my perspective, I estimated thirty to thirty-five feet. No human being had ever jumped that far. But she was as fast as a race-horse, could spring like a lion, and most of all, she was sure of herself.

The cat removed her boots. Stealthy and lithe, she cleared a running path. About forty yards from the moat, she set her stance, waved to us, and then burst into a full run. Planting her toes about a foot from the moat, she sailed gracefully over the molten rock, landing lightly on the crypt's base. That's when the monster moved. Cracks formed on its head and face; the mineral veneer flaked away. As it raised its arm, its stone skin wrinkled; chips and chunks crumbled to the tower's base. The cat could not see the gargoyle, but she could hear the cracking and breaking of its shell.

Beside the drawbridge, Adventure pulled the first handle; the securing chain clanked, loosening a corner of the structure. She hurried to the other side and reached for the second handle. High above, the gargoyle was free of stone and was now a flesh-and-blood creature. Its enormous wings spread wide as it leaped into the air. The cat tugged at the second handle, but it would not budge. The gargoyle circled high into the dark red sky and then swooped toward one of the boar-head pylons. With taloned feet, it kicked the sculpted head, knocking it into the lava. At the same time, a gush of molten rock poured from the neck of the pylon and flowed into the moat.

Both hands gripping tight to the drawbridge handle, the cat dropped her weight again and again; she tugged with all her might. Finally, the pinion gave way and the drawbridge clanked and rattled into place. At the same moment, the rock floor beneath us began to quake. Rubble slid down the walls of the gorge as we ran.

I was getting close to the bridge. Brutus and Golly followed just a few steps behind, their spears at the ready. Ignoring us, the airborne demon knocked over each boar head in turn. Molten rock flowed from each column. The moat was filling, the lava quickly neared the level of the bridge. As Adventure and I ran toward each other, she waved me forward. Above, the gargoyle banked and dove directly at us. The lava oscillated, splashing onto the wooden planks. The cat's eyes met mine as we passed on the bridge. I couldn't help but slow my pace. "Keep going!" she yelled. I listened. The next second, I was through the door.

Inside the crypt, a stairway with a banister led downward to a dimly lit chamber. Tiny creatures clung to the walls of the tunnel: greenish glow worms. There was just enough light to negotiate the stone stairway. After four or five steps, I stopped. On impulse, I turned and ran back. I crossed the bridge in a flash; as I did, lava flowed freely into the passage—closing the doorway forever. I paid it no mind, for in the near distance, the gargoyle hovered and touched down, clutching Adventure around the waist.

Golly and Brutus were charging with spears. Adventure scratched the monster's face and bit it on the arm; it dropped her. A resounding crack split the ground and shattered the acrid air; the thunder-like clap rumbled to a roar. As Golly and Brutus rushed to help the cat, a fissure opened beneath them, and they disappeared. The gargoyle leaped, flapped once, and touched down, blocking the path of its scampering prey. Adventure faked a run in one direction and then quickly cut back, trying to race past. The monster slapped her down with the back of its spiney hand. She sprang up and stood defiantly.

Throughout the gorge, small mounds erupted, spitting out flaming chunks, splashes of lava, and clouds of thick, black smoke. The monster backed Adventure toward a pit of sputtering tar. I frantically searched for a weapon. If I could plunge a spear into the gargoyle's leg or foot, Adventure would have a chance. Visibility came and went with the rolling smoke; it was getting worse. As I searched along the fissure that had swallowed Golly and Brutus, I could see it inching closed. Their spears must have fallen in with them. I heard their voices calling out for help. They were being squeezed to death by a volcanic vise and there was nothing I could do.

I called their names but heard no response. Explosions blasted the smothering air, which barreled forth like a fuggy wind. Suddenly, something flew up from the narrowing crack. Two objects bounced across the stone floor. The Orb slices—tossed up by the elf and dog man. I took one in each hand.

When I turned, Adventure was again in the gargoyle's grasp. Her arms were trapped. She kicked and writhed as the monster nudged its nose to the back of her head. Its cavernous maw grew wide, exposing huge, jagged teeth dripping with drool and venom. The gargoyle curled back its lips and readied a poisonous bite. I aimed the Orb wedges at its head, but the crystals remained dark and dead. When the creature chomped its teeth, Adventure slunk deeper within its grasp, and it bit nothing but air. Now the crystals in my hands moved. Vibrating faster and faster, they began to glow, brighter and brighter. I aimed at the creature's indigo eye.

The gargoyle loosened its grasp exposing the cat from the shoulders up. As the demon aimed its bite at Adventure's head, she wrestled her arms free and scratched ferociously at the monster's hands. I gripped the Orb wedges with all my strength and felt a radiating warmth. The gargoyle's Orb eye began to glow. As the cat twisted in the monster's grasp, it bit down, sinking its toxic grinders deep into her arm and shoulder. The gargoyle raised its chin and screamed. Adventure dropped to the ground, rolled away, tried twice to stand, but finally collapsed and lay still. The demon reached down to take her in its claws again.

The crystals in my hand trembled with vengeance and blazed like tiny suns. They blistered and burned my flesh, but I held on. A violet sheen emanated from the Orb, copiously flowing, and bathing the chasm from end to end, while the indigo eye in the monster's skull glowed ember red. As the glow intensified, a whirring sound resonated. My hands were burning up; blackened bone was showing. The gargoyle shrieked as the Orb eye blasted streams of energy across the gorge. In blotches and patches, its grotesque form returned to stone, breaking into chunks, and crumbling into bits. The charred glass eye lay upon the heap.

Startled by a sound from behind, I glanced around. Golly and Brutus had somehow ascended from the chasm. They were running toward me shouting and pointing, "Captain, Captain!

The cat! She's down!"

We rushed to Adventure's side. She had taken a nasty bite; her wounds were deep and bleeding. The gorge was burning and caving in around us. The crystals in the charred remains of my hands were cold and still. In the frozen abyss of my mind a thought glimmered, then ignited! I shouted, "The eye! Find the monster's eye!"

Brutus streaked toward the gargoyle's remains. With even greater speed he returned with the crystal. Golly lifted the cat and cradled her gently. I kept one slice of the Orb and gave Golly the other.

Then I saw a shape staggering aimlessly between the craters and crevices. It was Parnie, the toad. I hurried through the suffocating soot, took his arm, and pulled him toward the others. As we huddled together, the three crystals hummed, flickered, and shimmered. As fissures split the ground around us, the crystals radiated in shades of purple and blue. Exuding a thermogenic aura, the Orb burst forth a light as bright as a nova. For a fraction of a second existence imploded and infinity perished. We were nowhere, we were everywhere; we were never, we were forever.

***

Gradually recovering our senses, feeling the hand of gravity tug at our bodies, we gasped in disbelief and gazed in wonder.

We were no longer in the decimated gorge. We stood on the nighttime lawn of the Morningtown Inn. Streetlamps shone like beacons of life. Golly knelt and placed Adventure's motionless form on the grass.

"There may still be a chance," I said, holding up a wedge of the Orb. We formed a triangle around the cat, extended our crystals over her and touched them together. Tiny vibrations hummed and flecks of light appeared. The crystals quivered and glowed. A little brighter, a little brighter. The violet glow held steady, but the cat did not move. Little by little, the vibrating of the wedges weakened, finally going numb. The light faded from lavender to pink, then went dark. Our hearts sank to the depths. The cat lay still. Sorrow pooled as drops of grief washed away all hope.

From out the darkness, a hand reached out, touching its crystal to ours. Stanislaus held the southern slice. The wedges wriggled and slipped from our grasps. The four segments fused. An ember glowed deep within the globe. The Andean Orb was again whole. It drifted down and hovered over the cat's lifeless form. A shimmer of light, a rush of warmth, a twinkling sound. The Orb was gone.

Beneath a misty veil, the body on the ground stirred. But it was no longer the halfling form of the Adventure Cat. It was a woman with long, dark hair. She rose slowly, stretched and yawned, as though she'd been asleep for a century. Before our

dazzled eyes stood an Ultranian knight. Her name was Katherine.

"What are you all staring at?" she said. Brutus gasped, "You're
beautiful!"

# Chapter 27:
## Secret of Stanislaus Korkunia

Seven cuckoos from an old Bavarian clock at the Morningtown Inn announced the morning hour. We gathered in the dining hall and found places around the table. A hearty breakfast was on the way. Logs burned brightly in the hearth. Stanislaus walked to the northside window and drew back the curtains to reveal an early winter snow. Prissy cats pranced, rowdy dogs romped, and little children adorned jolly snowmen.

Stanislaus addressed the assembly. "To let you know. The elves have taken the toad man, Parnie Wermbom, to the infirmary. They'll give him a good looking over and he'll be afforded the proper care." He then signaled to an elf standing near the kitchen door. "Now, hor d'oeuvers for all of our dear friends."

Hot coffee and blueberry muffins broke our days-long fast. Pancakes, gooseberries, and poached eggs were yet to come. The surrounding elves were all ears as Golly and Brutus recounted their last minutes in the gorge. In truth, it was more of a performance, which included melodrama, sweeping gestures, and high-fidelity sound effects.

"The ground went right out from under us," said Brutus. "Deep into a crack we fell."

"Nothin' we could do," said Golly. "Nothin' but look up at a strip o' red sky."

"The shaking wouldn't stop. And the rocks shifted. Then the walls started closing in on us."

"We tried bracin' the spears between, but they snapped like toothpicks."

"Then, a light shined in—a pink-and-purple of sorts."

"Up we went," said Golly, "like a huge hand scooped us up and gently set us down."

Brutus concluded, "As my mother used to say, 'it might have been haints, it might have been saints'. But to my thinking, it must have been the strange, netherworld magic of that bloomin' Orb."

Arms out, palms up, shoulders shrugging—for once, Golly and Brutus were lost for words.

I offered, "Once those Orb crystals began to glow, it was as though they had come to life—lots of things started to happen. In fact, all the things we wanted to happen happened. In the end, it felt like we were sort of dissolving. We were no longer in the gorge—we were no longer anywhere." I held up my hands to display my palms. "Both palms had been severely burned, blackened and seared to the bone. When we arrived outside on the lawn, both hands had completely healed."

Katherine said, "And there's not a mark on my arm and shoulder where I'd been bitten by the horrible beast. Everything's become clear again. And though I now remember it all so well, it's like none of it ever happened. It's all so very strange."

I turned to Stanislaus. "What do you suppose happened to the Orb, Burgomaster?"

"Call it magic, a life force, something of the netherworld, or a natural event we simply don't understand. What we do know is the Orb does exist—at least it did. Where did it come from, where did it go . . . will it ever return? For now, the indigo crystal remains a mystery."

For a long moment, we all sat wondering about the wonder of it all.

Eight cuckoos cuckooed. At long last, the main course was served. Bowl after platter were laid upon the table. As we dined, Stanislaus led the conversation. "And so, my wandering knights—what lies ahead?

"I'm told a new barn needs buildin' for Widow Morley," said Golly. "Back to cobbling and odds and ends," said Brutus.

Katherine stood at the window, watching the snow. She began singing a folk song that had been a favorite of mine since childhood. When she turned, she wore a shy smile. We applauded. "Watching the Myna River," she said, "reminded me of the River Tura, near my home in Ultrania. I've sung those words many times while sitting on the bank, my thoughts flowing with the current as the waters rolled out to sea."

"It was a beautiful rendition," I said. "How did you learn such a song?" I asked.

"It's from a legend," she said. "Many years ago, long before I was born, a man came through the Coverture. He wore a wide-brimmed hat and funny pointed boots, and he carried a weapon, like Professor Winkleheimer's shooting pistol. He loved riding horses and singing that song. It's called 'Shenandoah.' It reminds me of home, my friends and family."

"It was very lovely," said Stanislaus. "Sweetly sad, warm and wandering." All murmured in agreement.

"The man from the Coverture," I said. "He sounds like a cowboy from the old American West. What happened to him?"

The Ultranian knight shrugged and turned to watch the snow. She sighed, "No one knows, Captain. He rode his mount back through the Coverture. Perhaps, like you and me, he simply longed to be home."

The burgomaster asked, "And what of you, Katherine? What lies ahead?

Katherine turned and approached the table. "For one," she said, "I've decided I do very much like the name Adventure.

And since any Katherine may rightly be called Cat, I shall keep Adventure Cat as my familiar name. Furthermore, I now consider myself a knight in the service of Morningtown as well as Ultrania."

Whistles, cheers, and applause arose and lingered, finally diminishing to convivial mutters and mumbles.

"And with that, knighthood has been granted!" said Stanislaus. "So, does the Adventure Cat have any adventurous plans?"

She clasped her hands behind her back and strolled around the table. "During my first encounter with Captain Newman, we discovered a pathway through the Coverture connecting north and south. All too soon, I must return home. I must make my way to the Aurium Mountains to join the Knights of Vindicar. Through vows of honor and sense of justice they are bound to free King Yegor from exile and restore him to the throne. The Vindicar are the finest and bravest men and women of the land—the elite of the Ultranian Kingdom. And I assure you, that usurping witch, Piranda, greatly fears their order."

"What stays their hand?" asked Stanislaus.

"Discretion. The Vindicar are relatively few in number," said Adventure. "And above all, they are resolute to avoid a civil war."

"Commendable," said Stanislaus.

"I fully agree," I said. "The strongest weapon is the open hand of friendship. No war is ever won."

"My eyes have always been open, but I've never truly seen until now," said Adventure. "Winning justice for my homeland through peaceful means will be my next endeavor." She breathed deeply and sighed. "But considering the vile disposition of that charlatan of a witch, the carrots and sticks of the whole affair dangle quite precariously. And most perplexing of all, I've come to realize it's not power for power's sake Piranda desires. She simply wants to be loved."

"Your eyes see well, indeed," said the burgomaster.

"I'll approach the hive with honey, with hope and an open hand. Offered song, I'll sing. Offered kindness, I'll be kind. Offered joy, I'll rejoice. But if I'm stung, I'll sting back—with staff, with arrow, and with sword."

The eyes of Golly and Brutus gleamed; they could not subdue their smiles. Together they said, "May we come along?"

"I was hoping the two of you might be of such a mind," said Adventure. "How about you, Captain?"

My words did not come easily. "An opportunity for my B list, I'm afraid. My battle with black magic and charlatans lies in the upper world. There's plenty to deal with—apathy, ignorance, corruption, prejudice, greed, deceit—among the mighty and among the mild. Wildfires, droughts, floods, horrific winds, and ravaging disease.

We've abused our world. We're destroying it—and we're harming yours in the process. The Earth is fighting back—it's fighting for its life. Joining Mother Nature in her fight to survive—this will be my next battle . . . I've got to find a way home."

Stanislaus said, "Since the first sunrise, good people have had to unite and stand against the wickedness, greed, and venality of those in power. A universal truism, the reason for which has baffled the most profound of minds and will likely do so until the most final of sunsets."

I said, "More and more, I'm coming to believe my last sunset is right before my eyes—and I've been blind to it, too busy tending to the little things in life to pay close enough attention to the big ones. It's the same for everybody, whether you live in Morningtown, Ultrania, or my home in America. Our world isn't changing—it has changed. It's no longer just people against people, ideas against ideas—that's all become frivolous. Compared to the dire needs of our planet, societal and political contentions have become moot and minor issues. We have to face the fact: We've built an oven around ourselves and we're still turning up the heat."

One of the elf elders raised his hand and bade the burgomaster, "Now may be the time."

Stanislaus nodded. "Very well, bring the etchings and notes."

An elf entered the room with several rolls of string-bound paper. Two others rolled a large easel up to the table. Stanislaus said, "The elves believe our world is getting warmer because of the shifting of the Earth's magma flows. There is nothing we can do. But stopping further contamination of the surface air is entirely possible through a magic so simple, yet so tragically elusive . . . sensible cooperation among people. All over the world, all machinery and factories must be redesigned or disabled until they operate cleanly and safely. If factories can be built that soil the air, machines can be built to clean the air. These are things the people of the oberlands can already accomplish if they truly desire."

I replied, "Yes, I believe so. And it's true, all the people in all the nations of the world must join in the effort. But convincing people of a danger they don't see or don't want to see is near to impossible."

"Nonetheless it must be done," said Stanislaus.

"It's been said so many times, in so many ways: The longest journey begins with a single step. But this is a journey for nearly eight billion —so there must be eight billion steps, and then eight billion more," I said.

Stanislaus offered, "One voice inspires two, two voices four, four inspire eight. Let a hundred tell a thousand, and a thousand tell a million . . ."

"But they must believe."

"Precisely." Stanislaus unraveled an etching and tacked it to the easel. "Our elves propose little factories that can clean the skies from within the skies."

Stanislaus pointed out the features of a flying machine much like a zeppelin. It was filled with warm air generated by the sun and the wind. One hundred percent clean energy. While the inner workings were far beyond the technology of their world, the elfin designers were convinced the upper world had scientists and engineers who could easily construct the mechanisms. Essentially, a turbine would create a vacuum drawing polluted air through a series of filters and elemental converters. The pollutants would be cleaned, compacted, and transported to beaches, deserts, and landfills. All coordinated and administered through mechanistic conduits (referring to the elves' elementary understanding of computer networks).

"Ingenious invention," I said. "Fairly simple in design. Easily manufactured. But it would take a whole lot of air balloons and mechanistic conduits to do the job."

Stanislaus countered, "It took millions of factories and automobiles to poison the sky. So, yes, it will take many, many little sky factories to restore it to health.”

One of the elves handed the burgomaster an envelope. He poured the contents onto the table. “Seeds,” he said, “from the Fever Jungles. Easily sown and tended. The hardy grasses reaped could draw massive amounts of wastes and contaminates from the air and store them safely within their shafts. Imagine gardens planted atop the hundreds of thousands of tall buildings and skyscrapers in each of your great cities, cleaning the air every minute, every second of the day.”

I nodded agreeably. “While the math and physics of it all flies high above my humble head, I’d be all for presenting such ideas if I could find a way home. Unfortunately, my best chance to get there is now buried under a million tons of molten rock.”

As I looked around the room, everyone in the place seemed to know something I did not. Somehow, I could tell by the looks on their faces. It was as though they had some sort of surprise in store for me. At that point, the only surprise I cared about was to find a way to place my feet on a sidewalk in Detroit. I finally spoke up. “OK, folks. My apologies, but I’m not in the mood for riddles.” It was a room full of glowing faces, shiny eyes, engaging smiles that seemed to be saying good-bye and offering best wishes. I was so enthralled by the throng’s fawning that I did not notice the Adventure Cat peppering a dash of slumber dust onto my right shoulder. Nor did I understand my sudden lightheadedness, my drooping eyelids, my dropping chin. The harder I fought against the sandman, the more the flitting fairy sprinkled winkies onto my noggin. Finally, I leaned forward and rested my forehead on my forearms.

I floated, lost in limbo, alone with my thoughts. There were no memories of the past, no actions for the present—only thoughts and fears about the future. A recent conversation with my friends in Morningtown was at the crux. In my mind, sinister seeds had been sown. They sprouted into visions of horrible things to come. The floods, the droughts, the famines, the deaths. The dense, toxic air; the endless acid rain; the ever-churning oceans; the towering, twisting winds. That was my last vision of the planet Earth as I floated off and away into the vastness of the Cosmos. That's all that was left.

Like so many of us, I'd been aware of the hubbub surrounding global warming and climate change, but I'd never taken the time to consider it in depth, to admit to myself the gravity of the situation. The Earth had been around for nearly five billion years. Things had changed for the better and for the worse, in cycles, and rhythms, and patterns since "In the beginning." In my own lifetime I had seen periods of extreme heat and extreme cold, times of famine and drought, times of storms and serenity, times of flourishment and decline. This was simply the way of life on Earth. And besides, I had my own life to live, and life is short. There were so many things I wanted and needed to do, and there always seemed to be so little time. Adrift in pondering and contemplation, my thoughts whirled and twirled.

I hadn't been paying enough attention to my own backyard, let alone the Earth as a living entity. A huge mistake—but not mine alone. The world was in trouble, big trouble. It was suffering and it was crying out. The temperature was rising—there was no denying that. The glacial ice was melting, and the seven seas were filling to the brim. Forests were burning and many animal species were dying out. The Earth was talking to us, and most of us weren't listening; it was dying, and we were killing it. These truths cannot be spoken often enough.

So now, finally, I was paying attention, and I was determined to do something. I wasn't sure what to do, or how to go about it, but I knew something had to be done. And I knew I was going to have ask for cooperation, and lots of it. The thing is, before I could get help, I had to find a way to get denying minds to listen. But how? Most unexpectedly, a memory drifted in. I was looking at a picture on a wall in my childhood home. A man in a robe stood in the faintest of light outside a humble dwelling. And there were the words: "Behold, I stand at the door and knock."

I reasoned: The beautiful blue planet needed our help. This was the greatest challenge ever to face humankind. If people genuinely listened, if they really paid attention and thought things over, if they came to truly understand how desperate and dangerous things really were—they would come together. They would let old wounds heal, set aside differences, and make the governments of the world listen. All would begin working together to save our world. They simply had to believe.

Hypnogogic awareness lured me from the depths of slumber. The next thing I knew, someone was jostling my arm. My eyes opened, but everything was dark. I was wearing a blindfold. When I reached up, someone touched my hand. I heard the voice of Stanislaus. "Don't touch the blindfold yet, Captain. You must not look until I've gone. Do I have your promise?"

"Yes. But what's going on? Am I in some sort of wagon? I can feel the cold air."

"You've had a ride in Morningtown's finest of crafts. A privilege bestowed on very few. And you'll be happy to know we've finally arrived. You are home. I'll come around and help you down." Within seconds, Stanislaus tapped me on the knee and took my arm as he guided me from the craft. "One step, second step—there you are now. Safe and sound, solid ground."

"The ground feels sort of strange," I said. "Yes, be careful. You're standing in snow."

I heard him walk around and get back into the craft. He said,

"Count slowly to one hundred before removing the eye wrap."

"I'm on my honor. I'll count nice and slow. I'll make sure you're out of sight. You know I keep my promises."

After giving me a ew final words of advice, the mysterious burgomaster said, "Very well, I bid thee good fortune and farewell."

As the craft departed, I heard a muffled drumming; there was a whisk of wind and a whispery sound. When my count reached one hundred, I removed the blindfold and looked in all directions. I was on the corner of a backstreet. Other than porch lights, the houses were dark. But the big full moon was beautiful; I hadn't seen it in so long. A sign under the streetlamp read Cherry Lane. Along the lane were the marks left by the mysterious vehicle of Stanislaus. The snow had been churned and there were two parallel lines, much like those left by wagon wheels. A picture formed in my mind—the flying chariot of Piranda the witch. So that was it, I thought, Stanislaus had a magical chariot too. I hadn't realized this at first because all had been so quiet. The horses had likely worn lined muzzles to shield them from the wind, and the freshly fallen snow had stifled the sounds of the wheels and hooves.

Another realization: Clearly, Stanislaus was no ordinary person. He was larger than life, perhaps some sort of long-lost wizard or sorcerer. Was he the one who had found the Orb in the Andes Mountains? Perhaps Piranda had chased him in a mad pursuit. Both at the reins of their flying conveyances, above the mountains, valleys, and seaways, they had raced all the way to the top of the world. They must have passed through the Coverture, one after another, with Stanislaus landing in the south and Piranda the north. It was a

fantastic notion, but it all made sense. Without intent, I suspected I had discovered the secret of Stanislaus Korkunia, Burgomaster of Morningtown.

When I turned, I was standing in front of a two-story brick house. The house number was 111 and there was a holly wreath on the door. As I trudged through the snow, I thought of what I might say. I had to find a way of explaining myself without giving away the location of the world beneath a world.

As I pondered the telling of my tale, I wondered whether such a place really did exist. It was possible I was swimming in the dazzling dream of a restless sleep. It was possible I'd ejected from the F-16 and was lying unconscious on a sheet of ice. It was possible I was in a hospital, hallucinating within the confines of a traumatic coma. Or I could have been locked in a rubber room laced in a straitjacket. Then again, maybe I really was just a little boy caught up in the vividness of a wandering imagination. And thinking beyond all physical law, was it possible I had crossed over into some unknown dimension? Had

I plummeted into some sort of parallel existence? After my recent experiences, reality seemed to have lost all meaning . . . Finally, in all fairness, I had to admit it was possible I had crossed over into the great unknown. I had to accept to the practical likelihood that I was dead.

Somewhere, in the depths of my heart, I hoped it had all been true. More than anything, I wanted to believe my amazing journey had taken place. I wondered whether Golly, Adventure, and Brutus were thinking about me. They were friends, they were family, and they were as real and genuine as anyone I'd ever known. I would never forget them. To me, all those dashes of dreams would live on forever. In the end, I decided it didn't matter how much of the story I told, and it didn't matter how much of it people were willing to believe— after all, I was only ten years old. The secrets of the unterlands would be safe.

Standing on the porch, I reached out to knock, then held back. Shining under the porchlight was an engraving on a plaque. It read Santa Nicole's Home for Children, EST. 1837. I rapped on the door just beneath the wreath. When the door opened, I felt the welcome warmth of the room. An older lady wearing a plush, lavender night robe smiled a kindly smile. "Hello, young man," she said. "It's very late, almost midnight. How can I help you?"

Just then, a cat brushed past my legs and ran into the house—

a striped tabby cat wearing a bright blue collar. "Goodness, Katrina, where have you been?" sighed the lady. She looked at me and said, "That rascal of a cat, always running off. The boys have been worried sick about you, Katrina."

"Boys?" I asked.

"Yes, they took her in as a stray. Gregory, he likes to be called Golly, and little Bartholomew, Brutus as he calls himself. They do worry about her so when she sneaks out. I always tell them she's just off on some glorious quest."

All at once, a tintinnabulation filled the air—the ringing of tiny bells. I saw the lady look over my head, up into the sky, and I turned and looked as well. A darkish shadow flowed from behind a cloud, and a silhouette crossed the moon's yellow face. Prancing reindeer pulled a man in a sleigh. Swirling away, they faded into the starlight.

"Looks like a few clouds to the north." She winked. "It may snow before morning." Just then the cat raced back outside with a tinkly jingle-bell toy. "Katrina!" the woman called. "Katrina! Come back here!" We watched the animal bound through the snow and out of sight.

Again, the woman sighed. "Oh well, she'll always be a free spirit. I suppose that's why the boys call her Adventure."

Confounded and confused, I entered a room where colored

lights and mirrored orbs lit up a tinseled tree. The boxes below were red and green, and all tied up with bows. The star atop was silver and gold. Stuffed stockings hung from the mantle of an old, brick fireplace.

Reaching out, the lady smiled and said, "Here, let me take your coat."

Still feeling unsettled and a little lost, I hesitated, but finally relented. As I removed my heavy parka, I remembered there was something in the pockets. Reaching deep, I removed a sealed tube of drawings; a wax box marked GRASS SEEDS; and a penknife—a gift from a soul mate.

Shards and fragments of the past were gone. Dreams and imaginings of the future would wait. The moment was in the present. A feeling of acceptance, a sense of belonging settled over me. The grandfather clock in the corner tolled a dozen times. The sound was resonant, solemn, and peaceful. It told me my wondrous journey had ended. It assured me . . . I was home.

# John William and the Omnipotent Indigo Orb

## "Howard R. Gorrell"

*Thank you for buying this novel.*